'I must say I envy Hensleigh,' murmured her unwelcome guest.

Lucy stiffened, but continued polishing so that the table wobbled noisily.

'Lucky fellow,' he went on, 'having a wench willing to clean his lodgings *and* warm his bed.'

Everything inside her stopped as well as the polishing rag. And the temper her grandparents had tried so hard to curb slipped its leash. Slowly she straightened and faced him, the dusting rag clenched in her fist. 'Wench?' She restrained the urge to throw the rag in his face.

His brows rose. 'A poor choice of words,' he said. 'You could do better than Hensleigh.'

'Really?' Rage slammed through her, but she kept her voice dulcet. 'You, for example?'

He smiled. 'If you like. If you tell me where he is.'

'They say it's a wise child who knows its own father,' she said, her stomach twisting.

James wondered if he'd been hit on the head with a brick as the implications slammed into him. No one had suggested that the woman in Hensleigh's lodgings was his *daughter*!

Author Note

This story takes place a little earlier than the rest of my stories, in 1802. Some years back I wrote a short story called *The Funeral*, and for various reasons needed an earlier setting. This was the genesis of James and Lucy's story. A throwaway line about her father's gambling debts gave me the lead into this book. I hope you enjoy it as much as I have enjoyed finding out more about them.

Readers familiar with the late eighteenth and early nineteenth century will recognise James's godfather, Charles James Fox. Fox's real-life love affair with the courtesan Elizabeth Armistead is one of the world's great love stories, and I was delighted to be able to include them in this book.

IN DEBT
TO THE EARL

Elizabeth Rolls

First published in Great Britain 2016
By Mills & Boon, an imprint of HarperCollins*Publishers*
1 London Bridge Street, London, SE1 9GF

Large Print edition 2016

© 2016 Elizabeth Rolls

ISBN: 978-0-263-26292-6

Our policy is to use papers that are natural, renewable and recyclable
products and made from wood grown in sustainable forests.
The logging and manufacturing processes conform to the legal
environmental regulations of the country of origin.

Printed and bound in Great Britain
by CPI Antony Rowe, Chippenham, Wiltshire

33885303

Elizabeth Rolls lives in the Adelaide Hills of South Australia with her husband, teenage sons, dogs and too many books. She is convinced that she will achieve a state of blessed Nirvana when her menfolk learn to put their own dishes in the dishwasher without being asked and cease flexing their testosterone over the television remote.

Elizabeth loves to hear from readers, and invites you to contact her via email at books@elizabethrolls.com.

Books by Elizabeth Rolls

Mills & Boon Historical Romance

His Lady Mistress
A Compromised Lady
A Regency Christmas
'A Soldier's Tale'
Lord Braybrook's Penniless Bride
A Magical Regency Christmas
'Christmas Cinderella'
In Debt to the Earl

Mills & Boon Historical *Undone!* ebooks

A Scandalous Liaison
A Shocking Proposition

M&B

Royal Weddings Through the Ages
'A Princely Dilemma'

Visit the Author Profile page
at millsandboon.co.uk for more titles.

For Sharon.

We share a birthday and a love of tea.
You share your daughters with me, and
we've stood beside too many soccer pitches
to count, cheering each other's kids on.
This one is for you.

Prologue

March 1802

'**D**amn it, Paget.' James, Lord Cambourne, stared down at the battered, unconscious face of his young cousin, Nick Remington. 'What the hell happened? Has the doctor been?'

Nick's manservant, Paget, nodded. 'Yes, m'lord. I sent for the doctor immediately. He's just left.'

'And?'

Paget tucked the blankets more securely around his young master. 'Just bruising, a cracked rib and a knock to the head.'

'*Just?*' James took exception to the servant's soothing tone. 'For God's sake, Paget! You're taking it mighty calmly! Does the boy make a habit of this?'

'No!' Paget glanced at Nick, who shifted restlessly, and lowered his voice. 'My lord, if we might go into the sitting room? Doctor Greaves said he ought to sleep—'

'James?' The voice was barely a whisper. 'That you?'

The blue eyes, one distinguished by a black eye of impressive proportions, were open, if bleary. Under the scrapes and bruises, his face was nearly as white as his pillow.

'Yes,' James said. 'What the devil have you been about, you idiot?' Relief roughened his voice.

'Being an idiot,' Nick got out through a split lip. 'Did Paget send for you?'

'Well, of course I did, Master Nick,' Paget said. 'You were attacked!'

'What?' James had been assuming a falling out of friends that had got out of hand. 'Attacked?'

Nick's gaze fastened on Paget. 'Tell me you didn't send for the mater and pater. Please.'

'No, sir.' Paget's tone was soothing. 'Just his lordship.'

'Thank God.' Nick attempted to sit up and the bedclothes fell back, revealing his naked torso, even as he sank down cursing.

James's eyes widened and he swore savagely. Nick's body was livid with bruises.

'Looks as bad as it feels, does it?' Nick managed a weak grin.

'Stay on the damn pillow.' James enforced the

command with a gentle hand on his cousin's shoulder. 'I can't blame you for not wanting to see your parents, but unless you wish me to send for them, you will do as you are told.'

'Bully,' Nick said with a half smile.

'Believe it,' James said. 'Who beat you?' Because that was what it looked like—a deliberate and brutal beating.

Nick grimaced. 'Did I mention that I was an idiot?'

'You did,' James said. 'Unnecessary, but you did mention it. Go on.'

'Well, I lost a bit of money.'

'How much is a bit?' James asked.

'Er…quite a bit. A couple of monkeys.'

James bit back several choice remarks. No doubt Nick was already thinking them anyway. 'A couple of monkeys.' His voice expressed polite interest. 'You lost a thousand at— What? Cards? Dice? A horse?'

'Cards,' Nick said. 'The thing is—'

'You couldn't pay.' James failed to keep the sarcasm out of his voice. A thousand was more than Nick's entire annual allowance.

'No.' Nick's voice was weary, his eyes closed. James glanced at Paget, who gestured to the door. On the whole James agreed. Nick was safe and the story could wait. But Nick's eyes opened again.

'I couldn't pay and he sold my vowels.'

'Who?'

'Chap called Hensleigh. Captain Hensleigh,' Nick said.

'Never heard of him,' James said. But Captain Hensleigh was going to hear from him. 'Navy or army?'

'What?'

'What sort of captain?' James asked.

Nick grimaced. 'Oh. Sharp, I should think.'

A Captain Sharp. Wonderful. Nick had come up to town for the first time, lost more money than he could pay to a professional card cheat and been beaten up.

James glanced at Paget. 'Is there any coffee?'

'I roasted and ground beans earlier,' Paget said. 'But Mr Nick fell asleep. It won't take long.'

'Thank you,' James said.

'Sorry,' Nick mumbled. 'Should have offered.'

James snorted. 'We'll just assume your manners have gone begging in the same place as your wits.'

'Get the coffee, Paget,' Nick said. 'There's a good chap.'

'Yes, sir.'

James turned back to Nick. 'Any chance those bruisers are coming back? Where did this happen?'

'Off Fleet Street, near the Strand.'

'What in God's name took you down there?' James demanded.

'Looking for Hensleigh,' Nick said. 'He gave me a week and it wasn't quite up.' He met James's gaze. 'I couldn't pay. I knew that and I was going to ask for more time.'

'What? And stop in at St Clement Danes on your way back up the Strand to pray for a miracle?' James asked.

Nick flushed. 'No. I was going to come to you and…and ask for advice. But I didn't find Hensleigh and I ran into my attackers on the way back.'

'My advice would have been to stay out of gaming hells in the first place,' James said. 'However, that's done. Why the hell didn't you stop when the play got too deep?' A question for the ages, that one.

He watched as Nick swallowed. 'I…I thought I could win it all back. You…you see, I *did* win at first. Quite a lot. And then—'

'And then you lost a bit. Not much, but a bit,' James said. It was a familiar story.

'Yes,' Nick said. 'And I won it back quite quickly, but then—'

'Then you really started losing,' James finished for him. 'Haven't you played enough salmon in your time to know when *you're* being played?'

'Apparently not.' Nick fiddled with the bedclothes. 'What do I do now? I can't pay this debt and even if I could, I wouldn't be able to pay for my lodgings, or eat, or—'

'Precisely,' James said. 'Did you enjoy it?'

'What?'

'The cards. The play. The excitement.' He needed to know if he was going to be wasting his money. He'd bail Nick out this first time, regardless, but if the boy was a bred-in-the-bone gamester, he needed to know. As things stood, Nick's father, William, was his heir, with Nick next in line.

'Oh.' Nick grimaced. 'No. Not much.'

'Really?' Was the boy just giving the answer he must know his cousin wanted?

'Well, winning was fun,' Nick admitted.

'Winning is supposed to be fun,' James said.

'Yes, but I have more fun, say, steeplechasing,' Nick said. 'Even if I don't win, the ride is fun.'

'And gaming isn't?'

Nick shook his head. And winced. 'No. I felt sick most of the time.'

Relief flooded James. 'Come down this summer and we'll race. There's a colt you can try out for me. He's not up to my weight.'

'If the pater ever lets me off the leash again,' Nick said. 'I'll have to write to him. Tell him what I've done and—'

'I'll sort it out,' James said. 'No need to upset your parents.' William and Susan were good people, but the boy would never hear the last of it and he suspected Nick had learned his lesson. Learned it the hard way, but at least he *had* learned it. Many never did. Also, William couldn't afford to settle a debt like this. James could.

'What? *No!*' This time Nick did sit up, swearing at the pain. 'Curse it, James!' he went on, when James had helped him back against the pillows. 'I wanted advice, not your money!'

'If I didn't believe that, you wouldn't be getting either,' James said. 'Listen, you aren't the first youngster to make a fool of himself in London, and—' he grimaced slightly at the memory '—I don't suppose I was either.'

'*You?*' Nick sounded as though he could as easily have believed St Paul's had heaved itself up off its foundations and walked away on chicken legs.

James reminded himself that his cousin was nineteen. 'I wasn't born staid and respectable,' he said. Far from it.

Nick flushed to the roots of his hair. 'I didn't mean *that*! It just seems unlikely that you could have done something this stupid.'

He'd been a great deal more stupid. 'Believe it or not, you don't have a monopoly on idiocy,' he said. 'But that's beside the point. The point is that someone bailed me out and never let me repay her.'

Nick stared. '*Her*? Who?'

James cleared his throat. 'What I'm saying is that I'll sort this out and consider that I've done something towards clearing an old obligation.' He was fairly sure Elizabeth would see it that way.

'Now I feel like a worm as well as an idiot,' Nick muttered. 'I *will* pay you back, whether you like it or not.'

'Fine,' said James, knowing better than to tell the idiot boy that the money didn't matter. If it mattered to Nick, so much the better. 'Now, you'd better tell me who and where I have to pay. And while we're at it you can furnish me with Captain Hensleigh's direction.'

Nick blew out a breath. 'I don't know it, but you'll find the Cockpit easily enough.'

'The Cockpit? Is that the hell?' James asked.

Nick nodded. 'Yes. It's in an old cellar. Used to have cocking there, apparently. He's there most nights.' He frowned. 'You don't need him, though. Fellow called Kilby bought the vowels. One of his bullies let the name slip, but they said to ask at the Maid and Magpie tavern with the money.'

Paget's return with coffee gave James a moment to think. He sat down on a chair by the bed and sipped. The first thing was to pay off the debt. Before Nick got another beating from this Kilby's enforcers. After that...

James's jaw hardened. Then he'd go after *Captain* Hensleigh.

'James?'

He looked at Nick. 'Hmm?'

'You aren't planning something stupid, are you?'

'No.' The lie came easily. 'I was thinking that your parents are due in town soon.' He ignored Nick's groan. 'You can go out to my place at Chiswick for a couple of weeks until you look less like something the cat coughed up and that rib has a chance to heal.'

Nick smiled weakly. 'Nice try. And you don't think Mama will just pop down for a visit? Chiswick isn't *that* far out of town.'

James shrugged. 'Not if I hint to your father that you took a woman with you.'

Nick sank even further into the pillows and James noted with some amusement that under his bruises the boy was blushing. 'Damn it, James! They'll think I'm in the petticoat line!'

James suppressed a grin. 'Aren't you? Well, it's your choice. Do you prefer your mama clucking over you like a hen with one chick?'

Nick groaned. 'All right, all right. I take your point. Thank you.'

'You can go in my carriage when the doctor says you can travel,' James said, sipping his coffee. 'This is excellent, by the way. Do you think Paget might confide his secret to my cook?'

Chapter One

Three weeks later

James blinked across the table at his opponent. 'I make that a thousand pounds, Hensleigh. Time to settle up, don't you think?' He spoke with extra precision, as if without care his speech might have slurred. With seeming clumsiness, he knocked his glass of burgundy. 'Oops,' he said absently.

Hensleigh smiled broadly as he righted the glass. 'Oh, come now, Cambourne! *I'm* no faint heart. The merest reverse! You must give me at least a *chance* to recoup my losses. Double or nothing on the next hand? Winner take all?'

James would have preferred to end this farce right there and then, walking out with his winnings, or at least Hensleigh's vowels. Frankly he thought he'd spent enough time in the Cockpit.

Finding the hell had been easy. Getting in had been trickier, even with the password Nick had given him, but a crown to the doorman had worked a minor miracle. He'd noted Hensleigh on his first visit, a tall, bluff, open-faced sort, with thinning ginger hair, but hadn't approached him. Instead he'd played dice at another table, careful not to win or lose too heavily, once he'd worked out how the dice were weighted. He'd dressed carefully, making sure he looked and behaved like a well-heeled squire fresh from the country—a pigeon ready for plucking. He'd also introduced himself as plain Mr Cambourne. In this situation his title would be a hindrance. He'd watched the card play, come to the conclusion that Hensleigh was far from the only Captain Sharp in the room, and planned accordingly.

Sure enough, the first time he'd played whist, he'd been allowed to win. Easily. Afterwards, when Hensleigh had come up to congratulate him, he'd grumbled that his opponent wasn't skilled enough to make it entertaining. The second time he'd lost a little, but won more, swaggering away two hundred pounds to the good. Tonight Hensleigh had approached him, all "hail, fellow, well met" and "care for a hand or two?" Apparently tonight was plucking time.

James considered. Double or nothing would end the affair and he wanted it over. The dingy, smoky hell, with its complement of the desperate and the dangerous, bored him. Several women, their profession—and assets—very obvious, prowled the room, only too ready to relieve a man of his winnings if the professional card sharps at the tables failed to do it. Occasionally a woman would leave with one or more of the players. It could not be said that they slipped away. Nothing so discreet. A few times James had heard the price agreed on.

He veiled his contempt with a bleary stare. 'Double or nothing?' he said. 'That would make your losses two thousand pounds, Hensleigh.'

The fellow smirked. 'Oh, well,' he said, with another broad smile, 'What's life without a little risk? Shall we have a new deck for it, eh?'

James raised his brows. 'Why not?' He sat back as Hensleigh signalled.

'A new deck here, my man,' Hensleigh said to the servant who came over. 'And a cloth for this mess. Mr Cambourne and I have agreed to double or nothing. Winner take all.'

The servant's gaze sharpened. 'Aye, Cap'n.' He scurried away.

'Another glass of wine, Cambourne?' Hensleigh suggested, his hand hovering by the bottle.

'Why not?' James plastered a vacuous grin to his face. Hensleigh had been pouring glass after glass of wine for him with a fine appearance of generosity. No doubt he assumed James was at least verging on foxed, if not well beyond it. In fact, most of the wine had been surreptitiously poured on to the carpet.

James lounged back to wait, as another servant wiped the table.

The first servant brought the new deck and glanced at Hensleigh, who held out his hand. 'Thank you, my man.' He cut the deck.

James waited until he began to shuffle, straightened and said quietly, with no trace of impairment, 'It's my turn to deal, Hensleigh.'

Several cards slipped from the man's hands, as his gaze flew to James's face. 'Is it? I am sure you must be mistaken.'

James raised his brows. 'No, Hensleigh, I am not.'

Hensleigh's eyes narrowed, flickered to the glass of wine.

James smiled. And shook his head. He reached out, swept up the fallen cards without taking his eyes from Hensleigh's face, and waited.

After a moment, expressionless, Hensleigh handed over the rest of the pack.

'Thank you,' said James, shuffling with an expertise he hadn't used earlier. Hensleigh's mouth tightened, but he said nothing. James ignored him, continuing the shuffle with unconcerned ease. Carefully he tilted the cards just so, as they ran through his fingers, catching the light. He didn't really need to see, but he wanted Hensleigh to sweat.

The man's eyes widened.

'Is this what they cashiered you for, Hensleigh?' James asked.

Hensleigh swallowed. 'The devil you say?'

'The army,' James said. 'It was the army, wasn't it? They don't like Captain Sharps in the army. Or the navy, but you don't strike me as the seafaring sort.' He continued to shuffle. 'Or perhaps I'm insulting the army and you invented your rank. Horse Guards didn't know anything about you when I enquired.' He smiled humourlessly as Hensleigh paled. 'Rather clumsy, the markings on this deck,' he went on. 'I can feel the wax lines on the backs quite easily. The other deck was less obvious.'

Hensleigh rallied. 'You are mistaken, sir. But we can call for another deck.'

James shook his head. 'No. We settle up. Now.'

'You agreed to double or nothing—'

'With an unmarked pack,' James said. 'All bets are off now.' He gathered the cards with a practised flick. 'Do we leave quietly, or shall I make it public?'

Hensleigh looked around nervously and clenched his fists. 'Damn you.'

James shrugged. 'Just sign your vowels, Hensleigh, and we'll have them countersigned by the management.' He wouldn't put it past the swine to disavow them if he thought he could get away with it. 'And don't even think about playing here again until you've paid me,' he added.

Hensleigh glared. 'You were stringing me!'

James bowed. 'Absolutely.'

Two weeks later

Trying not to breathe any deeper than absolutely necessary to support life, James trod up the narrow, creaking stairs. The aroma of last night's fish—hell, possibly last year's fish—and over-boiled cabbage followed him with putrid tenacity. Another flight of stairs and he tried to persuade himself that the smell was losing heart.

A week after their card game, Hensleigh—surprise, surprise—had neither turned up at James's house to settle his debts, nor returned to the Cockpit. After a further week of hunting, courtesy of a chance sighting on the Strand, James had found his prey's bolt-hole. The bolt-hole, according to what he'd been told, where Hensleigh kept his woman.

Third landing, the landlady had said.

Haven't seen 'is nibs, but the girl's up there.

The landing creaked, sagging ominously under his weight. He could see the announcement in the *Morning Gazette*… "Lord C met an untimely end collecting on a debt of honour by falling to his death when a landing gave way…"

He glanced around, wrinkling his nose; the rancid fish was just as odoriferous up here as down below. He might not need the money Hensleigh owed him, but by God he was going to break him. By the time he was done, Hensleigh wouldn't be able to keep himself, let alone any sort of woman. If Hensleigh wasn't home, then his mistress could deliver the warning that his vowels were about to be sold on.

He rapped sharply, noting with faint surprise that the door was actually clean...

The door opened and a girl enveloped in a grimy apron and clutching a rag stared at him. A few coppery tendrils of hair had escaped from her mob cap and brushed against a creamy-fair, slightly flushed cheek. A familiar odour that had nothing to do with fish drifted from the apartment. He sniffed—furniture polish? Yes, and something else, something sweet and indefinable that drifted through him.

'Are you looking for someone?'

James's world lurched a little at the slightly husky and surprisingly well-bred voice. His gaze met wary green eyes and an altogether unwelcome heat slid through his veins. How the hell did pond scum like Hensleigh acquire a woman like this one? Even as he wondered, the girl began to close the door. 'You must have the wrong address.'

He stuck his foot in the door. 'The devil I do.'

* * *

Lucy wondered if several foolish and altogether unlikely daydreams had become tangled with reality. The dreams where a tall, dark-haired, handsome gentleman came and swept her away into a life of safety. Only in her dreams, when this gentleman appeared at the door, she was somehow garbed in the latest fashions, with a dainty reticule dangling from her wrist. Not clad in a worn-out gown and grubby apron, and clutching a polishing rag. Nor in her dreams did the gentleman have cold, storm-grey eyes that looked at her as if she were something stuck to his shoe. Nor did he scowl. Her dream gentleman went down on one knee and offered her his heart. She wasn't holding out for a prince, however, just a kind, respectable man who didn't gamble and had a comfortable home. Nor did she insist on the glass slipper, which she thought would be most uncomfortable, but clearly, if she had a fairy godmother at all, the fairy's wand had a slight flaw.

'I'm looking for Hensleigh.'

For a moment the deep, velvet-dark voice froze her so that she just stared dumbly. It wasn't so much that he was tall, although he was, but that there was something about the way he stood. The way he seemed to fill the landing. Perhaps it was his shoulders? They seemed very broad, much broader than Papa's. Whatever the reason, her mind had scrambled.

She cleared her throat. 'I'm sorry, sir. There is no one—' Her mind cleared and her stomach chilled at her near mistake, at the cold eyes that raked her. 'That is, he's not here.' She clutched the polishing rag to steady the sudden trembling of her hands. *Hensleigh, not Armitage.* Papa had drummed it into her years ago not to use their real name. Ever. The name he used changed periodically, but it had been Hensleigh for weeks now. Before that it had been Hammersley and before that…well, something else starting with *H*. According to Shakespeare, a rose would smell as sweet by any other name, but she thought the rose might find it confusing to be re-named every few months.

Cold eyes narrowed and her pulse beat erratically. His voice, lethally soft, curled through her. 'Of course a rose by any other name may smell as sweet.' She flinched. Was the man a sorcerer? 'Although I'm sure it does become confusing.'

She bit her lip. *Neither confirm, nor deny. Explanations are dangerous.* There was only one reason such a man would be looking for her father. *How much this time?* A question that was none of her business even to think, let alone voice.

'He isn't here, I'm afraid. Please move your foot.'

She wished she hadn't used that word, *afraid*. It nudged too close to the truth.

The visitor cocked his head to one side. 'And when do you expect his return?'

His foot didn't move. Lucy forced breath into her lungs. A cold knot, not entirely composed of hunger, twisted in her belly. 'I…I don't know.' And for the first time in a very long while she wished that her father were about to walk through the door. This man had every nerve prickling the way he looked at her…as though he didn't believe her.

'I'll wait.'

Let the wolf over the threshold? Alarm bells clashed.

'No. He's—'

Powerful hands seized her shoulders, lifting and dumping her out on the landing. Her breath caught and her senses whirled in panic, as he stalked into the apartment. For a moment she considered leaving him to it and racing downstairs to the relative safety of Mrs Beattie's kitchen. *Coward! Find your backbone, for God's sake!* He'd dumped her out here like yesterday's rubbish! Anger drove out the fear and common sense flooded back. A man with designs on her wouldn't have pushed her out on the landing. Ergo, she was safe. Gritting her teeth, she went after him.

'How dare you! I don't care who you are! Get out!'

His glance flicked over the room and back to her. 'How do you propose to make me?' he asked, as if he really wanted to know.

She had no idea how, but— 'This is my home!' she retorted. 'I have every right to ask you to leave!' As homes went it was pathetic, but that didn't mean she had to accept this…this thug's presence in it.

Amusement crinkled the corners of his eyes. 'Your home, madam? Not much to defend, is it? Or are you defending Hensleigh? Or is it Hammersley this week? Where is he?'

She had spent the morning dusting and polishing. The floor was clean. Every stick of furniture gleamed. And she had never been so bitterly aware of the rickety table and chairs, the chipped looking glass over the fireplace, the bare floorboards or the threadbare curtain hiding the corner where she slept, as that scornful gaze raked the room.

'I already told you, I don't know!' That he knew the last name they had used sent a chill slithering down her spine.

'So you did,' he said. 'Are you going to invite me to sit down?'

'No.'

He shrugged and sat down anyway on the battered chair by the cold, empty grate. There hadn't been a fire in it for weeks. There was barely enough money for food, let alone luxuries.

She dragged in breath and let it go again. There was nothing she could do to shift him and she refused to rail at him like a Billingsgate fishwife. She stuffed her fury behind a solid door and slammed it shut.

'You will excuse me if I continue my work,' she said calmly and swiped her polishing rag back into the open jar of beeswax on the table. She could not afford more, but despite that she started all over again in the corner furthest from the fireplace, taking her time, hoping he would get bored and leave if she ignored him.

Unfortunately *he* didn't ignore *her*.

That grey, assessing gaze remained on her as she re-polished the table with painstaking thoroughness.

'I must say I envy Hensleigh,' murmured her unwelcome guest after a few moments. She stiffened, but continued polishing so that the table wobbled noisily. 'Lucky fellow,' he went on, 'having a wench willing to clean his lodgings twice in one morning *and* warm his bed.'

Everything inside her stopped as well as the polishing rag. And the temper her grandparents had tried so hard to curb slipped its leash. Slowly she straightened and faced him, the dusting rag clenched in her fist. 'Wench?' She restrained the urge to throw the rag in his face.

His brows rose. 'A poor choice of words,' he said.

'You're certainly a cut above wench-dom, even if your taste in men is execrable. You could do better than Hensleigh or whatever his name is this week.'

'Really?' Rage slammed through her, but she kept her voice dulcet. 'You, for example?'

He smiled, reminding her of the wolf down at the Royal Exchange. 'If you like. If you tell me where he is.'

'They say it's a wise child who knows its own father,' she said, her stomach twisting. 'It would be an interesting set of circumstances that permitted her to choose him.'

James wondered if he'd been hit on the head with a brick as the implications slammed into him. No one had suggested that the woman in Hensleigh's lodgings was his *daughter*! He had assumed...

'But,' the impossible girl continued, 'if you are prepared to acknowledge me as your natural daughter I'll be very happy to have it so. Although...' she looked him up and down in a way he found oddly unnerving '...you must have been a rather precocious child.'

James collected his scattered wits and found his tongue. 'You're his daughter, not his—' He stopped there. If she was Hensleigh's daughter—

'Correct.' The chill in her voice would have shaken an iceberg.

'Do you expect an apology, Miss... Hensleigh?'

Hell's teeth! Men did have daughters, even Hensleigh could have one. But—

She stared at him. 'What? Do I *look* stupid?'

He took a careful breath. Delicate features, and the small fist gripping the polishing rag as though she'd like to shove it down his throat was gracefully formed, if grubby. She looked furious, not stupid. And her voice was well bred, even if it had an edge on it fit to flay a rhinoceros, and there was something about the way she held herself, and that damn polishing rag—an air of dignity. He'd meant it when he said that she could do better than Hensleigh. She was not a beauty, not in the strictest sense of the word, but—those eyes blazed, and the mouth was soft and lush—or it would be if it weren't flat with anger. Damn it! There ought to be nothing remotely appealing about her! She was a redhead with the ghosts of last summer's freckles dancing over her nose, the whole shabby room smelt of furniture polish, and the truth was that he didn't *want* to believe that she could be Hensleigh's mistress. Which was ridiculous. It didn't matter a damn if she was Hensleigh's mistress or not. Or did it? Stealing a man's mistress was one thing, seducing his daughter quite another. And selling Hensleigh's vowels if it might condemn this girl to an even worse situation was yet another thing.

His gaze fell on a narrow door on the other side

of the room. Had he been so intent on the girl he'd nearly missed that? Without a word he rose and strode across, shoved it open and looked in.

'He's not here!' The girl's voice was furious now. No fear, just raw fury. He had to admire that.

A neatly made bed, washstand and small chest were the only furnishings. He closed the door and turned back to the girl.

'Are you satisfied now?' she demanded. 'Or would you like to look under the bed?'

'One bed, ma'am?' he asked. 'And where do *you* sleep?' Talk about stupid! He'd damn near believed her!

Her eyes spat green fire in an absolutely white face. She stormed across the room. 'It's none of your business, but—' Reaching the far corner he'd assumed held a chamber pot, she flung back the curtain across it.

His shocked gaze took in a thin, narrow pallet on the floor, covered with a totally inadequate blanket. A folded nightgown lay on top of the blanket and with it what looked like a violin case.

It convinced him as nothing else could have. Any man with this girl for a mistress would have her warming his bed, not shivering there in the corner.

'You sleep there?' It was all he could find to say. What sort of man let his daughter sleep in a draughty corner on a pallet that would scarcely do for an unwanted dog, while he took the relatively comfortable bed?

She jerked the curtain back into place. 'As you see.' Her cheeks were crimson. 'I don't care what you think of me,' she went on, 'and I doubt you care what I think of you, but you have forced your way into my home, insulted me in every conceivable way—I would prefer it if you left. I will tell my father you called.'

'But you won't tell me where he is.' *Why would she? The man is her father, for God's sake. Even if he doesn't look after her.*

'I don't *know* where he is.'

He cocked his head. There was something there in her voice. Fear?

'Would you tell me if you did know?' he asked gently.

'He owes you money, doesn't he?'

He stiffened. No, she wasn't stupid. But neither was he. If he told her the truth, what were the odds that he'd lose his quarry? 'So quick to assume the worst, Miss Hensleigh?' he said. 'The boot might be on the other foot.'

She stared. 'You owe *him* money?'

He hesitated only a moment. 'Is that so surprising?' It wasn't a lie. He hadn't said outright that he owed Hensleigh money. His conscience squirmed regardless.

She looked at him uncertainly. 'I see. Well, I still don't know where he is or when he will return. But if you leave your name I will let him know that you called.'

And the instant Hensleigh heard his name, he'd bolt again. However, at least he could be fairly sure now that she really didn't know where her father was. 'Remington,' he said. Another half-truth. He quashed his conscience's mutterings with the reminder that neither she nor her father had seen fit to share their real name, either. Remington was his family name, after all. Unless she described him, hopefully he'd think it had been Nick. No one would view Nick as a threat.

'Very well, Mr Remington. Good day to you.'

'You really don't know where he's gone?' James pressed. 'Your landlady mentioned that she hadn't seen him for several days.'

Scarlet washed into her cheeks again. 'No. At least, not exactly. He may be with a…a friend.' She dragged in a breath. 'There is a woman he visits, but—'

'What?'

Her chin went up. 'A mistress. I thought you knew all about mistresses!'

He cleared his throat. 'I know what a mistress is for!' It was the concept of a father who didn't keep that sort of knowledge from his daughter that startled him. And the concept of a daughter who didn't pretend ignorance of such things. Although he supposed under the circumstances that would rank with stupidity.

'Quite.' Her voice spat scorn. 'I don't know her name, or where she lives. If you knew he wasn't here, why bother coming up?'

She was quick enough, he'd grant her that. 'Because your landlady might be mistaken, or you might have known where he was.' He rose. 'I'll call again, Miss Hensleigh.'

There was no point staying any longer. He had as much information as he was going to get on this visit.

James reached the bottom of the stairs without falling through them. The stench of cabbage and fish had gained ground while he'd been upstairs. Or perhaps it was the contrast with the beeswax. Plain beeswax. Mama had always insisted on a touch of lemon in the furniture polish…his grandmother had favoured lavender.

There was no reason, logical or otherwise, why a girl wielding a beeswax-scented polishing rag should interfere with his plans to destroy Hensleigh. He was not responsible for the fate of Hensleigh or his daughter.

He stepped out into Frenchman's Yard. A shabbily

dressed man snored fitfully in a doorway, an empty bottle beside him, while several ragged boys played some sort of game with pebbles. One of them eyed him hopefully. 'Got a copper, yer worship?'

Aware that it might be a monumental error of judgement—men had probably been mugged for less—James fished out a sixpence and held it up. 'Information first.'

The sight of this untold wealth had the attention of all the boys. They crowded around and James kept his other hand in his pocket, firmly on his purse.

'Hensleigh. Anyone seen him recently?'

The boys exchanged glances. One of them, clearly the leader from the way he stood forward a little, spoke. 'The cap'n, you mean?'

James let that pass. 'Yes.'

The boy shrugged. 'Not for three, mebbe four days. Lu bain't seen 'im, neither.'

'Lu?'

The boy's eyes narrowed and he glanced up at the window of Hensleigh's lodgings. 'You was up there with her long enough. She's 'is daughter. Lucy.'

'Right.' If she was anything else, these boys would know it. And then there was the hair. Hensleigh's fading ginger hair must once have been red. Those few tendrils drifting from the confines of the girl's mob cap had shimmered copper.

'Fitch might know where the cap'n is.' One of the

smaller boys spoke up. 'Fitch's real friendly with Lu. Gives 'er money sometimes, 'e does.'

Without looking, the leader cuffed the boy on the head. 'Stow it.'

'Fitch?'

But the small boy took one look at the other boy's face and shook his head.

The leader shrugged. 'Just a cove.'

James reminded himself that it was none of his business if Miss Hensleigh was real friendly with anyone. Even a cove who gave her money sometimes. It happened. Yet in his pocket, his hand balled to a fist.

From above the sound of a violin being tuned floated down. James listened, arrested as first the G string was tuned, then the D and A in turn were coaxed into harmony. Finally the E string. A moment's silence and then the instrument sang, a lilting, dancing tune that somehow brightened the dingy yard even though the sun sulked behind its gloomy defences.

Dragging his attention away from the music, James tossed the original sixpence to the leader, plucked another out of his pocket and gave it to the small boy who had mentioned Fitch.

'If anyone does know where the captain is, I'd be interested.'

'Took a bag, 'e did,' volunteered another boy. 'Saw 'im wiv it right down on Fleet, by the Bolt.'

'Did you see him get on a coach?' James asked. The Bolt-in-Tun, on Fleet Street, was the departure point for some of the Bath coaches. Bath would be a very likely destination for a card sharp looking to recoup his losses.

The boy hesitated, finally shrugged. 'Nah. Just happened to see 'im there. Wasn't that int'rested, was I?'

James fished out another sixpence and flicked it to him. 'Apparently not. And you're also clever enough not to tell me what you think I want to hear. Thank you.'

The lad nipped the coin out of the air with startling dexterity. 'Could nick down there an' ask around if you like, guv.'

James considered that. 'No. Never mind. Does the name Kilby mean anything to you?'

The boys went very still and furtive glances were cast at their leader. He shrugged. 'Nah. Never heard of 'im.'

James nodded. 'Thank you.' Fairly sure he had just been lied to, he strolled out of the yard and headed west, towards Fleet Street and the Bolt-in-Tun. The lilt of Lucy Hensleigh's fiddle remained with him long after it had been drowned by distance and the rumble of wheels and hooves.

* * *

Lucy played until the light slid away from the window, leaving her in the shadows. Wrapped safely in the music's enchantment, she could pretend for a little while, hold out the terrifying reality of her life. She played from memory. He had sold her music months ago, along with her last three books. The only reason he hadn't sold the violin as well was that she had been out with it when he came home looking for things to sell. Slowly she let the spell unravel, knowing that even music could not keep out the world for ever. Shivering a little, she set the instrument back in its case and closed the window. She had practised for long enough and Fitch would be along soon.

Her stomach growled.

If only Papa had been home when Mr Remington called! Then they'd have some money. Money for the rent, money for food. Unless he owed it all to someone else. Over the four years that she'd been with him after Grandma's death the gentleman's code of so-called honour had been drummed into her—debts of honour were paid first, no matter if your daughter was hungry and you weren't using your real name.

Perhaps he wasn't out of town after all. Surely he wouldn't have gone right away if someone owed him money...*unless he owes more to someone else...*

The gaming was a disease, holding her father in a fevered grip. Nothing else mattered to him. No logic, no reason could reach him. Nothing but the game. He was charming about it, naturally. Papa was always charming. Even when he was lying. In fact, especially when he was lying. He had reassured her at first. There was nothing to worry about. Everything was quite as it should be. All proper gentlemen played. He would stop as soon as he had made their fortunes. And she had believed him. Or perhaps she had just wanted to believe him. That he would stop. Just one more game to set all right, get the dibs in tune. Always just one more game. To get the dibs in tune. To oblige a friend. A matter of honour. Just one more.

She supposed she had wanted to believe him. What sixteen-year-old girl, with nowhere else to turn, wanted to believe that her father had them on an irreversible downward slide to destitution?

She looked at the worn-leather violin case. Thank God she'd had it with her the afternoon Papa had sold her books and music. He'd been furious that the violin had not been there to sell as well.

Luckily he had won that night and had forgotten about selling the instrument the next day. Now she either took it with her or hid it. And she hadn't told her father the truth—that, courtesy of Fitch, she had found a way to earn enough money to feed herself.

Chapter Two

Jig waited as Kilby's pen scratched across the big ledger. Wonderful it were, how the man could write so quick an' all. Not that Jig had any use for book learning—he did all right. Too much book learning could make a fellow soft. But there was no doubt that Kilby had kept his edge, right enough.

The pen slowed and sand was sprinkled across the page.

Kilby looked up. 'Your report, Jig.'

Jig, so named because he'd narrowly escaped dancing a hempen jig as a boy, shifted under Kilby's flat stare.

'Found 'is nest, guv.'

Kilby stretched his arms and set his hands to either side of the ledger. His smile, to Jig's way of thinking, weren't real encouraging. Nor his fingers, drumming on the desk. Jig watched, narrow-eyed. The left hand it were—the one near the knife. Word was that Kilby drumming his fingers meant he was annoyed. Further word said that the first a man knew of Kilby reaching for the knife was the realisation that his difficulty breathing had to do with the knife buried in his windpipe. Nor a smart cove didn't discount the pistol near Kilby's right hand neither.

'Two days since I set you on to find Hensleigh, Jig,' Kilby said. 'Two whole days. I note you only say you've found his nest. But perhaps that's just your roundabout way of saying you have found the man himself?'

Jig swallowed. 'As to that, guv, I ain't found 'im as such. Seemin'ly 'e's away. No one ain't seen 'im.'

The fingers stopped drumming and Jig breathed a mort easier. Kilby was usually open to reason.

'Away?'

'That's it, guv. Can't find a cove who ain't there, but I got 'is hole.'

Kilby nodded. 'But if he's left his hole, Jig, then it is no longer his hole. Wouldn't you say?'

'Reckon 'e's comin' back, guv.' Cold sweat trickled down his spine. 'Got a girl there.'

This time the fingers of Kilby's right hand—the one near the pistol—started drumming. 'Jig, men abandon women all the time. What makes you—?'

'Reckon this is different, guv.' Jig cleared his throat. 'Seems the wench is 'is daughter.'

Kilby's fingers stilled. 'A *daughter*? He's kept that very quiet.'

Jig relaxed a little. 'Yeah. An' it ain't hard to see why, neither.' Remembering the tasty-looking little redhead, he licked his lips.

'Ah. Pretty, is she?'

'Ripe as a plum ready for pluckin',' Jig assured him. He'd been tempted to do a bit of plucking himself, but he knew better than that. More than his life was worth if the wench turned out to be of interest to Kilby.

'Hmm.' Kilby leaned back, frowning. 'The question will be, has someone plucked the plum already?'

Jig said nothing. For himself he didn't much care if a wench were already broke to saddle. But an unbroken ride was worth a mint in some quarters.

'Well, never mind.' Kilby said. 'Since Hensleigh has a saleable asset I'll get back the money he bilked me of with the Moresby boy's vowels. You can go now, Jig.'

Jig hesitated. The rest of his information might not be so welcome, but information was information. Kilby liked to know everything. 'Got a bit more, guv.'

'What?'

'There's a gent sniffin' around.'

Kilby sat up slowly. 'Sniffing where? Not here?'

'Nah.' Jig shook his head. 'Heard him askin' around about Hensleigh. That's how I tracked Hensleigh.'

'After the girl?'

Jig scowled. 'Could be. But he found out Hensleigh mighta gone to Bath.'

Kilby raised his brows and Jig expanded. 'The gent asked some lads. Got told Hensleigh'd been down the Bolt. So I follered 'im and sure enough 'e goes down there an' starts askin' round. Seems Hensleigh or a bloke like 'im took a ticket for Bath.'

Kilby let out a breath. 'The odds are high Hensleigh owes him money, too.' He considered. 'Or he might just be after the girl.'

'Might be both,' offered Jig.

Kilby nodded. 'Yes. He might have come looking for his money and now be wondering if he should just take his winnings out of the girl's hide.' He rubbed his chin. 'Check at the Cockpit who Hensleigh lost to recently. And watch his lodgings. If the same gentleman shows up again, find out where he lives, or get a name.'

'Aye, guv.'

'Anything else?'

'Asked about you, he did.'

Kilby's hands clenched to fists. 'Did he now?' His voice was very soft and Jig tensed. 'Did he get an answer?'

Jig shook his head. 'Nah. No one said nothin'.'

Kilby nodded. 'Very wise. Anything else?'

Jig hesitated. This went against the grain, so it

did, but he valued his life and folks that held out on Kilby tended to find that their lives ended unexpectedly. 'The boy—Fitch.'

'What about Fitch?'

Jig shuffled. 'Seemin'ly 'e's hangin' around the wench, too. Heard one of they lads say as how 'e gives 'er money.'

Kilby's fist clenched. 'Is he now? Isn't that interesting? It might be an idea to keep an eye on him, as well. His earnings have been down recently. Find out why.'

'Aye, guv.'

'You've done quite well, Jig,' Kilby said. 'I'm impressed.'

It was probably a waste of time to call at Hensleigh's lodgings again. James told himself that as he strolled along the north side of the Strand the next day. His visit to the Bolt-in-Tun had netted the information that Hensleigh had bought a ticket for Bath. James had discarded the notion of driving down himself. Tracking Hensleigh would take time and might alert him. The last thing he wanted was for the fellow to run altogether.

The man had to return sooner or later to his daughter. But he wouldn't wager a farthing against Hensleigh finding another bolt hole, so keeping a close eye on said daughter made complete sense.

Lucy.

He lengthened his stride. Her name was no concern of his. Nor was she, or her soft coppery curls, any concern of his. Except that she was damnably inconvenient. She might not be any concern of his, but he couldn't quite put aside the niggling question of her fate if he brought her father to utter ruin.

Fitch's real friendly with Lu. Gives 'er money sometimes, 'e does.

He gritted his teeth. It was highly likely that Lucy Hensleigh had already guarded against being tangled in her father's fate in the form of the friendly Fitch. Not hard to imagine what a man would give her money for.

You could do better for her than the sort of protector she'll have picked up around here...

He pushed the thought aside. It would be tantamount to blackmail. *'I'm going to ruin your father. Bed with me and you won't go down with him.'* Charming, and he was damned if he wanted an unwilling mistress. He doubted Miss Lucy Hensleigh liked him above half, anyway. There was no reason why she should like him and she would like him even less if she uncovered his deception. He didn't much like himself for having done that.

She'd like you well enough if you were getting her out of the gutter...

As it was...the merry, dancing sweep of a violin

scattered his thoughts. He slowed, glanced around and spotted the fiddler on the other side of the narrow street near a corner. And frowned. It was a lad. But the sound of that particular fiddle, and the dancing, jigging tune seemed familiar. He looked more closely at the lad.

A mere stripling, barely breeched from the look of him, he wore an ill-fitting shabby coat and a cap hid his hair. A pale cheek was tucked lovingly against the mellow timber of the instrument as he stroked magic from it. Another cap lay at his feet. As James watched several people tossed in coins. Another, smaller boy hovered nearby.

Dodging between the traffic, James crossed to the south side of the street. He felt in his pocket and found a coin. Not seeming so much as to glance at the fiddler and his companion, James dropped the coin in the cap as he passed.

Lucy watched Mr Remington go as she continued to play. Her stomach had tied itself in knots. Why, she had no idea. It was no bread and butter of his if she kept herself from starving by playing in the street. Although, since he already owed Papa money, she supposed he might be annoyed if he'd realised whose cap he'd dropped money into. She glanced down and her playing faltered. A crown gleamed fatly amongst the pennies and farthings—more than she'd earn in a week.

'Fitch—'

He was already scooping it up. It disappeared safely into some fastness in his clothing. Sometimes people would pretend to lean down to put money in, but actually take money out. Fitch's watchful eye prevented that, for which she gave him a share of the take. The crown meant money for the rent and a hearty meal for both of them tonight.

'Generous cove,' he said.

'He's the one I told you about.' Lucy kept playing.

'Right.' He stepped back, leaning against the wall again.

Lucy changed the tune, sliding into a sentimental ballad she'd heard someone singing the week before. She played with the melody, embellishing it here, tweaking it there. A few people stopped to listen and more coins tinkled in the open case. She smiled, nodding thanks as they moved on, and slipped back into a dance tune.

'Bloke's comin' back,' Fitch muttered.

Her breath caught as she played, watching from the corner of her eye as Mr Remington passed on the other side of the street. This time he didn't glance their way and the twisting knot in her belly loosened. Clearly he'd gone to her lodgings, found her not there and left.

She played on, smiling as people left coins, keeping a watchful eye on the weather, trying not to think about Mr Remington. He meant nothing to her. She had to think of important things—such as how to climb out of the hole her father was digging for them.

You could write to Uncle Bertram—Aunt Caroline might write you a reference. She might know someone who needs a governess, or a companion.

Four years ago, after Grandmama died, they had forced Papa to take her away, since they had not wished to house her. A reference would not cost them anything. Except of course they would probably refuse to pay for the letter she sent them.

A chilly breeze skittered along the pavement, fluttering skirts and awnings, bringing with it the steely scent of rain. Thunder rumbled a warning in the distance. She looked up at the sky; heavy clouds threatened.

'Reckon it's time to pack up.' Fitch was watching the sky, too. 'No folks'll be willing to part with a groat if 'n it comes on to rain like it's makin' to.'

Lucy was already loosening her violin strings. She wouldn't risk a drenching for her elderly instrument. She slid the violin and bow back into the case propped against the wall behind her and fastened the hinged end.

She looked at Fitch. 'Are you hungry? I am.' A

slight understatement, that. She was starving. Last night's dinner had been scanty and there'd been nothing for breakfast either this morning or yesterday.

'Yeah.' Fitch scooped up the day's take.

'Well,' Lucy said, 'we could break that crown buying dinner and split the remainder.'

The boy nodded. 'No one won't notice you in them clothes if we go to the Maid an' Magpie. Not if you don't speak too much.'

Lucy's stomach flipped. No one ever seemed to notice that the 'lad' playing fiddle was in fact a lass, but she'd never gone into a tavern.

'Walk into the Maid in yer own clothes an' you'll get yer bum pinched or worse,' Fitch said. 'An' if you do go back an' change there'll be more folks in there. Come *on*,' he urged. 'Be raining frogs in a coupla minutes.'

She dragged in a deep breath. 'All right. Let's go.'

He gave her a cheeky grin. 'It'll be fine. You'll see. The Maid does a bang-up steak-an'-kidney pie.'

The bang-up steak-and-kidney pie warmed Lucy as she hurried home along the rain-slicked street. As well as her fiddle, she had more food tucked under her arm. She had taken off her coat and swathed the violin case in it and she broke into a run as the tunnel leading into Frenchman's Yard came in view.

In addition to the bread and cheese she had bought for breakfast, and the treat of a bag of jellied eels for supper, there was a whole shilling left over for the rent. Tomorrow she could earn more money, although she couldn't hope for such luck as had favoured her today.

She ducked into the shelter of the tunnel and eased back to a walk, catching her breath. For once no one was snoring off a pint of gin in the putrid passageway. She held her breath and hurried through, coming out blinking into the relatively fresh air of the yard.

Although the rain had eased, the wind had turned bitter, slicing to the bone, and she dashed across the yard and into the lodging house. Her landlady did not look out from the kitchen door at the back of the dingy hall and Lucy hurried up the stairs, ignoring the ominous creaks.

She dug into the pocket of her breeches for the key and pulled it out, juggling her fiddle and the package of food. Her cold fingers fumbled the key into the lock and turned it. Lord, she'd be glad to get out of these icy, sodden clothes. Perhaps when she gave Mrs Beattie the extra shilling, the woman would let her dry them, or even herself, by the kitchen fire. Sometimes Mrs Beattie could be obliging about things like that. And sometimes not. Although an extra shilling was an excellent sweetener for the woman's uncertain moods.

Closing the door, she breathed a sigh of relief. Home. Such as it was. With a shilling and supper.

'A profitable day, Miss Hensleigh?'

Her breath jerked in on a startled gasp as she dropped the key and whipped around, bobbling her belongings. Somehow she saved the violin, grabbing it frantically as it slipped, but the food scattered on the floor.

Back pressed to the door, her eyes adjusting to the gloom, she saw Mr Remington rise frowning from the chair by the empty grate. Sick fear swooped through her with understanding. He'd recognised her. Known she was out and deliberately let her see him leave. Then he'd circled around to wait, realising that she'd never come home alone knowing he was here.

She found her voice through the choking fright. 'Mrs Beattie will come up if I scream.' She hoped. Mrs Beattie ought not to have let him in.

Mr Remington's frown deepened as he came towards her. 'Why would you scream now, if you didn't when I startled you?'

Was he an idiot? Or simply so arrogant he thought she'd welcome his attentions? She reached behind her for the door knob just as he bent to pick up the fallen loaf of bread. She stared.

'What are you doing?' Her voice was barely a squeak.

'Picking up your—ah, bread.' He straightened. 'Where should I throw this?'

'*Throw* it? Just put it on the table, please.'

He stared at her. 'It's been on the floor! Surely you aren't—'

'I can't afford to be quite so nice in my notions as you!' Anger swept away fear. 'Place it on the table, if you please.'

His jaw dropped. 'You're still going to eat it?'

'Unless *you've* walked something in, the floor is clean enough.' For heaven's sake! She'd swept and scrubbed yesterday. Her cheeks burned with humiliation as, saying nothing, he put the loaf on the table.

She set the violin down and scooped her supper of jellied eels back into its bag.

'I'm sorry.'

At the sound of his deep voice, she nearly dropped the eels again.

'What?'

'Is it so hard to believe I'd apologise for startling you into dropping your supper?' A shade of annoyance crept into his voice.

She looked up. 'Oh.'

'Although,' he went on, picking up the cheese, 'I'm damned if I know why you thought you needed to scream afterwards. You know why I'm here.'

'Do I?' she asked. 'You sneak back here and wait for me in the dark, despite the fact that my father obviously hasn't returned, and wonder why I think I might need to scream?'

Even in the bad light she saw two spots of scarlet spring to his cheeks as he stared at her. For a moment he said nothing. Then, 'That, Miss Hensleigh, is insulting. You thought I'd assault you?'

'The possibility occurred to me,' she said, refusing to back down, even though his outrage was obvious and she was fairly sure she'd been mistaken. But something niggled at her. If she was mistaken, then why *had* he come back? 'It's not as though I know you at all,' she pointed out. 'Let alone well enough to judge your character!' And given the foolish attraction she seemed to have for him, it was doubly important to be on her guard. Why had he come back?

James reined in his anger, forced himself to see her side. She had come home to find a near-stranger waiting in the dark. And it wasn't as if he had a particularly good reason for waiting. He gritted his teeth. She wasn't to know that while he might seduce a willing woman, he certainly wouldn't assault or force one.

'I apologise.' That made two apologies inside of five minutes. 'So your father hasn't returned?'

'No.'

He waited, but she said nothing more, merely got a dish from a shelf and the—what was that mess in the bag?—jellied eels on the table and put them with the bread and cheese he'd salvaged. The plate rattled a little as she set it down and he looked closely.

Damn it, she was shivering, her lips nearly blue. 'You should get out of those wet clothes,' he said, trying very hard not to notice the long, lovely line of her legs in the breeches and wrinkled stockings. Or the way the damp sleeves of the rough shirt clung to her slender arms. He could only thank God that she wore a waistcoat. 'Tell me where the fuel is and I'll light the fire.'

Her chin lifted. 'There's no need.'

'The devil there isn't,' he said. 'You must be half-frozen.'

Her soft mouth set in a stubborn line he was coming to know. 'I'll be perfectly fine once I change. Which I'll do when you've left.'

'You need a fire,' he insisted. 'Where is the fuel?'

'There isn't any,' she said at last. 'I...I forgot to order it.'

Colour stained her cheeks again and at last the truth sank in—she couldn't afford fuel. Her bastard of a father had left her high and dry to shift for herself and she couldn't afford fuel. That was why she'd been playing on the street.

He strode to the door.

'You're leaving?'

He paused with his hand on the latch. Did she have to sound so damned relieved? 'I'm getting fuel,' he growled. 'Change while I'm gone.'

Lucy stared at the door which had shut with something very like a bang. Who did he think he was, ordering her about? Was she a child? Incapable of thinking for herself? She wasn't answerable to him.

But somewhere inside, beyond the reach of chilly clothing, there was a comforting warmth that someone cared enough to scold about wet clothes and insist on a fire. Even though he'd find it impossible to obtain wood or coal at this hour, it was kind of him to try. Although if he were planning to wait and see if Papa showed up this evening, he might be thinking of his own comfort.

She glanced around. She daren't change in her curtained-off corner in case he came back. Shivering, she collected her gown from its hook in the corner, holding it out at arm's length to keep it dry, and hurried into the other room.

By the time she had peeled off her damply clinging clothes, rubbed herself down briskly and dressed again, she'd heard the door open and close. Assured footsteps sounded. She was still cold. Not the bone-numbing cold of before, but cold. A fire would have been lovely, but a dish of jellied eels later would do.

She sighed. Good manners dictated that she offer bread and cheese to her unwelcome guest.

She opened the door to the parlour. At least he wouldn't have found fuel, so she wouldn't have to pay him for—

A heaped bucket of coal stood beside the hearth with a pile of kindling and Mr Remington was crumpling up old newspaper. She swallowed, saying farewell to the rent money.

'Where did you get that?'

He kept crumpling. 'Your landlady.'

'Oh. Er…thank you. I'll pay her in the morning.' And there, right there, was a lie—she didn't have enough money. She steeled herself. 'How much was it?'

'I've paid her.'

'Paid her?'

'Yes. Come and sit down.' He began to set kindling on top of the paper with a quick efficiency that surprised her. Not at all like her uncle or cousin, neither of whom had ever laid a fire.

He'd set the chair for her and—she blushed at the sight—he'd placed the blanket from her pallet on it. Something in her trembled at the thought of him touching her bedding.

Idiot! He probably handled it with his gloves on to avoid catching anything!

'How much do I owe you?' She kept her voice

steady, but Papa would be furious if it came out of his winnings.

'What?' His voice was brusque as he reached for the tinder box she'd had no use for in weeks. 'Wrap that blanket around yourself.'

'I can look after myself,' she said, sitting in the chair and tucking the threadbare blanket around her shoulders.

'Then next time, don't stay out so long that you risk taking a chill,' he answered, setting the touch-wood to the paper.

She choked back the urge to explain herself. She owed him no explanation—only whatever he had paid Mrs Beattie for the fuel.

'I owe you money for the coal. How much?'

There was a moment's silence except for the crackle as the fire took hold. 'Don't worry about it,' he said at last, standing up and stepping back from the fire.

'Sir—Mr Remington—'

'It doesn't matter,' he said. 'How often do you perform in the street?'

That was none of his business either, but she supposed there was no harm in answering. 'Every so often.' The warmth from the leaping fire reached her, seeped into the chill.

'I suppose you think the clothes are a disguise.'

She glared up at him, holding out her hands to the blaze. 'No one else has ever noticed!'

'You think?'

The sarcasm stung, but she ignored it. 'They didn't even notice in the tavern we—'

'*Tavern?*' Grey eyes bored into her. 'What the hell were you doing in a damn tavern, dressed as a boy no less?'

'Eating my dinner,' she shot back.

'In a tavern,' he repeated. 'And how do you know you weren't noticed?'

'Because,' she said without thinking, 'no one pinched my bum!'

There was a moment of stunned silence she could have cut.

'Your—*what?*'

She gritted her teeth. Her grandparents, Grandpapa in particular, had spent years teaching her to curb her temper and think before she spoke. This man somehow undermined her hard-won self-control. Well, she'd said it and there was no use pretending she hadn't. Or that he hadn't heard, and probably said, worse. Gentlemen did. Even her grandfather had used a few choice words when his favourite mare stepped on his foot.

'My bum,' she said. 'Fitch said if—'

'Fitch?'

'The boy with me. He said if I—'

'*That* was Fitch?'

'*Yes*. He said it was safer to stay in the boys'—' His tone of voice registered and fear curled through her. He'd sounded as if he knew something of Fitch. 'Why are you interested in him?' She could think of any number of reasons to be interested in Fitch. Especially if you carried an expensive watch and chain, and a purse that dripped crowns...

'Someone mentioned him as a friend of yours.' He sounded angry.

'Is there something wrong with that?' she demanded.

The hands that had built the fire so easily curled to fists. 'Apparently not. I'm sure your father approves.'

She snorted. 'Papa's never laid eyes on Fitch.'

James reined in the rising anger. None of this was her fault. Not even the fact that he didn't know whether to be relieved or worried that her supposed protector was a mere child. It was none of his concern. So why had he gone down and fronted the grimy Mrs Beattie to buy fuel for the girl? Why the hell was he still here? His body had a very obvious answer and it wasn't one he entirely liked.

'Where does he live?'

Overhead something creaked and the girl's gaze flickered upward as she frowned.

'Something up there?' James asked.

'I hope not another leak,' she said. 'It's probably a cat. They fight on the roof. Are you going to leave?'

'Soon enough,' he said. 'Where does the boy live?'

'Hereabouts,' she said eventually.

'Where?'

'Nowhere, really. He's an orphan. He picks up a living where he can.'

James bit back an oath. It didn't take much intelligence to work out what that living would involve. And it wasn't uncommon for pickpockets to use a street performer as a cover. 'Hell's teeth, girl! Where have your wits gone begging?' he ground out, fear clawing at his belly. 'If he plies that trade while you're playing your fiddle, you'll both hang!'

'He doesn't!' she flared.

'Oh, for God's sake!' At least she wasn't pretending not to know what he meant. 'It's—'

'Not while I'm playing,' she insisted. 'He promised and I give him half the money anyway.'

Something about the very quietness of her response convinced him. 'Half the money?' he demanded. 'Why?'

She rolled her eyes. 'Because I'd lose at least half of it to people pretending to put money in, of course!' she explained as one who states the obvious, as he supposed it was.

'And Fitch stops that.'

'Yes. And other…that is, pickpockets, stay away.'

She hesitated, then said, 'Because they think it's his pitch.'

'If he's a thief,' he said bluntly, 'you're a damn fool to associate with him.'

Her chin came up. 'He's my friend,' she said. 'And *he* doesn't swear at me.'

James cleared his throat. '*Bum* is a word not usually learned in polite circles,' he pointed out.

'Well,' she amended, 'I don't think he does so deliberately.' The bright eyes narrowed. 'You seem to have learned it.'

'But not in polite circles,' he said, fighting a grin at the neat way she'd turned the tables on him.

She shrugged. 'Since I'm clearly not in polite circles here, I can't see that it matters. Let me assure you that I wouldn't have said it in my grandmother's drawing room.'

'Your grandmother has a drawing room?' Had Miss Hensleigh just implied that she didn't think he was polite?

Her mouth tightened. 'She did when she was alive.'

That didn't really surprise him. Hensleigh's manners and speech were those of a gentleman. He hadn't been born in the gutter, even if he was damn close to ending in one and dragging his daughter with him. And there was the nub. After two brief meetings, James couldn't stomach the thought of Hensleigh taking the girl down with him. Damn it, she shouldn't be eating in a tavern with a pickpocket, or living in these shabby rooms. She shouldn't know such things exist—

He looked up as the roof creaked again.

She glanced at the window uneasily. 'You should go,' she said.

He scowled. 'For God's sake! If I had designs on your virtue I'd have it by now!' And could have kicked himself as she flushed. It wasn't quite the truth, either...

'No.' She rose and walked over to the window. 'But it's getting dark. The streets aren't safe around here at night.'

She was worried about him? No, she just wanted him gone. But her warning had reminded him of something. 'Do you know a fellow called Kilby?'

Her brow knotted. 'Kilby? No.' She didn't sound entirely sure. After a moment, she said, 'At least, Papa knows him, I think. I heard him mention the name once to someone who came home with him.'

'He brought someone home?' It hadn't been easy finding out where Hensleigh lived. That the man was fool enough to bring anyone home surprised him.

'Not exactly. It was more like the other man had followed him. Papa never brings anyone home. I was asleep at first. I think he caught up with Papa at the door. They argued and I woke up. The man asked for time, but I remember Papa saying that since Kilby had them, it was too late. That he, the other man, should make himself scarce—'

'Vowels.' James muttered it, almost to himself. From what he'd learned, Hensleigh was in the habit of selling debts on to the mysterious Kilby. Kilby bought them at a discount and charged the full amount, plus interest.

'Gambling debts?'

He glanced at her. 'What else? Your father probably sold the fellow's debts to this Kilby. Did he see you?'

'Who?' She looked rather puzzled at first, but then her brow cleared. 'Oh, the man who followed Papa home? No. I told you. I was asleep. And it wasn't here anyway.'

'Not here?'

She went very pink. 'We've only been here a couple of months. It was just before we moved.'

A ball of tension unknotted in his gut. He'd seen enough of the men Hensleigh associated with to feel cold all over at the thought of any of them knowing about this girl. Apparently the man had the sense to change his lodgings every so often to throw any pursuit off the scent. 'Good,' he said.

She was watching him, an odd expression on her face. 'If you're going to take the money for the coal off what you owe Papa, he won't like it.'

'What?' For a moment he had no idea what she

was talking about. 'What I owe—?' Too late he realised that he had tripped himself up. 'Look, the coal was nothing. It doesn't—'

But her eyes had narrowed. He could see her putting it together. He braced himself.

'If you owed him money,' she said finally, 'there was no reason to come back today, let alone wait.' Her voice was very quiet. 'You could hardly suppose he wouldn't call on you as soon as he returned. But if he owes you money—' she bit her lip and he knew an urge to reach out, stroke away the small hurt '—then there was every reason to return and wait, wasn't there?'

'Yes,' he said. There was no point denying it, even if he could bring himself to lie to her again.

'So you lied to me,' she said, as if being lied to was perfectly normal. 'How much?'

His mind blanked for a moment. 'How much for what?' he countered. What sort of idiot couldn't keep a lie straight in his head? Somehow this girl unravelled his wits and scattered them to the winds.

She swallowed and the silent jerk of her throat stabbed at him. 'How much does he owe you?'

He didn't know whether to be disappointed or relieved that she wasn't offering to barter herself for the debt.

He hesitated. She was already pale, her mouth set as if braced for a blow. A blow he didn't want to strike. He clenched his fists, gritting his teeth. The time for lies was past. Well, almost. 'One hundred pounds.' He could not bring himself to tell her the full amount.

It was a shameful fact that Lucy had never, not once in her life, come close to fainting. Her cousin Jane had prided herself on her ability to faint dead away with becoming grace at the slightest provocation, be it a spider, a snake or the admiring glance of an eligible gentleman. Jane had been as much admired for her exquisite sensibility as for her beauty. Lucy never felt so much as dizzy. Spiders didn't bother her, she thought the occasional snake she saw was far more scared of her than she was of it and gentlemen never noticed her.

But now the abyss along which her father had skirted, week after week, month after month and year after year, gaped at her feet, a black, fathomless pit that threatened to swallow her whole. Her vision greyed... She couldn't really be off balance, because there didn't seem to be a floor to be off balance on, and she was falling...and then, not.

For a blinding instant she was conscious of the power of his arms, the sheer strength of his body, as he caught her, steadied her. For one wild, insane moment she knew the urge to remain there. *Safe.* Then, with a fierce wrench, she fought to free herself, shoving away from him, willing her head to stop spinning, her knees to hold and her lungs to draw air. *Safe?* Whatever else this man might be, he wasn't *safe*.

'Let me *go*!' She struggled, but he held her tightly.

'Don't be an idiot, Lucy!' he said. 'You damn near fainted on me!'

'I don't faint!' Somehow she was sitting in the chair he had vacated, his hands still gripping her shoulders. 'And I have not said you may call me Lucy!'

He snorted. 'What else should I call you? We both know Hensleigh is not your real name.'

That struck home. She said quietly, 'Please let me go.' If he didn't—

He let her go and she reached up to rub her shoulder where he had gripped her, where the shock of his touch shivered in her flesh.

His brows snapped together. 'I'm sorry,' he said stiffly, as though the words shamed him. 'I didn't mean to hurt you.'

She couldn't explain that he hadn't hurt her. She couldn't explain that shivery feeling even to herself. Her throat worked. 'One hundred pounds.' The words jerked out all anyhow. 'How? When?' Clearly Papa was not with his mistress—one hundred pounds was a fortune and Papa had run.

And he didn't take you. Didn't even bother to warn

you. Heat pricked behind her eyes. With that much money she could—

'That amount shocks you?'

The bitter tone, more than the words, did it. Inside her something shattered into molten shards, drying her eyes in the white-hot blaze. What did he have to be bitter about? Her father might or might not come back. All the money he had won a few weeks ago was gone. At best he had left town to play elsewhere until he had enough to pay off—

'I suppose Remington is not really your name, sir?' she forced out.

He looked annoyed as he pulled out an elegant silver card case. 'Cambourne.' He handed her a card. 'Remington is the family name.'

Family name? She looked at the card. Cambourne. And not merely *Mr Cambourne*, but *Lord* Cambourne, a belted earl, no less. No wonder Papa had run. There would be very few places he could play profitably in London without having paid off this debt. Fear choked her. She knew her father's code. A debt like this would be paid before all else. Before the rent for their lodgings, before food—well, food for her. He'd buy himself a meal on the way home, give Mrs Beattie a shilling to keep her sweet and tell his daughter there was no money. Why on earth had she ever thought she owed him the least vestige of loyalty? And yet…he was her father. She remembered him from her childhood before Mama died, kind when he was at home, often bringing her a present, a sweet or a cake. Once a painted wooden brooch—a bird perched singing on a twig. *And he sold the jewellery Grandmama left you.* Her fingers went to her chest, felt the locket through the threadbare gown. Not quite all. Just what he'd known about. Sold it and pocketed the money. Sworn he'd make their fortunes. He'd made that fortune, all right. She'd been dazed, dazzled, sure that at last she was safe, that she'd have a proper home. And then he'd lost most of it the following week.

Lord Cambourne said nothing and she fought to ignore his presence. One hundred pounds. Papa had won five times as much a few weeks ago. He'd let her have some money that time. Enough to buy food, the beeswax and pay off the arrears on their lodgings. Otherwise Mrs Beattie would have kicked them out. There was nothing left of what he'd given her. And with what she could earn, she would be lucky to have enough to eat for a week if she ate one meal a day, and only then if Mrs Beattie didn't insist on being paid again next week.

'I don't know where he is,' she said again. Folly to keep repeating it. Either Lord Cambourne believed her, or he did not. There was nothing she could do about it.

He was watching her. Those dark-grey eyes

seemed to look right through her and see things she preferred to keep hidden. She lifted her chin, praying that the choking fear was not apparent. Praying that he would leave so that she could *think*.

'You should leave.' Pretending that Mr Remington, or Lord Cambourne, or whatever he wished to call himself, was a welcome visitor was beyond her.

James hesitated. There was no reason to linger. Any more than there had been reason to stay this long. And yet he didn't want to go. Lucy Hensleigh, or whatever she called herself, bothered him. The idea of her going out alone, performing in the street for pennies, didn't exactly shock him; that twisting in his gut wasn't shock. Oh, there was shock all right. But it was shock at how he was feeling about her. How he felt about her being here alone, her father having seemingly abandoned her. And shock at the feel of her slender body in his arms a few moments ago. He hadn't wanted to let her go.

Hell's teeth! If a debt of one hundred pounds had rattled her that badly, how would she have taken the truth? Or that his intention was to sell the debt on?

It wasn't James's responsibility. He'd bought coal so she'd have some warmth. She had food. And he was due at a late supper back in St James's, after which he had a ball to attend. Not that it would matter overly if he were late... Damn it to hell and back! How safe was she here?

'Beyond the man who followed him home, your father's friends don't call?'

She shook her head. 'No.'

Relief breathed through him. He hoped it would stay that way.

'And you've really no idea when he will return?'

The soft mouth turned mulish 'No. There's no point asking again. You either believe me or you don't. He's disappeared before. Never for more than a few days.'

The roof creaked loudly and she jumped.

'Miss Hensleigh, are you sure you don't mind being here alone?' James asked gently. He couldn't blame her for being nervous. *And what can you do about it? Offer to remain with her?*

'I'm not alone,' she pointed out. 'You're here. And I don't like it!'

James clenched his fists. *He* was making her nervous? He let out a breath. He couldn't blame her for that. Reluctantly, he walked to the door. 'I'll bid you goodnight.'

She stared at him. 'You're actually leaving?'

'Yes. Bolt the door behind me.'

She rose, graceful even in her shabby gown with a threadbare blanket around her. 'I always do at night.'

'Good.' The door wasn't strong enough to keep

anyone out who really wanted to get in, but at least the noise would warn her.

James opened the door, turned and held out his hand to her. 'Goodnight.'

After a moment's hesitation she placed her hand in his, slowly, as if she doubted the wisdom of doing so. His fingers closed over hers gently, he felt them quiver, heard the soft intake of breath as his clasp tightened. Such a small hand and so cold in his. A steel band seemed to clamp about his chest as startled green eyes met his, her lips parted slightly, and he fought the shocking urge to lean forward and taste them, find out if they would tremble in response.

Heat licked through him at the thought, but instead he covered her hand with his other one. 'Promise me that you'll sit by the fire long enough to warm up properly.' The thought of her cold and so alone haunted him. She ought not to be left alone, but he couldn't stay. Didn't dare. Damn her father to hell for leaving her like this.

Her chin lifted, revealing the slender column of her throat. 'Do you think I can't look after myself?'

He doubted it. Not if some bastard decided to help himself. He ignored the urge to behave like one of the aforementioned bastards and trace the ivory line of her throat with one finger, discover the swift pulse beating beneath silk-soft skin… His fingers tightened on hers. 'I think that you shouldn't have to,' he said at last. Wanting her was bad enough, the warring urge to look after her, keep her safe even from himself, make sure she was never cold or hungry ever again, was more than foolish—it ranked close to insanity. There was no point elaborating on the dangers; those wary eyes told him that she knew them already, recognised him as one of them. And if she considered him a danger she was not interested in becoming his mistress. She had not even tried to influence him or buy him off with a little flirtation, or by making play with wet lashes over her father's debt. He had to respect that.

Reluctantly, he released her hand and stepped back. 'Bolt the door behind me,' he repeated. Somehow he got the door open and shut with himself outside it before his resolution failed. He waited, heard the squeak and thud as she shot the bolt with what sounded like unwonted vigour.

His brows rose. 'Goodnight to you, too, Miss Hensleigh.'

There was a moment's silence. Then, 'Goodnight, sir.' Stiff, reluctant. Rather as if she would have preferred to consign him to Hades.

Chapter Three

Lucy listened to the steady steps and accompanying creaks as he crossed the landing. Heard him descend the stairs and heaved a sigh of what ought to have been relief, and felt frighteningly like regret. Shivering, she lifted the hand he had held to her breast. The strong pressure of his fingers, the enveloping warmth, lingered. He had held her hand as if he cared about her.

He held your hand for a moment in farewell. It meant nothing. Less than nothing to him.

He was gone. So why did the bright edge of tension still score her? Why did it matter that he had held her hand? Worse, why did she wish he was still holding it? She'd been wrong about his motive for waiting; he wanted Papa, not her. Lord! He'd been insulted at the very suggestion. And yet he'd held her hand in that odd way. Tenderly. As if he hadn't wanted to let her go.

He was kind, that was all. Buying fuel, lighting the fire.

Why? Papa owes him a small fortune.

Suspicious cynicism was not one of her more attractive traits, but she couldn't afford naivety. In the last four years she'd learned to be wary of seeming kindness. People, especially men, wanted something in return. She'd learnt very quickly what men usually wanted from a girl—something that meant less than nothing to them, but would spell disaster for her. Papa had also realised that very quickly. It was why he never brought anyone back to their lodgings if he could avoid it. Just the young man who had followed him a couple of months ago and now Cambourne.

He ought to be your enemy. Remember what Grandpapa was used to say? Beware of Greeks bearing gifts.

She wasn't sure about the origin of the quote, but thought it might be Homer. Someone had been suspicious about the Trojan Horse, as well they might. She had not been permitted to read Homer, of course. Grandmama had frowned on young girls reading anything more inflammatory than a book of sermons and Homer definitely counted as inflammatory.

The roof creaked loudly and she hurried to the window. She pushed the casement open and stepped back. A moment later Fitch swung through the window, to land catlike and dripping.

'What the hell did his nibs want?' he demanded. 'Bit of a dolly roll?'

'No,' Lucy said. At least she hoped not if Fitch meant what she thought he meant.

Fitch snorted. 'Right.'

'He wants my father. I told you.'

The boy gave a shrug as he dripped his way over to the fire. 'Just bet he does. But that ain't to say he can't chase a bit of tail on the side.' He held out his hands to the blaze. 'Nice. You buy fuel with the extra shilling?'

'He bought it,' Lucy admitted.

Fitch's eyes narrowed. 'Did he now? An' you reckon—'

The stairs groaned under a heavy, uneven tread. The two of them froze.

'Mrs Beattie,' Lucy whispered, panic clutching at her insides.

Fitch made for the window, but voices floated up from the yard. 'Damn!' he muttered, hesitating.

'The bedroom!' Lucy said. 'She's no reason to go in there!'

Silent as a hunting cat, Fitch disappeared into the other room.

Lucy unbolted the door, then sat at the table and strove to appear unconcerned as the steps waddled over the complaining landing. The door rattled under the less-than-genteel knock.

'Come in!' She put on her best welcoming voice.

Mrs Beattie came in, eyes darting about. 'Gorn, is he?'

'Yes.' *As if you didn't know!* Very little got past the eagle-eyed landlady. 'And I would prefer it if you did not permit strangers to wait for me.'

Mrs Beattie shrugged. 'Called yestiddy, didn' he? An' this afternoon, lookin' for yeh.' She scowled. 'Not but what I didn' know he'd slipped back this evenin'. Not till he come lookin' for coal.'

'Oh. I see.' Getting past Mrs Beattie unnoticed was nigh on impossible, but given the woman's annoyance, apparently Cambourne had done it. 'Can I help you with something?'

Mrs Beattie scowled. 'In a manner of speakin'. You an' me need to have a little talk about money, missy.'

Lucy's stomach lurched. 'The rent is due Friday. And I understood the coal was paid for.'

Mrs Beattie's lips pursed, and Lucy could almost see her wondering if it was worth trying to gouge a little extra on the coal.

'It was,' the woman admitted and Lucy let out a breath she hadn't realised she'd been holding. 'It's the extra rent you an' me got to talk about.'

'Extra rent?' The words felt thick on her tongue.

The landlady wiped greasy hands on her apron. 'Aye. Yeh can bring a trick up here, long as yer quiet. But usin' the rooms fer business, that's extra rent.'

James strode back along the Strand towards Whitehall. He was going to be late to supper if he didn't hurry. He kept an eye open for trouble and a hand on the loaded pistol in his coat pocket.

The streets aren't safe around here at night.

Nor during the day for that matter. Not for a woman alone. And yet she traversed them daily. Unbidden, the image of her in boys' clothes, slender legs encased in breeches, came to him. The threadbare, poorly fitting clothes had hidden everything. Perhaps he'd only known because he'd recognised the sound of her violin. Then he'd looked properly, seen the delicate line of her jaw, watched the slender hands coaxing magic from the violin. No one else had spotted the graceful girl hiding in the shabby suit. Even in the tavern. Ill-lit and crowded, she must have passed unnoticed. But it bothered him.

She ought not to be performing in the street.

So is she supposed to starve in ladylike silence to suit your notions of respectability?

Her father is damn well supposed to look after her! Not leave her earning pennies playing the fiddle.

And there was the rub. Her father. The man who

owed him a thousand pounds. Who'd set the mysterious Kilby's enforcers after Nick and left Lucy to shift for herself. The man he'd sworn to ruin.

'Good God! What brings you down this way, Cambourne?'

James stared at the gentleman descending from a hackney cab. 'Montgomery.' He acknowledged the viscount with a cool nod. 'A business matter.' He didn't bother to ask what brought Montgomery this way. The man had an unsavoury reputation for preferring the brothels down here. Brothels that were fussy neither about the age nor willingness of their girls. Or, it was whispered, how the customers treated them.

'Business? Down here?' Montgomery looked amused and slightly disdainful. 'My man of affairs deals with anything to do with the City.'

The cab driver coughed. 'Beggin' your pardon, milor'—'

Montgomery turned, scowling. 'Yes, yes, my good man. Really, such a fuss over a paltry shilling or two.'

The jarvey said nothing, but James saw the anxiety underlying the scorn in his eyes.

'The man has his living to earn, Montgomery.'

Montgomery sighed, produced the fare from his pocket and handed it over. 'Really, Cambourne. Next you'll be telling me that you pay your tailor when he duns you!'

'Not exactly,' James said. 'He doesn't dun me, because I pay when he bills me.'

Montgomery looked pained. 'How very respectable. Well, I'm off to partake in the joys of the flesh. I've a nice, fresh game pullet reserved. Care to come along? I'm sure we can find something for you.' The smirk suggested he knew what the response would be.

James didn't bother to hide his distaste. 'Thank you. No.' He glanced at the jarvey, who was easing his horse away from the curb. 'I'm going back to Mayfair. Do you want the fare?'

The horse stopped at once. 'Glad of it, guv,' said the jarvey.

'Thank you. I won't hold you up.' He swung open the door and stepped into the cab.

Montgomery shuddered. 'Really, Cambourne! You don't thank a jarvey.'

James leaned on the open window. 'Is that so? I find thanking people ensures better, more willing service. You might try it with your game pullet.'

Montgomery's laughter was unpleasant. 'Willing? I'm not courting an heiress, man. This one's bought and paid for. Willing doesn't—'

The rest was lost in the rattle of hooves and wheels

as the cab set off. James sat back, frowning. Montgomery always left a nasty taste in his mouth.

A moment later the trap opened. 'Beggin' your pardon, guv. Old horse took off afore you'd finished your chat.'

'An intelligent beast,' said James drily. 'Tell him to take me to Berkeley Street.'

'Righto, guv.'

The trap shut and James leaned back on the squabs. Damn it. If he ruined Hensleigh completely, then Lucy would be on her own. He let out a breath. Perhaps he didn't have to break Hensleigh, or Hammersley, or whatever his name was, entirely. He saw again Nick's battered face and swore.

Lucy had no idea what *trick* meant in this context, but the phrase 'place of business' gave her the clue.

'Lor— Look, Mrs Beattie, you're mistaken.' Instinct warned her against revealing too much about her visitor. 'The gentleman is a friend of my father's.' That was a stretch, but it would do. 'He was looking for him.'

Mrs Beattie gave a snort. 'Listen, dearie, when you an' your pa moved in I was all set to charge 'im for business, but he insisted you was his daughter, an' he weren't selling tricks.' She sniffed. 'Can't say as I really believed 'im at the start, but I gave 'im the lower rate on trial as you might say. But I warned 'im.'

'Warned him?' Lucy scowled at the woman. 'About what?'

Mrs Beattie crossed her arms over her ample bosom. 'Warned 'im if I so much as smelled a suspicion of a trick up here, he'd be paying more.'

Speechless, Lucy stared at her and she went on. 'Now, I dunno if he didn' tell you, or if you just thought you could sneak yer fancy man past me, but—'

'He is *not* my fancy man!' Lucy's face flamed.

The snort this time was of equine proportions. 'Right. An' I'm the Queen o' France,' Mrs Beattie said, with a fine disregard for the fact that the last French queen's head had fallen under the guillotine some years previously. 'It ain't no never mind o' mine, long as you pay up. Mind you...' She looked around. 'Flash gent like that, you play 'im right, you oughta get a nice little house to yerself.'

Outrage bubbled up. 'Mrs Beattie! I am *not*—' Not what? Not playing tricks? 'Not selling myself!'

Mrs Beattie scowled. 'Well, yer a fool, givin' it to him for love. Anyone can see 'e's well-breeched.'

'He came to see if my father had returned!' Lucy insisted.

'That don't take half an hour, nor it don't need no coal,' said the lady with unarguable logic. 'Three shillings a week extra, missy.'

'And does that include coal for business purposes?' Lucy demanded.

The landlady scowled. 'S'pose I could throw in some coal,' she said grudgingly. '*When* you pays the extra.'

Lucy blinked. Clearly sarcasm was wasted on Mrs Beattie. Still, if she was going to be bilked for extra rent this week, she might as well get something out of it. Hopefully, once Mrs Beattie realised her mistake, and that Lord Cambourne was not continuing to call, the rent would drop back.

Mrs Beattie, evidently concluding that she'd completed her business, stumped to the door. Reaching it, she looked back. 'Three shillings extra. Payable Friday.' She went out, closing the door behind her with a triumphant bang.

Lucy sank on to the chair, staring at the closed door as fear choked her. She barely had enough money left to buy food. Now it was Tuesday night. She had no idea if she could earn three shillings for extra rent, as well as eat, between now and Friday. If only she'd stayed out longer, so that Cambourne had given up and gone away without alerting Mrs Beattie. Or even if she hadn't indulged in dinner at the tavern, so she had more money towards the rent, or—

'Well, now there's the devil to pay.' Fitch came out of the bedroom and cast a disgusted glance at the door. He stalked to the fire and held out his hands to the blaze. 'You sure his nibs don't want a roll?'

'A—' Lucy swallowed. 'A roll. Is that like a trick?'

He nodded. 'Yeah. You has a quick roll, or turns a trick.'

Lucy stowed the information away. More knowledge unsuitable for the drawing room. But she wasn't in a safe, protected drawing room.

'He's just looking for my father,' she said. If he'd wanted anything else, there had been nothing to stop him taking it. Although there had been nothing to stop her grandmother's cat killing a mouse instantly, either.

'Might get some rhino from him,' Fitch suggested. 'Since you reckoned as he owes your pa money, he could pay you some on account like.'

Lucy shook her head, flushing at the thought of begging from his lordship. 'No.' Anger rose again. 'He lied about that. Papa owes *him* money. And—' she clenched her fists '—he lied about his name. He isn't Mr Remington at all. He's Lord Cambourne— an earl.'

'Ah.' Fitch scowled. 'Makes more sense, him comin' back, then.' He didn't push it, apparently accepting that a fellow already owed money was an unlikely touch.

'Well, that leaves yer fiddle,' he said. 'Did well enough today.' He hesitated. 'Lu, you know I'd never flam a mark while you're playing the fiddle, don't you?'

She blinked. 'Of course I know that. You promised. Why do you ask?'

He shrugged. 'No reason. Just thinkin'. S'long's you know.'

Memory tugged. 'Did you hear what Lord Cambourne said?'

He scowled. 'Heard that. He said it loud enough.'

She reached out and touched his hand. 'I told him you'd promised. That you wouldn't do that. It will be all right, Fitch. As long as I can earn enough for this week, once she sees Lord Cambourne isn't calling all the time, she'll realise I'm not his...his—'

'Dollymop,' Fitch supplied. He looked sceptical. 'Yeah. Drop the rent right back, she will. Being as how she's so generous an' all. Look, you want me to go away? The old bitch realises I'm sleeping here, it'll be another three shillings.'

'No. Don't go.' Knowing that she wasn't completely alone at night allowed her to sleep better. And she knew that he was off the streets, safe for a few hours.

He cocked his head. 'You sure?'

'Yes. Are you still hungry?' She changed the subject. 'Have some bread and cheese.'

He cut bread and a chunk of cheese to go with it, passed them to her, then cut some for himself.

Munching, he crouched down by the fire. 'Least you flammed some coal outta her for the extra rent,' he said through a mouthful. 'With that an' what his nibs bought you'll starve all nice an' cosy.'

She grimaced. A thought occurred to her. 'Fitch?'

'Yeah?'

'Do you know someone called Kilby?'

He went utterly still, wariness in every line. 'Where'd you hear that name?'

'Lord Cambourne, and I think Papa knows him.'

There was a moment's silence. 'Don't go askin' no questions about Kilby,' Fitch said at last. 'Better if you'd never heard the name. Safer.' He swallowed his mouthful. 'His nibs asks again, tell him you don't know nothin'. Safer,' he repeated.

Kilby was still at his desk when Jig reported to him, but Jig noted with relief that, far from drumming his fingers, the man was eating.

'Jig. What have you got for me?' Kilby bit into a chicken leg.

'Still no sign of Hensleigh, guv,' Jig said, trying not to stare at the rest of the chicken.' His stomach rumbled.

'Girl might be covering for him.' Kilby spoke through a mouthful.

Jig shook his head. 'Don' reckon, guv. Sounds like

she ain't got no money an' the gent come a-calling tonight.'

'Did he now?' Kilby set the half-eaten chicken leg back on the platter. 'Anything on him?'

Jig swallowed spit. God, that chicken smelled good. 'Got a name—Remington.'

Kilby's hand froze halfway to the tankard. 'Remington?'

'Yeah. Struck me, too,' Jig said. 'But it ain't *him*, guv.' Like he wouldn't reckernise a bloke he'd helped beat bloody? Weren't blind, or dicked in the nob, was he?

'No. Of course not.' Kilby took a swallow from the tankard. 'You can describe the fellow?'

Jig nodded. 'Tall. Taller'n me. Well set-up cove. Moves like 'e'd strip to advantage. Real easy on 'is feet. Dark hair. Dresses like quality. Not real bang-up new, but quality.'

'Probably tupping the girl.' Kilby sighed. 'Pity.'

'Woman owns the lodgings reckons that's the way of it,' Jig said. 'Been flapping her mouth all over. But I ain't so sure.'

Kilby stared over the rim of the tankard. 'And what engenders this extraordinary optimism, Jig?'

Allowing that he didn't understand any of them breakteeth words, Jig got the idea. 'Well, you wanted me to find out why young Fitch's earnings was down.'

'Yes?'

'So, I seen 'im hangin' round a lad playin' the fiddle. Right crowd there was.'

'So Fitch *should* have had easy pickings.' Kilby's fingers drummed in such a way that Jig reckoned Fitch had better watch out for himself. 'The little rat's holding out on me, is that it?'

'Not ezackly, guv.' Jig went on. 'Far's I could tell, he weren't picking pockets at all.'

'*What?*'

'No. Just makin' sure no one else helped theirselves to the takin's.'

Kilby sat back. 'Maybe we'd better have a word to this lad with a fiddle.'

'Well, now,' Jig said, 'funny you should say that, guv. I ain't sure it is a lad—'

'What? You said—'

'Reckon it's the girl. Hensleigh's girl, playin' for pennies. And—'

'And why would she be doing that—' Kilby said, looking interested.

'If she's givin' rides to a toff,' Jig finished. 'It don't make sense.'

'No,' Kilby said. 'It doesn't. Get word to Fitch that I want his takings *up*. Nothing else. No word of this. And he's to be given a couple of night jobs.'

'An' the toff? You want me to find out more?'

'No. Keep an eye on the girl.' Kilby's eyes bored

into him. 'I don't have to tell you that she is to remain untouched, do I?'

The party at Aldwick House was in full swing when James arrived. He ran into his host in the first of the open salons.

'Ah, Cambourne.' Viscount Aldwick held out his hand to James. 'Didn't see you in the reception line.'

James shook his hand. 'My apologies to you and Lady Aldwick, sir. I'm afraid I was rather late.'

Aldwick smiled briefly. 'Never mind. As it is, I wonder if you might just slip along to my library. It's not generally open tonight, but someone there would like a word with you.'

The library was lit only by the fire in the hearth and a single branch of candles on the chimneypiece. Shadows filled the room.

'Cambourne?' A dark figure rose from a wing chair by the fire.

James knew the quiet, deep voice. 'Hunt? What the devil are you doing here?' He moved towards the fire. 'How—?' He grimaced. 'I'm sorry. There's no point asking how you are—I saw the notice in the papers about your brother's death. If there's anything I can do…?'

Close enough now to make out Huntercombe's features, he could see lines carved in the older man's face that hadn't been there six months ago. Deep lines and a shadow in the eyes that had nothing to do with the darkness of the room.

Huntercombe smiled briefly. 'Kind of you. I wondered if I might have a word?' He glanced around the library. 'I knew you'd be here tonight, so I sent a note around to Aldwick this afternoon and he told me to make myself at home. I'm not actually invited this evening, at least, I suppose I would have been, but—' He shrugged.

James nodded. A man deep in mourning for his half-brother didn't normally attend balls. The Marquess of Huntercombe was only in town to attend the House of Lords. 'You didn't have to come out like this. I would have come to you.'

Huntercombe reached for a decanter on the wine table beside him. 'I know. But I thought it better to be a trifle circumspect. Brandy?'

James took the chair on the other side of the fireplace. 'Thank you. Circumspect about what?'

'I heard young Remington had a little trouble recently. With a certain Captain Hensleigh.'

James leaned forward. 'How do you know about that?'

Huntercombe's eyes closed. 'Don't worry—it's gone no further. Your cousin's man and my valet happen to be brothers. Is the boy really all right?'

'Bruised, battered. He appears to have learnt his lesson, thank God,' said James.

Huntercombe's eyes opened. 'Then he was luckier than Gerald.' He took a swallow of brandy. 'If, as my valet seems to think, you're hunting Hensleigh, or Hammersley, as Gerald knew him, I have some information for you.'

An hour later, James was still staring into the dancing fire, his mouth set in grim lines. Huntercombe had left thirty minutes ago, but he had no inclination to join the silken, perfumed crowd in the main rooms. Instead he poured another brandy and breathed the heady fumes before sipping.

Huntercombe had said Nick had been lucky. James's fingers tightened on the heavy glass. That was an understatement. There was no longer any question of merely ruining Hensleigh—he was going to use him to get to this mysterious Kilby. And then he'd destroy both of them.

And Lucy? He hardened his resolve. He'd keep her safe, but Huntercombe's story changed the game. Pursuing Lucy gave him the best of all reasons for continuing to call at those shabby lodgings…as long as everyone thought he was after the girl no one would question his visits.

But beyond that, he needed advice from someone who knew the shadowy world he had stumbled into.

* * *

Lucy dreamed. Dark grey eyes smiled at her with inexpressible tenderness. Strong arms held her secure against all threat of danger. Even held her warm and safe from the rain. She nestled a little deeper into the warmth and safety…until the drumming of the rain penetrated.

Literally.

Lucy woke to an icy trickle of water leaking right over her head. With a muttered curse she scrambled out of bed, dragging the thin, lumpy mattress and blankets out of the way.

She stared up at the sagging matchboard ceiling. God only knew where the water was getting in and it didn't matter. What mattered was convincing Mrs Beattie to get it mended.

Five minutes later she was dressed, had the bed shoved against the wall and a bucket under the leak. Catching her cloak off the back of the door, she wrapped it around her and went into the other room. The curtain that hid her usual sleeping place was open, the pallet and blanket empty. The closed window suggested that Fitch had taken his leave by the stairs well before first light to avoid Mrs Beattie.

Lucy's heart sank a little, but she pushed the melancholy aside and cut bread and cheese. The fire had gone out long ago. Briefly she considered relighting it, but dismissed the idea even though there was plenty of coal left. She needed to save it for when she was cold, not waste it on luxuries like toasted cheese. Munching, Lucy looked out of the window. Grey rain swept the yard, battering relentlessly at sagging walls and boarded-up windows.

Rain before seven, fine by eleven...

Armed with this unwarranted optimism, Lucy went downstairs to do battle with Mrs Beattie.

Mrs Beattie puffed up the stairs, grumbling that she'd see for herself. Confronted with the leak, she glared first at it and then at Lucy, as if wanting to blame *her* for it.

''Tain't *my* fault,' she said at last. 'Dessay it'll ease off when it ain't raining.'

Lucy blinked. 'I'm sure it will.'

Mrs Beattie squinted at the leak again. 'Don't reckon as it needs mending,' she said at last. ''Course, you want to put a bucket there, you can.'

'Of course, Mrs Beattie,' said Lucy meekly. 'Would you like me to tell Mr Wynn downstairs why his ceiling is leaking, or will you?'

Mrs Beattie scowled. Mr Wynn had lived in the rooms below for years. He paid his rent on time and extra to eat his dinner in the kitchen. Mrs Beattie would not want to offend him. 'S'pose I can speak to someone about it. 'Tain't my fault,' she repeated, and stumped off, banging the door behind her.

When the bells of St Clement's struck eleven the world still wept and a bitter wind whipped through every crack it could find and drove the rain ruthlessly against the window. There was no point going out, she told herself. She'd be lucky to earn a penny. No one would want to pause to listen to a fiddle in this weather, even if she could find a sheltered spot where her violin and bow would not be ruined.

Three shillings... She was two short.

She changed into her boys' clothes and pulled her shabby old cloak on over them.

She tried a shop awning, the shopkeeper having decided against setting out his wares on a pavement running with water. She had barely played a note before the shopkeeper charged out.

'Here! Be off with you! There's no begging here!'

'I'm not begging, sir.' Lucy kept her head down. 'I'm just playing. If people give me a penny, that's—'

'Hah!' The indignant shopkeeper brandished a heavy stick and swung it at the violin.

Lucy pivoted, taking the blow on her right shoulder to protect the instrument. She cried out, going down on her knee. The man struck again, nearly sending her sprawling.

'Go on! Or there's more of that.' The shopkeeper smacked the stick into his hand. 'Summon the magistrate, I will!'

'All right!' Her shoulder throbbing, Lucy grabbed the case. Fear choked her. If he struck again, hit the violin or bow... She fumbled, struggling to pack the instrument away. Another blow landed and she nearly dropped the violin.

'Hi! Leave 'im be, ya big lummox!'

And Fitch was there, dancing between her and the shopkeeper. 'Got a cloth ear, cully?' the boy demanded, weaving about, dodging a strike from the stick. 'Doncha like a tune? Might bring a few folks into yer scummy shop, it might.'

'Why, you little gutter rat!' The shopkeeper swung at him again.

Fitch leapt out of reach and Lucy had the case closed. She struggled to her feet.

'Come on!' Fitch caught her free arm. It was her right arm and she gasped as he tugged her away.

'And don't come back!' said the shopkeeper. 'I know your sort! Be bringing all your thieving mates next!'

Fitch got her around the corner. 'You all right?'

She nodded.

'Looked like he caught you a good one,' Fitch said, frowning. 'Look, I can't hang about. Gotta work.'

'Fitch!'

He scowled. 'No choice. I'm bein' watched. Bloke I have to hand my take reckons Kilby ain't happy with me.' He glanced around and muttered, 'Gotta go. Said I was off to get food.' He reached out and touched her shoulder. 'That all right?'

She swallowed. 'Don't worry about it. Just be careful.'

He flashed her a cocky grin. ''Course.'

Her stomach clutched in fear as he ran off, turning down an alleyway.

By the end of the day Lucy had sixpence for her efforts and her right arm throbbed with each stroke of the bow. To add to her misery the rain had turned to sleet. Crouched shivering in the entrance to a yard, Lucy packed her instrument away while the wind howled through the dark tunnel behind her, raking her with icy claws.

Tired, cold and wet, she went home, buying a penny loaf on the way.

The Parburys' saloons overflowed with silk, superfine and Bath coating, gossip, wine and scent. Crystal chandeliers flung dancing light on the guests and hothouse flowers bloomed in a battalion of vases.

James worked his way through the knots of people, pausing here and there to greet a friend, nod to an acquaintance. He ducked behind a potted palm when one of his aunts, Lady Callington, hove into view.

Once she had disappeared, he emerged and continued. The last thing he needed was Letty to begin her customary discourse on the disadvantages of his ongoing bachelor state in a room stuffed to the gills with hopeful young ladies and their even-more-hopeful mamas.

Snatches of conversation wafted after him as he navigated the sea of familiar faces.

'Really, I cannot think what dear Jane was thinking to wear that yellow gown. It makes her look so dreadfully...'

'Heaven knows, Mrs Repton's drawing-room curtains are so shabby, one wonders how she receives a guest without blushing for shame...'

'The dinner? Oh, it was dreadful. *Far* too much oil and the asparagus not *quite* fresh, my dear...'

James accepted a glass of champagne from a passing footman and continued, trying not to see a girl in a shabby suit of boy's clothing crouched on the floor of her run-down lodgings, rescuing her dropped supper.

It had rained all day. At least she wouldn't have been out on the streets playing that blasted violin, but had she eaten? He could call on her tomorrow evening, make sure she was all right, and—and see if her father had returned, he reminded himself. Lucy, little though he liked it, had become a means to an—

'James!'

He swung around and there was Nick grinning, his bruises all gone. For a moment he just stared at his cousin, Hunt's shattered voice in his head.

They broke him to pieces, Cambourne. And it was my fault. I told the boy I'd pay no more gaming debts.

James pulled himself together. 'Nick.' He held out his hand, and looked him over critically. Forced himself to speak normally. 'You look a great deal better than the last time I saw you. How was Chiswick? My people looked after you?'

Nick laughed. 'Lord, yes. I was cosseted to within an inch of my life, and—' He broke off. 'Oh, good evening, sir.' He gulped. 'How are you? Is Mama here?'

James turned and smiled at his older cousin and heir, Nick's father. 'William. I thought I'd see you here.'

William Remington nodded at him. 'James.' He surveyed his son. 'Hear you've been out of town, boy.'

Nick flushed and James adopted an air of world-weary experience.

'Just down to James's place at Chiswick, sir,' Nick muttered. 'Er…rusticating, you know.'

William cleared his throat. 'I dare say. No doubt it was inevitable. Still, no need for your mama to know.' James hid a grin. William imagined his wife to be blissfully ignorant of that sort of thing. James doubted that Susan Remington was anything of the kind. William continued. 'I persuaded her that there was no need for her to rush down after you the moment she arrived in town.' He gave James a friendly elbow in the ribs. 'Boys will be boys, eh, James?'

'They will indeed.' James tried hard not to laugh at Nick's scarlet cheeks. The boy could scarcely be more embarrassed if he had gone out of town to enjoy the company of a harem.

'Wild oats,' William said charitably, 'are perfectly natural in a young man. Your mama is in the next saloon, Nick. She will like to see you, I dare say.' He turned to James. 'I called this afternoon, but Penfold said you were out. Susan and I would be delighted if you came to dinner tomorrow night.'

James opened his mouth to suggest another night, but William smiled comfortably.

'Penfold let me in and I had a glance at your engagement diary. You're supposed to be attending the Manningham ball tomorrow night. Plenty of time for dinner.'

As James mentally cursed his butler, William patted Nick on the shoulder and strolled on.

'Hell,' Nick muttered, burying his nose in his champagne glass. 'I wonder what my mother *does* think! Are you going to dinner?'

'Probably, yes,' said James, biting back several curses on the subject of William's managing disposition. That would make it two days running he was unable to visit Lucy. He had a parliamentary committee meeting tomorrow. 'And your mother thinks that you went out of town with a mistress,' he continued. 'I shouldn't think William fooled her for a minute. Consider it the wages of sin and be grateful that she won't actually ask you about it.' Instead, she'd ask *him*. And he'd have to lie through his teeth so that Susan never suspected that her eldest son had come damn close to being murdered.

Nick choked on his champagne and James thumped him on the back.

'Ah! Cambourne. This is more your usual milieu.'

The urbane, amused tones had James turning slowly.

'Good evening, Montgomery.'

Nick looked slightly embarrassed. 'Evening, Monty.'

Montgomery smiled, including Nick. 'How do you do, Remington? Do you know, I found your cousin in a deuced odd place the other evening.'

'Did you?' Nick gave James a quizzical look.

James swore mentally.

Montgomery smirked. 'Yes. The Strand, of all places. Hard to imagine what could possibly tempt Cambourne down there.'

'Quite.' Nick sounded as though his back teeth were clamped together.

Montgomery favoured them both with a nod and strolled on.

James stared at Nick. 'Monty?'

Nick flushed. 'Never mind that. The Strand? What the hell were you doing down there? Damn it, James! I learned my lesson. You don't need to—'

'It had nothing to do with you,' James said. 'Or at least very little,' he amended. 'I wanted to know more about Hensleigh.'

'Why?' demanded Nick.

'Because he sold your vowels on to a man he must have known was dangerous,' James said quietly. 'I discovered you weren't the first. A few discreet enquiries netted the names of several other young fools who couldn't pay.' He hesitated. 'And then last night I was told about one who wasn't quite as lucky as you.'

Nick stared. 'What?'

'Gerald Moresby died,' James said. 'Huntercombe's younger brother. It happened a couple of months ago.'

'Died?' Nick had paled. 'But, what was the point of that? I mean, he couldn't pay if he was dead!'

James shrugged. 'He was beaten twice. The first time was probably a warning, but he still couldn't pay. The second beating killed him.'

Nick clenched his fists. 'If you knew it was that dangerous, why are you going after Hensleigh?'

James didn't say anything at first. Originally he'd simply wanted to destroy Hensleigh for putting Nick in danger. It was more now. 'I didn't know at first, but now? Now I don't want it happening to someone else,' he said at last. 'One of your younger brothers, for example.' Kit and Jasper were still at school and he saw again Huntercombe's weary face, the grief, the self-blame.

Nick let out a breath. 'I didn't think of that.' He scowled. 'Damn Montgomery.'

James stilled. 'What?'

Nick looked uncomfortable. 'He told me about the Cockpit— Oh. Good evening, sir.'

James turned to find a very portly and somewhat untidy middle-aged gentleman smiling at them from under heavy dark eyebrows. A smear of what might have been gravy adorned his cravat.

'Nick, m'boy. Heard you had to rusticate.' The bushy eyebrows rose as Nick turned scarlet and the newcomer clapped him on the shoulder. 'Well, well. Mum's the word. And James. How d'you do?'

James held out his hand to his godfather. 'Fox. I'm very well. And you, sir?'

'Oh, well enough, boy. Well enough.'

'I'll be off, James.' Nick sketched a bow. 'Servant, sir.'

'Delighted to see you, Nick. Give my best to your papa, won't you?'

'William will have apoplexy,' James said, as Nick disappeared into the crowd.

Charles James Fox, ex-roué, ex-man-about-town, member of the Commons and self-confessed admirer of Napoleon, snorted. 'Wasn't me lending his precious boy a whole damn mansion to entertain a bevy of bawds.'

James choked on his champagne. 'Who the hell told you that?'

Fox grinned comfortably. 'Never you mind. I hear most things eventually. Funny thing, though—' He took a pinch of snuff. 'What I can't hear is who was the lucky girl. Or girls, as the juicier gossip would have it.'

James cleared his throat. 'Fancy that. Some things are sacred after all.'

Fox put the snuffbox back in his pocket. 'Precious few. What was it all about, James? I've been hearing some odd things.'

Letting out a breath, James considered his godfather. Fox had all sorts of odd acquaintances and contacts. It was possible that he might help. 'May I call on you, sir?'

Fox favoured him with a baleful stare. 'We'll be offended should you *not.*'

James grinned. 'Sorry, sir. I didn't mean it quite like that. I meant, I'd rather not talk about it here, but if you don't mind I'd like to ask your advice.' He realised that Fox had said *we...* 'Is Elizabeth with you?'

Fox nodded. 'She is. We think of going to Paris in the summer, so I persuaded my Liz to come up to town for a few days. I am sure she will like to see you.'

James hesitated. Fox raised his bushy brows. 'Don't tell me some of William's prosiness has rubbed off and calling on my Liz is beneath you, boy.'

James stared. 'What? No! Of course not.' Elizabeth Armistead had been Fox's mistress for nearly twenty years. She had abandoned her position as one of London's most celebrated courtesans to rusticate with Fox out at Chertsey. Not for money. Fox had gambled away his considerable fortune long before meeting his dearest Liz. Conventional wisdom might mock at it, but Elizabeth had committed the grandest of follies for a courtesan: she had fallen in love. Worse, she had fallen in love with a penniless gamester and followed her foolish heart.

Although she was twenty years his elder, James

considered Elizabeth one of his dearest friends. And if Fox would permit it…

'I need her help, sir. Some questions she might be able to answer.' James grimaced. 'Only you might not like it.'

Fox's dark eyes gleamed and he rubbed his hands together. 'A mystery, eh? Come along, then, and tell me over a hand of cards.'

It was James's turn to raise his brows. 'Cards, sir? With you?'

Fox grinned. 'We'll play for love. My Liz would be very cross if I fleeced you.'

Chapter Four

The next morning Lucy struggled to dress herself. She could scarcely use her right arm and the bruising was livid. Sweating with the effort of getting into shirt and breeches, Lucy stared out at the rain. At some point in the night it had stopped and she had hoped today would be fine. Instead it was nearly as bad as the day before.

It didn't matter; she had to go out. She needed three shillings by the end of the week and she was a shilling and sixpence short. No. A shilling and sevenpence. She'd bought a penny loaf yesterday.

Biting her lip against the pain, she wriggled into the waistcoat and jacket. Sweat dripped into her eye and automatically she raised her right hand to wipe it away...except she couldn't lift her arm. Breathing hard, she used her left hand instead.

How will you lift the bow?

* * *

Fifteen minutes later, she accepted the truth; she couldn't play. Not properly. Not even close. And outside the skies had closed in with a steady, pitiless downpour that drove against the window in bitter gusts.

Defeated, Lucy tucked the cloak, a blanket and the counterpane around her and curled up on the settle. There was no point struggling out of the boy's clothing. She had half a loaf of bread and clean water to wash it down. She wouldn't starve or die of thirst. But tomorrow she had to pay the rent. If she couldn't use her arm by then, there was only one thing left to sell.

The knock on the door pulled her out of a light doze. She'd heard the bells a little while ago and knew it was after midday. Mrs Beattie had been up about then to check the leak.

'Who is it?'

'Cambourne.'

She shut her eyes. Mrs Beattie was never going to believe these visits were innocent. 'Go away. He's not here.'

The door opened anyway.

James stared at Lucy, curled in a counterpane on that miserably uncomfortable settle. No wonder she was wrapped up—it was freezing in the little room.

With a muttered curse he stalked across the room. 'Why haven't you lit the fire?' A glance at the bucket by the fireplace gave him the answer. There was less than half a bucket left.

He dropped his parcel and a closed basket on the table and scowled at Miss Hensleigh. 'You'll freeze.'

'Rubbish. I'm perfectly comfortable with the blanket and counterpane. I'll light the fire later. Why are you here again?'

'My parliamentary committee meeting was cancelled.' He didn't believe she wasn't cold. Her face was pale and there was a pinched look to it.

'And you didn't have anything better to do than annoy me? My father hasn't returned.'

James sat down in the chair. 'I'm glad you aren't out in the rain today.'

She said nothing. He gestured to the parcel. 'There are some books in that parcel. And some music.'

Ah. At the mention of books and music, her eyes glowed, the lips softened and parted. His breath shortened. Lord, she was lovely. Then the gates slammed shut, her mouth flattened. 'Why would you do that?'

'Because I thought you might enjoy them. The music I bought for you. The books are from my library. A loan. There's a small chess set in there as well. Do you play?'

'A little.' She sat up, the counterpane and a blanket falling back to reveal that she was also bundled up in a cloak. Because she couldn't afford to light the fire. Damn it. What else couldn't she afford? He pushed the question aside for now.

'Should you like to play?'

'You came all this way to play chess? What if I didn't play?'

'Then I suppose I would have to teach you.' He took the set out. 'If you wished it.'

Green eyes narrowed. 'I asked you to go away. My wishes don't appear to come into it.'

He placed the set on the table. 'You don't get that wish. At least, not yet.' He hated thinking that she was cold. 'Is your landlady in?'

'I've no idea. Why?'

'I'll buy more coal.' No point asking if she was cold again. She'd lie through her teeth even if they were chattering.

'No.' She straightened, eyes wide. 'There's no need. I have enough for later.'

'But not enough for now.'

There was a beat of silence. 'No. Not for now. And I don't want you to buy me coal!' Judging by her voice, he suspected that somewhere under the cloak and counterpane, she had clenched her fists.

'Then having invited myself to play chess with you, I'll buy it for me. However cosy you may be under there, *I'm* cold.' His greatcoat, muffler and gloves were keeping him reasonably comfortable. But let her think him arrogant and whatever else she liked. The thought of her shivering under the counterpane and not enough blankets ripped at him. If he had to use her to get to Hensleigh, at least he could look after her while he was doing it.

He crouched before the cold grate and lit the fire, watched the golden flames crackle and dance as it caught. Glancing up, he smiled at her. 'There's a plum cake in that basket. Why don't you cut some for us while I fetch the coal? Make a pot of tea.' There was a battered-looking teapot on the shelf above the fireplace.

Something flickered in her eyes, instantly quelled. 'Thank you. I'm not hungry. And I've…I've run out of tea.'

He stood up. 'Whatever else you may be, Miss Hensleigh, you're a terrible liar.'

When he came back with the coal the cake was cut into slices and the chessboard was set out. Lucy glanced up, bit her lip as she saw the bucket of coal. 'You saw Mrs Beattie?'

'Yes.' He bent to put more coal on the fire. 'She didn't mind selling me the coal, but I thought the better of buying tea from her.' He'd looked at the woman's tea, sniffed it and shuddered. God only knew what it was, but it wasn't tea. Not as he knew it.

'No doubt.'

He frowned. There was something in her voice that he couldn't quite put his finger on. Resignation? He looked closely at her, but he could read nothing in her expression.

The chess set was a very small one and the light poor and uncertain, so he sat beside her on the settle and gave the board a quarter-turn. 'Do you prefer black or white?'

Several moves in he realised Lucy had been overly modest when she'd said she played *a little.* She was his match.

'Who taught you?' He watched narrowly as she declined to take a knight he had set out temptingly and thus avoided his trap.

'My grandfather.' She didn't glance up, but kept her gaze on the board, her face still, utterly focused. She leaned forward a little as she moved a pawn and a stray curl brushed her cheek. Firelight sparked along it and his fingers itched to touch it, to slide into the coppery mass and feel it tumble free and silken over his wrist… He took a careful breath. What if his pursuit of Lucy Hensleigh was not pretence?

'We forgot to set a wager,' he said. 'Name your stake.'

Her head came up, eyes blazing, and he waited for the set down.

'My father's debt.'

He should have seen that coming, and cursed silently. His plan to destroy Hensleigh chanced on a single game of chess he wasn't at all certain he could win. Only she thought it was one hundred pounds. He let out a breath. Having offered a wager and told her to name the stakes, he could not, in all honour, refuse. Nor could he wriggle around it by saying he would cancel one hundred pounds. 'And if I win?'

It was as if he had doused a fire. The blaze died from her eyes and his stomach lurched. Beside the chessboard, one small hand clenched to a fist. 'That was stupid of me. I've nothing to set against the debt if I lose. No stakes. Can we not just play for…for the game?'

Last night Fox had refused to play for money. *We'll play for love.* 'We could. But a bet, a small bet—'

'One hundred pounds is a *small* bet?'

'It could be larger.' He made his move, redeploying the knight she had spurned. 'A kiss from you.' He wanted a great deal more, but he'd settle for a kiss.

Wariness flared. A kiss against a debt of one hundred pounds. She schooled herself to stillness, not to betray her surprise by so much as a flicker. He wasn't even looking at her, but at the chessboard, considering his next move. Clearly the kiss wasn't important, but he had offered a wager, asked her to name the stakes, and now honour would not permit him to back away. He knew she had no money, so he'd proposed a different stake.

How do you know that you can trust him to take only a kiss?

She didn't. But if he decided to take more than a kiss there was nothing to stop him, whether she was willing or not. And if he reneged on cancelling the debt? Well, nothing ventured, nothing gained. If he won, she would have lost a kiss. If she won and he held to his word, then life would be safer. *Until Papa loses again.*

She stared at the chessboard, seeing only a firm mouth, the hard angles of jaw and cheekbones. She couldn't stop her father gambling. She knew that. But she could win a brief respite. Not for *him*. She would not have risked a button, let alone a kiss, for *him*. But if she could win this wager, perhaps she could gain enough breathing space to escape from the trap that had closed around her.

A kiss. It was only a kiss and only if she lost. She had been kissed before. She had been assured then, by her cousin Warwick, and afterwards by her uncle, that it meant *nothing*, men needed their amusements and took them where they found them.

In other words, *she* was nothing. A kiss could not be important...at least, not to him, and certainly not to her. But—

She risked a look at him. 'What about your wife?'

'My *what*?'

'Your wife. Would she—?'

'I heard what you said.' He shook his head. 'What in Hades makes you think I'm married? Why is that important to you?'

Men and their amusements. She gritted her teeth. 'Men have one code of honour. Paying gambling debts before the tradesmen or the landlady. That sort of thing. Mine includes not taking something that isn't mine!'

'And if the kiss is not important to me, or to my wife, always supposing that I had one?'

She dragged in a breath. Why argue over a kiss she might not have to give? And why did it hurt to hear that the kiss wasn't important to him? 'Because it's *my* kiss.' Which sounded absolutely stupid.

'Very well. I'm not married.'

For all she knew, he was lying through his teeth. 'All right. A kiss, then, against my father's debt.'

The corner of his mouth tilted. 'I could be lying.'

Was the wretched man a mind-reader? 'Yes. But that's your responsibility. However,' she continued, 'I would be sorry for your wife.'

'My non-existent wife.' His gaze narrowed. 'You

tried to trick me, didn't you? The way you phrased your question.'

Her breath shortened. 'Yes.'

A laugh shook him. 'Very clever. If I *did* have a wife, I probably would have said something stupid to give it away.' Smiling grey eyes held her gaze. 'Do we have a wager?'

The friendly smile scared her more than the thought of the kiss. 'Yes. If I win, you forgive my father's debt. If you win, I'll give you a kiss.'

Cambourne inclined his head. 'Done.'

She had lost. She knew, had recognised almost as soon as she had made the move, the mistake that had led to the fall of her king. So. No respite. No breathing space.

'My game.'

'Yes.' She braced herself to pay the wager.

He rose, went to the fire and put some more coals on it.

She stared at his back, the broad shoulders, tapering to narrow hips and—heat not due to the fire slid through her—his backside. It had never occurred to her that a man's backside could be attractive. Young ladies were not supposed to think about such things, and Grandmama had always insisted that it was how and what one thought that defined a lady, not circumstances... 'Do you want that kiss, or not?' Perhaps he didn't. Perhaps he was married after all and had changed his mind.

He stood up in one smooth, lithe action and turned to her. 'Oh, yes.' His soft voice stroked every nerve ending. 'I want it.'

Her pulse stood still, then picked up, pounding erratically. She dragged in a breath. Better to get it over and done with. She rose, letting the counterpane and blanket fall to the settle.

Cambourne's brows shot up. 'You're wearing boys' clothes?'

She looked down at the shabby trousers and coat. She'd forgotten. 'Oh. Does it matter?'

The corner of his mouth quirked. 'I suppose not. Nothing like novelty to pique the appetite.'

'Novelty?'

That mouth twitched again. 'I don't think I've ever kissed anyone who wears boys' clothes.' His brows drew together. 'Were you going out to play?'

'Yes. But my… It was too wet.' She didn't want to say anything about her injured shoulder.

She took another unsteady breath and walked towards him.

Again those brows rose. 'What are you about?'

She eyed him in confusion. 'Coming to kiss you. Or do you want me to blow you a kiss?'

His smile did strange things to her insides. 'No. That won't meet the terms of the wager at all. Very well.' He spread his arms out in a gesture of surrender. 'Have at me.'

Reaching him, she stood on tiptoe, lifted her left hand to his shoulder for balance and brushed a kiss against his jaw. A little scratchy, he smelled of sandalwood soap, and some dark, underlying scent that must be him. Hot, dangerous, it lured her. So easy to lean in, to kiss him again, on the mouth this time... What was she *thinking*? She stepped back quickly. There. That was done. And he'd never know she'd nearly...

His eyes opened. 'Just what was that?'

She scowled. 'A kiss. That was what we agreed.'

He shook his head. 'Oh, no, it wasn't. *That* was a peck on the cheek. Or rather, the jaw. Not something I'd wager your father's debt against.'

Panic bubbled up. 'It was a kiss,' she insisted.

'If you were my sister, or maiden aunt, it might be,' he agreed. 'I suppose I'll have to show you.'

She forced herself to hold her ground, not to back away as his arms came around her, slowly, inexorably, drawing her closer as she stilled utterly. His warmth enveloped her as surely as his arms. Instinctively she brought her hands up and rested them against him. She could feel his breath lifting his chest, feel its soft huff against her temple. He smelled so...*male*. It tugged deep inside so that she hardly dared breathe in case she could never get it out of her head.

And then a light caress, warm, firm lips at her temple. Heat flooded her and her lungs seized, refusing to do their duty. Beneath her hands, beneath his coat, his chest was hard, solid. Strong. His arms tightened and doubt slid through her.

What if he wanted more than the kiss?

His arms eased and gentle fingers traced the line of her throat. Sensation shot through her as her pulse leapt and quickened.

'Look up, sweetheart.'

She met the fierce blaze in his eyes and her breath jerked in.

Her breath shuddered out as he murmured against her temple, 'Just a kiss. I promise.' Then that wicked mouth curved into a smile and whispered its way past her ear, along her jaw, tickling, teasing. He lingered where her pulse danced in her throat, then found the corner of her mouth. And still his arms held her gently, as slowly his mouth closed over hers.

James's control shuddered at the reality of her inexperience. What had he expected? Of course she didn't know how to kiss. Every nerve, every muscle and sinew lusting for more, he kept the kiss light. Gentle. Sweet. Wondering what she would do, he opened his mouth against hers, traced the trembling curve of her lower lip with his tongue. Her lips parted on a gasp and he tasted her shock, tasted *her* as he took possession gently, deepening the kiss on a slow surge. Her taste filled him, spicy sweet, all heat and startled innocence. Before she could draw back, he released her mouth.

'Now,' he murmured against her lips. 'My kiss.'

Senses reeling, Lucy pulled back a little and stared. His kiss? What had that been, then? 'But... I just kissed you.' He'd put his tongue in her mouth and she'd *let* him. Her insides melted at the memory, at the lingering wine-dark taste of him.

Again that wicked smile that shredded all reason and common sense. 'No, you didn't. I showed you how. Now *you* kiss *me*. Like that.'

That kiss had been a *lesson*? She clenched her fists. 'And if I don't?'

The smile deepened. 'I'll be disappointed.'

She could live with that. But why didn't he just take what he wanted?

She already knew the answer: he wanted *her* to kiss *him*. Oh, he could take a kiss, and anything else he wanted. But he wanted more than that. He wanted her to give it. Freely.

It's just a kiss.

Only, it wasn't. Not now. She could refuse, and he wouldn't insist. But a very unladylike part of her wanted to kiss him. Wanted to see if she could re-

duce him to quivering idiocy as he had with her...
wanted to taste him again.

James waited. She was going to tell him to go to—

'Very well.'

His certainties shook. She looked more like a mar-
tyr facing the lions than a woman about to give a
kiss willingly, but she was going to kiss him. And
he'd promised that he'd take only a kiss. He took a
careful breath. Only a knave would take more, but
he was going to need the strength of a saint.

Small hands, one on his shoulder, the other at his
waist as she stood on tiptoe again, reaching up to
him, wobbled a little. Obligingly he lowered his head
and her eyes closed as their lips met. He waited.
After a moment her lips moved tentatively in what
had to be the clumsiest, sweetest kiss he'd ever received. Fighting the urge to take the reins and kiss
her, he moved his own lips in gentle response. His
groin tightened, not so gently. And then it came, her
tongue, shy and damp against his lips. Heat spread
through him, urgency slid around his control.

A kiss. Only a kiss.

He could do that. But his arms went around her,
drew her against the fierce ache of his body. She
yielded on a gasp of shock that he tasted as he
opened his mouth to accept her kiss and return it.

He was no green boy to be taken by surprise and
ambushed by feminine charms. Kisses were pleas-

ant, charming, perhaps even arousing. Never had the sweetness of a kiss shuddered through him like an earthquake, tearing at his control.

Her mouth, her taste, was sweet beyond all understanding. He slid his tongue past hers, stroked, teased and shook as a moan trembled through her and she responded. Her tongue danced with his, still shy, a little clumsy, and yet a kiss had never aroused him more. And that slender body, delicate curves and softness, pressed against him. His hands moulded her back beneath the shabby clothes. More. He wanted more. Everything.

He broke the kiss, reaching for control as he rested his brow on hers.

There were rules against seducing innocents. Damn good rules. Rules he must not break, despite the hammering in his blood and the fire in his loins. And if he hadn't known that she was an innocent before he kissed her, he knew it now.

He looked down at her. Misty green eyes, dazed with the kisses they had shared, gazed back. His heart shook. Her cheeks were flushed, her mouth damp, swollen from his. Even as he watched, her lips trembled, tempting, soft, ready to yield, and if he kissed her again he'd never be able to stop.

Her chin lifted, exposing the delicate line of her throat. 'Is…is that it?'

Part of him howled, *No*. 'Yes.' A wager. Agreed in

honour. He had to let her go. But his arms remained around her, one hand resting on the supple curve of her waist, the other at her nape, caressing the vulnerable skin there, fingers sliding into the silken curls that tumbled over his wrist. One shuddering breath and he stepped back, letting her go.

Lucy forced herself to breathe. He had stopped and it felt as though something inside her had torn apart.

He walked away, spoke with his back to her. 'Miss Hensleigh—if you wish, I can take you out of all this. You would be safe with me.'

Heat flared on her cheeks. 'Are you asking me to be your mistress?'

'Yes.'

'That kiss. Those *kisses*.' Her breath shuddered out. 'You promised. Just a kiss.' And he'd taken at least two. How were you supposed to tell where one kiss ended and another began? And there was no *just* about his kisses. They were the sort that made you forget all sense. The sort that enticed one to madness and made it seem sane.

He swung around. 'I said a kiss only and I meant it.'

'You were trying to seduce me!'

'No.' He pushed a hand through his hair. 'At least, not intentionally.'

Not intentionally? 'You've just asked me to be

your mistress!' How much more intentional could a man be?

'Yes,' he admitted. 'But I'm not seducing you right here and now.'

She stared.

'I want more than a quick tumble.' His mouth hardened. 'Otherwise, if you weren't an innocent, we'd be in bed by now.'

'Why does that matter to you?'

'Don't insult me.' Fury simmered in the deep voice. 'I play by the rules. I don't seduce innocents.' He took a deep breath and his voice gentled. 'If you don't want to be my mistress, you say so and that ends it. If you aren't sure, then I'll give you time to think. I won't seduce you into it, or offer you lies about love.'

She took a deep breath. Honesty. He was at least offering her honesty. And safety for a time. All she had to do was agree...

James wondered if anyone had ever made such a mess of a straightforward offer. He might as well finish the job. 'One other thing I'm not offering.'

'Marriage,' she said. 'Don't worry. I'm not *that* innocent.'

Marriage? 'I was referring to your father's debt. That's not negotiable. It stands, whether you become my mistress or not.'

'Then why wager on it? Or were you that certain of winning?'

His mouth flattened. 'No, I wasn't. But I offered a wager, told you to name the stakes. You did.'

He told himself that he couldn't allow the justice he sought for Hunt's brother to be compromised that way. And he was lying to himself. Even without that, he would have refused. Because if that was the only reason she'd consent—it would be a sort of rape. Even if he had been willing to cease his pursuit of her father, he wasn't going to hold that over her head. If she was going to come to him it had to be willingly. For herself. Apart from desire, which was a low burn in his gut, it would bring Hensleigh to him.

He walked over to the window, away from the temptation to take her back into his arms and kiss her into agreeing. He gritted his teeth against the urge. And found himself venturing on to the boggy territory of explanations instead.

'I asked you to be my mistress. Not to let me bed you in settlement of your father's debt. If you choose to be my mistress, you are choosing for yourself. It would be an arrangement between you and me. I won't blackmail you.'

It would still bring Hensleigh to him, but she'd be safe under his protection. She deserved better, a woman who had worried that he might be married before agreeing to a wager for a kiss. 'You would have a small house. Servants. Clothing. Jewels, pin money. An allowance.'

The Lucy Armitage who had been so carefully brought up by Grandmama would be fainting dead away, after weeping tears of shame at being offered such an insult. The girl who had become Lucy Hensleigh, as well as Lucy Hammersley and several other names in the past four years, was unbearably tempted.

Oh, not by the promise of jewels and clothes, although she supposed some new clothes would be inevitable, and not even just by the prospect of being safe for a little while. She was tempted by his honesty, his gentleness and, in a queer way, his honour. And those three things told her he would keep her safe.

Safe? He's offering you what Grandmama called a fate worse than death!

But then again, she didn't think Grandmama had ever been truly hungry in her life, nor faced the prospect of life on the streets. And she wouldn't be his mistress for always. She knew enough to know that men tired of mistresses eventually. Forewarned was forearmed. Another of Grandmama's sayings. Knowing in advance that her time with Cambourne would be limited by his interest, surely she could save enough money to buy an annuity? Enough to live on simply.

And what if there is a child? Will you risk bringing an innocent into this mess?

'Are you wondering if you can trust me?' His voice, clipped and brusque, ought to have been the very opposite of reassuring. He continued, 'If you agree, a contract will be drawn up to protect you, and provide for any child.'

He was reading her mind again. But he had addressed her worst fear to a degree. A child would be looked after.

A shiver rippled through her. She ought to be refusing. Indeed, she ought to have refused already, not be questioning if she could trust him. A man who offered to take a girl as his mistress was clearly not to be trusted. Except he wasn't trying to trick her into it. He was being very direct about it. He hadn't offered undying devotion, let alone marriage, only to renege later. He'd offered to take her as his mistress.

'No.' She clenched her fists, as if that way she could strangle the little voice pointing out all the advantages of his offer. 'Thank you,' she added, thinking that she had been very blunt.

He blinked. 'That's it? "No, *thank you*"?'

Irritation flared. 'What am I supposed to say? Explain my decision?'

A smile tugged at his mouth. 'I might have expected a set down for suggesting such a thing to you, rather than a polite refusal.'

She might have known he would mock her. 'I do apologise if you feel short-changed, my lord. Offers, dishonourable or otherwise, do not come my way every day.'

His mouth hardened. 'They could. Very easily.'

'Is that a threat?'

'A warning. Have a care to yourself, Lucy. I won't pester you any longer, but bid you good afternoon.'

An unnamed emotion coursed through her. It should have been relief. Relief that he wasn't going to push the point. She couldn't convince herself that was it at all.

'Does this mean you'll stay away now?' Mrs Beattie might accept her assurances that it was all a mistake, that she had not taken Cambourne as her lover, and drop the rent back...

'No. I'll call tomorrow. But I won't pester you about this.'

'Because I said no?'

'Because you said no.'

It must be relief that she felt.

'However,' he added, 'should you change your mind, you have only to say so. The offer remains open.'

Slowly, giving her every chance to back away, he lifted his hand to her face, traced the line of her jaw with fingertips that were barely there. Her breath caught, as that featherlight touch drifted to her throat, lit fires that whispered through her whole body. Everything in her ached, yearned…and she was a fool. A fool tempted by a dream.

She stepped back, forced her knees to steady and her lungs to function. 'Goodbye, my lord.'

'Au revoir.' He bowed and was gone.

Still trembling, his touch still echoing in her blood, she listened to his footsteps on the stairs, heard the door to the yard close and resisted the temptation to rush to the window. It was unnecessary. Already she knew exactly what that tall, lean, broad-shouldered figure looked like. Knew the deceptively easy stride that spoke of effortless strength. The same strength that he could have used against her so easily. But he hadn't. Instead he was seducing her with a gentleness and forbearance that was far more dangerous than threats or blackmail. Had he realised that if he'd offered her father's debts in return for her consent she would have told him to go to hell?

She should have told him to go to hell anyway. But as long as she didn't permit herself to change her mind she was safe.

The day dragged on until evening fell and it was too dark to read. She toasted some bread for supper, saving some for Fitch. The fire Cambourne had lit glowed cheerfully, holding back the dark. She should have let it go out long ago, but there was little point saving the coal; if she could afford to pay the rent in two days then there would be more coal. If not, Mrs Beattie would probably have her tossed out.

Or you can become Cambourne's mistress. She swallowed. It would be so easy to agree. She wasn't even sure why she hadn't agreed then and there. She snuggled the counterpane around her more securely. Her shoulder wasn't as sore as it had been that morning. Soon she would be able to play again. Meanwhile she had one thing she could sell to pay the rent.

In the distance St Clement's struck ten and fear licked at her. Fitch wasn't coming. Two nights in a row. Was he even now in Newgate? She prayed. Prayed that he was safe and that she would think of some way of keeping him safe.

Chapter Five

'*A pound?*'

'Pound,' the old man said. 'An' dear at the price. Take it or leave it.'

Lucy's fingers closed, shaking, on the gold locket. 'It's worth much more than that!' She had been able to save this piece because her father hadn't known about it. After he'd sold the rest she'd worn it hidden under her gown.

Old Mr Jessup shook his head. 'Maybe to you, missy. Ain't worth more to me.'

'Why, the chain is worth more than that!' Lucy said, indignant.

He shrugged. 'Chain ain't only worth five bob to me.'

'Five shillings?'

'What I said, innit?'

For an instant outrage threatened to bubble over. But a calmer, colder voice suggested a compromise.

'Done.' Lucy unfastened the catch, removed the locket, and held out the chain.

'Eh?' Jessup stared.

'Five shillings. For the chain,' she said, tucking the locket away inside her bodice.

'Hang on!' he protested. 'Never said I'd pay that!'

'You said it was worth five shillings,' Lucy insisted.

The wrinkles chased themselves into a scowl. 'Didn' say that's what I'd pay,' he muttered. 'Be lucky to *get* five shillings for it.'

'You said that's what it was worth to you. Not what it might be worth to a customer.' Lucy held out the chain. 'I call that an offer. Five shillings.'

'Oh, all right,' he grumbled, fossicking in a metal box behind the counter. 'Five shillings.'

Some of the choking fear and despair curdling inside Lucy eased. She might only have five shillings, but she still had the precious locket with Mama's picture. Right now she could pay Mrs Beattie's extra three shillings and have money left over for food. And by next week she would be able to play again. She had managed for perhaps ten minutes when she had tried that morning. Not long enough to play for her supper, but it was better than it had been two days ago.

Jessup counted out coins and handed them over. She checked. 'Sixpence short, Mr Jessup.'

The scowl deepened, but he surrendered the six-pence. 'Got me living to earn,' he complained. 'Same as the next man.'

Judging by the coins in his cash box, Jessup had more than enough for *his* dinner.

'Thank you, sir,' she said, summoning a polite smile. 'Good day to you.'

He snorted. 'Think pretty words make up for rob-bing a poor man blind, do yeh, missy?'

She bit back a tart rejoinder; she might still need to sell him the locket if Papa didn't come home soon. There was no point in annoying the old man. She wasn't quite sure why he hadn't forced the price down from five shillings as he'd clearly wanted to do, but he hadn't. Perhaps the fact that he could be construed as having made an offer had been enough to bind him?

'No, Mr Jessup. I'm just grateful that you helped me with a fair price.' That nearly choked her and Jessup actually looked startled.

He fidgeted with the cash box. 'Take yourself off then, missy.' He lowered his voice. 'When yeh see that father of yours, tell him Kilby's lookin' for him.'

'Kilby?'

Jessup looked around hurriedly. 'No need to make the world a present of his name! Just tell yer pa. An' yeh didn' hear it from me.'

* * *

Fitch stayed close in the shadowed alley. He hadn't dared go near Lu the past couple of days. Kilby's bruiser, Jig, had made it clear the boss wasn't pleased and that if he didn't get back on the job there'd be trouble. An' he'd asked a few questions, casual-like, about Lu. Jig thought she was a boy, so he'd stayed away, just to be safe. He reckoned he was in the clear now, though. He'd made his take for yesterday and today, easy, and his pockets were empty. Jig had been keeping an eye on him. and as soon as he'd handed over the take he'd sloped off. Anything he got now was his and he was hungry.

Several marks strolled by, jabbering foreign. Frenchies, he thought, an' none of 'em takin' a blind bit of notice of anything around them. He could lift a purse and be gone before the mark knew he'd been robbed.

He didn't move. He just didn't feel so easy about lifting a purse now. Oh, a mark was still a mark. He didn't give a rat's skinny tail about the mark. But it just didn't sit right or something. Kept thinking of Lu's face the other night when she'd seen him. Relief. And if there'd been relief, then there'd been fear afore it.

Once he might have laughed that off. *He* wasn't afeared. What was he? A wet-behind-the-ears gowk?

But what Lu's flash gent had said the other night, that had given him that sick feeling in his belly while he listened on the roof. Hadn't been able to hear much, but he'd heard that all right. Made him think. Think about Lu getting taken up with him if he flammed marks while she was playing her fiddle—not that he would! But say someone thought he had? That Lu was part of it?

She'd go up the ladder to bed right behind him. And that gave him a sick feeling right to the stomach like when he'd seen that shopkeeper whale on her. He didn't know what would be worse, seeing her go up and drop, or knowing she was next after him.

Even thinking of her standing in the crowd crying because he was dancing on air to the tune of Jack Ketch was bad. She was frightened for him and now, at last, he understood. So maybe some pennies for holding a couple of prads might be better than lifting a purse or the timepiece that fat cove there had stuffed back in his pocket. He just didn' like to think of Lu being afeared, that was all.

And there, like his thoughts had whistled her up, there she was, Lu—coming out of Jessup the pawnbroker's shop. Several curses escaped under his breath. Things he didn't say around Lu. Not that she'd know what they meant, but still.

If she was coming out of Jessup's she'd been short for the rent, and the only thing she could have sold to that bloodsucker was the little gold locket with the painting of her ma inside. Useless stuff, gold. You couldn't eat it, could you? But it was handy for turning into other things. Like food, or drink.

But Lu set store by that gewgaw. Apart from the fiddle, it was the only thing she had left to remind her of her ma. He could hardly remember his own ma, just her voice, all gentle-like, and being held by her. He scowled. No point thinking about it. But Lu had sold her locket. All because of a gizzard-sucking shopkeeper, and, when you got right down to it, his nibs, thinkin' he owned everyone and...

Fitch's eyes widened and then narrowed. Speculating. Because there, strolling towards him out of Twining's Teas looking like the lord of all the earth, was his nibs. *Lord* Cambourne, if you please—or even if you didn't; the careless bastard who'd messed everything up for Lu.

Fitch wriggled his fingers, easing into the shadows. He'd have to be real careful. The mark knew him. Do it while he was crossing the street, p'raps. Thinkin' about not getting squashed by a dray or something. 'Course, shoving him under a dray would make the job a lot easier.

The mark strolled past, but Fitch waited. Two would get you one that the bleeder knew, or thought he knew, all about pickpockets. But he didn't know

Fitch. Ten yards behind his mark, Fitch sauntered out of the shadows all careless like.

Lucy's breath caught and her heart leapt oddly as she saw Lord Cambourne leave Twining's Teas on the opposite side of the Strand. His tall, straight figure was impossible to miss. Briefly, she wondered what on earth he had been doing in there. Surely he didn't buy his own tea? She could believe that he might visit a jeweller, or…or his tailor. But a tea merchant? An earl must have a score of servants to order his tea and anything else he desired. But there he was, tucking what looked like a pound of tea in his pocket in a way that quite ruined the set of his coat.

He'd bought it for her. And she doubted he'd bought one of the cheaper blends.

He turned right. Towards home. Her home. And her brain finally caught up with reality. He was seducing her with tea.

He hadn't called yesterday and Lucy had been hoping desperately that Mrs Beattie would have noted that.

She watched as he stepped back to allow a shabbily dressed woman, her head bowed, to shuffle past. *Manners maketh man.* Grandmama had said that. But Lucy had a notion that with Lord Cambourne, it wasn't just manners. Her father had beautiful manners—when he chose to employ them. But if he'd even noticed the old woman, he would have pushed past, thinking her beneath him.

There was a difference between company manners and being considerate, being kind.

Stop being a ninny. Are you going to become his mistress, or not?

She didn't have to. Not yet. She had enough for the rent.

And next week? If he keeps calling, you'll be paying extra rent again.

And Lord Cambourne was about to call on her at a time when Mrs Beattie was bound to notice, and heaven knew how many other people would be around to tell her if Mrs B. didn't see for herself.

You could explain the extra rent to him. He said he didn't want to blackmail you...

She braced herself as she set off, intent on reaching the crossing ahead of him. She'd only tell him as much as was absolutely necessary, and... Fitch.

He'd slipped from an alley, sauntering along the opposite pavement, hands in his pockets, as though he hadn't a care. And all the time drifting closer and closer to his lordship.

Behind her two dogs took exception to each other's interest in the same stretch of gutter and joined battle with noisy enthusiasm. Lucy, her heart in her throat, heard them only faintly.

No. He wouldn't. He couldn't be that foolish. And if he was then she'd make him give it back. Or she'd give it back.

The flurry of a dogfight on the other side of the street caught James's eye. And there she was—Lucy, in her girl's clothes. A tension he hadn't quite been aware of, an indefinable worry, eased. At least she hadn't taken an inflammation of the lungs after playing in the rain. But she was staring at him as though she'd seen her own ghost—and that knot of worry retwisted itself. She looked paler, thinner, damn it! And—and why the devil was she staring at him like that? Like…

The faintest hint of movement on the very edge of his vision warned him.

Time stopped for Lucy as Fitch's hand dipped into his victim's pocket and Lord Cambourne whirled, grabbing the boy. There was no thought. Only blind terror at the single, shattering truth—Fitch would hang.

She was not aware of making a decision, only of running, dodging a wagon, a brewer's dray. There was a roaring in her ears that had nothing to do with the shouts and swearing. A horse's shoulder barely missed her and she stumbled, but kept moving in her mad dash, all her being centred on getting to Fitch.

* * *

The wriggling thief in his grasp, James heard the yells and curses from the street. His heart slammed into his throat as he saw Lucy nearly go down under a horse. Even the boy stopped fighting and uttered a curse that was halfway to a terrified prayer.

And then she was across, panting and dishevelled, her eyes wild, clutching his arm.

'Let him go! Please, it was a mistake! Let him go!'

'It was a mistake, all right,' James snarled. 'His! The little rat tried to pick my pocket!'

'He's not a rat!' Lucy raged. 'He's a child!'

'He's old enough to hang!' James said and flinched at what he saw in her face.

'*No!* Please. I'll do anything!'

It was little more than a whisper and she was white. Bone white. As if a demon had taken every drop of blood from her. *Anything.* His heart lurched. Did she care that much?

'Too right that one's old enough to hang, guv,' said a man who had stopped beside them.

'Aye,' said another worthy. 'Ruddy pickpockets!' He flexed his hands. 'I'll help you get the young varmint to the magistrate, sir!' He reached for the boy, but found Lucy in the way. 'Here! Get you gone, doxy!'

Before James could say anything, the fellow grabbed Lucy by the shoulder and spun her away.

A cry broke from her and she went to her knees. 'Lucy!' Reaching for her, James lost his grip on the boy and swore, expecting him to run.

Instead the boy lowered his head and charged, butting the man who'd flung Lucy away solidly in the midriff. The fellow went down, winded, and the boy turned back at once, crouching beside them.

'Lu! You all right?'

Someone grabbed the boy, dragged him up.

'I got 'im, guv!'

James looked up from Lucy and frowned. The boy wasn't struggling now. Maybe he thought there wasn't any point, since he was surrounded with two burly fellows holding him and several more watching, but his eyes were fixed on the girl. The girl who'd risked her life coming to his defence. James swore under his breath. His duty was clear. The boy should be turned over to the authorities, but—

'My lord. *Please!*'

With a silent curse he helped her up and, keeping his arm about her, looked at the men holding—what was the boy's name? Fitch, that was it. The boy's eyes met his, defiant but somehow accepting, as if he knew he was done and that was that. And beneath that, the hint of a fear he'd never admit.

'Let him go,' he said curtly. 'It was a mistake, an accident. He stumbled against me. That's all.' He couldn't believe he was saying it.

'*What?*' The man Fitch had butted exploded. 'He's a thief, guv!' he protested. 'Stumbled my ar—' Catching James's eye, he broke off. 'Aunt,' he amended. 'And it's plain as a pikestaff the wench is in it! Playing you, they are.' He spat in the gutter. 'Pretty wench bats wet eyelashes and you let 'em get away with it. Bah!' Glaring at James, he released his hold on Fitch with a shove that sent the boy staggering and stalked off, muttering.

The other fellow held his ground. 'You'll regret this, your honour,' he said. 'Look, I'll help you get them both to the magistrate. Only thing to be done. At the very least the boy should swing, and as for the wench—'

'It was a mistake,' repeated James, feeling Lucy shudder in the circle of his arm. 'Thank you for your assistance, but I'll deal with this.'

Apparently recovering some of his bravado, the boy shook free and dusted himself off. He flung the fellow a cocky look at which the man let out a curse and stormed off. He eyed James suspiciously. 'What— Lu!'

James caught Lucy as she swayed and, with a curse, swung her up into his arms.

'Let her go, damn yer eyes! What're you doin' with her?'

'She's fainted!' James said shortly, horrified at the frail weight.

The boy stared. 'Lu don't faint!'

'She has now,' James said. 'Probably at the prospect of seeing you dance in mid-air!'

The boy bit his lip. 'She's…Lu's got a bad shoulder. Right one.'

James looked at him. 'What happened?'

He got a savage glare in return. 'Shopkeeper didn' like her playin' outside his shop t'other day. Hit her with a stick.'

Damn it! He'd *known* she wasn't safe in those boys' clothes. Oh, people might be blind enough not to see a girl, especially as thin as she was, but— He pushed the thoughts away. They didn't help. He started to walk with Lucy in his arms. Without bothering to look he knew the boy was at his heels.

Chapter Six

The landlady caught them in the hall. ''Ere! What's this?'

James cleared his throat. 'Miss Hensleigh is unwell.'

The lady snorted. 'I dessay, but—' Her eyes widened as she saw Fitch. 'You! Get out! Not havin' your sort sneakin' in. Steal summat, like as not!'

'He's with me,' James informed her.

The woman goggled, but didn't protest when Fitch darted up the stairs. By the time James gained the upper landing the boy had the door open and the settle pulled in front of the fireplace.

James lowered Lucy on to the settle. She didn't move as he started to undo the buttons of her bodice. His fingers shook, which was ridiculous. He'd undressed a woman before, for God's sake, and it wasn't as though he was undressing this one for any nefarious purpose. He swallowed as his fingers accidentally brushed against silken skin. She made a sound. A sigh. And his blood stirred.

'What the hell are you doing?' the boy demanded.

'Looking to see how bad her shoulder is,' James growled, angry with the unwelcome direction of his thoughts. Carefully, trying very hard not to see, let alone touch, the gentle curves and pale skin he'd revealed, he folded the fabric back. His fingers brushed silk again as he eased the gown off her shoulder... His eyes widened and his breath jerked in.

'*Hell.*' It came out in a strangled whisper. 'A shopkeeper did this with a stick? It looks more like he beat her with a club!' The bruising was livid, although from the yellowing about the edges he judged it had happened a couple of days ago.

'He got in a few swings afore I got there,' the boy said. 'Reckon she was more worried about makin' sure he didn't hit the fiddle. Bust it, that would.'

Probing with careful fingers, James thought it was lucky Lucy's shoulder hadn't been broken. 'Is there some water?'

Fitch shrugged. 'Prob'ly.'

James took out his handkerchief. 'Dampen this and bring it back.'

The boy glared. 'Don' take your orders, do I? Is it for Lu?'

'Yes.'

'Right. Otherways, you could stick it where the sun

don't shine.' Fitch took the handkerchief and dipped it in the jug on the table. 'You want it squeezed out?'

'Yes, please.' James held out his hand for the handkerchief. 'Thank you.' The boy shrugged and walked away. Gently James wiped Lucy's face and brow, and the tightness in his chest eased as her eyes fluttered. 'Don't try to get up. Just lie still, and—'

'Here.' James looked up. Fitch was back, a threadbare blanket in his arms, and a ratty-looking pillow.

'Good idea.' James tucked the blanket around Lucy, wishing it were thicker, softer. That he had something more comfortable, stuffed with feathers and horsehair, for her to lie on. He took the offered pillow and eased her down on to it. 'Stay there for a while.' Damn it. She looked so pale and small. A copper curl had escaped its bonds, drifting close to her eye. He stroked it back, felt the damp strands twine about his fingers. Everything in him tightened and his fingers curved over her cheek. Soft. Vulnerable. He still felt sick, remembering how she'd dodged horses and wagons crossing the Strand. To save the boy.

He stood up and beckoned to Fitch, gesturing him over to the window. Surprisingly, the boy obeyed without argument.

'Now,' James said to Fitch in lethally quiet tones, 'beyond the fact that Lucy begged for your life, give me one good reason why I shouldn't have hauled you in front of the nearest magistrate.' Apart from the simple fact that instead of taking his chance to run, the boy had stood his ground to protect Lucy.

'Because it's all your fault, you gizzard sucker!' snarled the boy. 'Coming around and pestering Lu, so that old bitch, Mrs B., reckoned as how she was turning tricks, an'—'

'Fitch! No!'

James turned. Lucy had struggled upright and sat looking dazed. He strode back to her, cursing, as Fitch swept on.

'An' then I seen her comin' out of old Jessup's an' I knew she'd sold her ma, and there you were.' His voice dripped scorn. 'Comin' out of Twining's with yer fancy char when Lu can't hardly pay the rent this week because of you!'

Not much of this made sense to James. 'Just stay where I put you,' he said, bending over Lucy to stop her trying to stand.

Fitch was at her other side. 'Don' get up, Lu. Scared a year off me when you went all funny like that.'

She stopped trying to rise and James settled the blanket back around her. 'What about the rent?' He didn't quite understand how that was his fault...*except of course that you scared her father out of town. Hell. She could have ended up on the street...* His blood ran cold at the thought. She'd already taken a beating from a shopkeeper.

Fitch barged on with his story. 'She can't pay the rent because the old bi—'

James cuffed the side of his head. 'Mind your language.'

Fitch scowled. 'Cow, then. The old cow put the rent up because she—'

'Fitch! Will you be quiet!'

James ignored her. 'Go on, Fitch. Because she what?'

'Because she said as how if Lu was turning tricks, she had to pay extra rent!'

'What?' He knew what a 'trick' was. But if Lucy had been that desperate... He'd *asked* her, offered to take her as his mistress, so...did she loathe him that much? Shaken, he turned to look at her.

'Mrs Beattie made a mistake!' It was a wonder her cheeks didn't ignite they were so red.

'How the devil did she make—?'

'Because *you* kept comin' round to see Lu!' Fitch said. His lip curled. 'She didn't believe you was just calling to see if Lu's pa was back.'

Several pounds' worth of pennies dropped with a resounding clatter.

He faced Lucy, struggling to find a delicate way to say it. 'Your landlady put up the rent because... of my visits?' It sounded feeble.

The boy gave a harsh crack of laughter. Apparently he thought it was pretty feeble, too. 'Dress it up nice, why don't yer, guv? An' now she's 'ad to sell her ma to that old goat, Jessup.'

James stared. The boy sounded almost as though he were crying.

'Fitch! I didn't sell the locket,' said Lucy. She reached into her bodice and brought out a small gold locket. 'Just the chain. I can buy a ribbon for it.' She tucked it away again.

'Bet that bloodsucker Jessup didn't give you much for the chain, neither,' muttered Fitch, rubbing the back of his hand over his nose. 'But least you didn' sell yer ma.'

'Stop it, Fitch,' Lucy said. 'None of this matters to his lordship!'

That slashed James's already raw conscience. 'The hell it doesn't! Is that why you were out playing the violin in the street? To make the rent?'

She flushed. 'Not the time you saw me. I just needed money for food. But after you left, Mrs Beattie came up and—'

'She thought I'd taken you already.' He managed to say it this time. It didn't make things any more palatable, but at least he wasn't hiding behind polite euphemisms.

Lucy had paled. 'Yes.'

He let out a breath. 'So you've been out playing the violin to—'

'No, she hasn't,' said Fitch. ''Cause that stupid shopkeeper bashed her so hard she can't lift the bow proper!'

Lucy shut her eyes at the expression on Cambourne's face. Hard. Angry. She shook her head to dispel the odd impression of gentleness that curled up from her memory. She didn't remember much between that dizzying blackness when it had become clear that he was not going to haul Fitch to the nearest magistrate and finding herself here on the settle. He'd been careful with her, that was all. Because, like a ninny, she'd fainted.

She stared at him. Had he carried her all that way? And up the stairs? He must have. Because she didn't see how else she'd got here.

'I'm perfectly well now. And my shoulder is much better. I could play a bit this morning. Thank you for bringing me home. And for…for—' How did you thank a man for not having your only friend hanged? 'Thank you for being kind to Fitch.'

He looked angrier than ever. Lucy scowled right back. She didn't know what he had to be angry about—always excepting Fitch's attempt to rifle his pockets—and she didn't much care. Now he knew everything and he could go.

She forced herself to sit up straighter. The blanket

fell to her waist and she felt the breath of cold air on her breast and aching shoulder. Her cheeks burning, she hauled up the open bodice, started to button it with clumsy fingers. He'd undone her gown...and she'd let him? Just lain there and *let* him?

'Please go.' She meant it to sound determined. A command. Not a shaken whisper.

'It's all right, Lu,' Fitch said. 'He wanted to see how bad yer shoulder is.' He eyed it professionally. 'Doesn't look too bad.'

'Not too bad?' Cambourne clenched his fists. 'She needs arnica on it and—'

'I'll put some on after you go,' Lucy lied.

He gave a harsh crack of laughter. 'You can't feed yourself or pay the rent and you think I'll believe you've got arnica tucked away?' He turned to Fitch. 'Here.' He dug in his pocket and brought out his purse. 'Pretend your ploy worked. You've got my money. Buy some arnica at the apothecary's and some dinner for both of you.'

Fitch shoved his hands behind his back. 'You mad? I go out there tonight with money like that an' they'll have me clapped up afore you can say *knife*! Prob'ly think I stuck you a good one, too!' He shook his head. 'Not me.' He shot Lucy an apologetic look. 'Sorry, Lu.'

James cursed. The boy was right. Having decided against having him arrested, sending him out on the streets tonight was pointless. But the boy knew where to find the apothecary, where to find a decent meal…

'Very well. We'll both go,' James said.

Fitch scowled. 'Might be all right. Long as you ain't just wanting to get me nicked when Lu ain't looking.'

'My word on it,' James said. 'As long as you keep your larcenous instincts under control,' he added.

'My *what*?'

'No thieving while you're out with me.'

'Right.' Fitch snorted. 'Like I'd try it on tonight, anyway.'

That logic James could accept. Far more easily than he would have accepted a declaration of repentance. 'Can you light the fire?' he asked.

The boy rolled his eyes. 'What? Think I'm half-witted? Yeah, I can light a fire.'

'Good. Get one lit for Lucy and—'

'I can light my own fire!' Lucy sat up.

'—meet me downstairs in ten minutes,' James finished.

'Where're you going?' Fitch demanded.

'To have a word with Mrs Beattie,' James said.

'What?' Lucy sounded panic-stricken. 'No! She'll probably double the rent if you—'

'She's going to drop the rent back,' James assured her. 'And you aren't going to light the fire.'

To his amusement the boy backed him up. 'That's right, Lu.' He started crumpling paper. 'This is men's business. You just sit.'

James risked a glance at Lucy. She was staring at him.

'What?' he asked.

'Why?' she asked quietly. 'Why are you doing this? My father owes you a fortune and—'

'That's nothing to do with you,' he said. A fortune? If she thought one hundred pounds a fortune, what would she call the truth? 'None of this is your fault.'

'It's not your fault either,' she pointed out. 'You should leave.'

'No,' he said. 'I shouldn't.' His actions, however unintentional, had caused her harm. The least he could do was put it right. He ignored the cynical little voice whispering that while his behaviour *might*, just possibly, be construed as chivalrous by the generously minded, only a fool would describe it as disinterested.

'You goin', guv?' asked the boy, now laying kindling on top of the paper. 'Acos I'll be done here afore you even find the kitchen at this rate.'

James rapped sharply on the door at the back of the hall.

'Who is it?'

'Cambourne.' He hadn't given the woman his title the other night and saw no need now. Better if she didn't know.

There was a moment's silence in which James had time to further tighten his grip on his temper.

The door opened to reveal Mrs Beattie, her face red, possibly from the heat of the kitchen fire, but just as likely from the reek of gin on her breath.

'What? She want more coal?' The woman wiped her hands on her apron. 'Need to see the rent afore—'

James stalked past her into the kitchen, wondering how long it was possible to hold his breath and live. An elderly man sat at the kitchen table, a bowl of something before him that might just possibly be soup.

He stared at James. 'Entertainin' the Fancy, now, Mrs B.?' he asked.

Mrs Beattie snorted. 'Not me. The captain's girl.'

The old man's eyes narrowed and he looked James up and down, as a man might a prize bull. 'Done right well for herself, then.'

His wheezing chuckle dried up under James's blistering glare and he addressed himself once more to his soup with noisy appreciation.

James turned his attention to the landlady. 'Apparently you are labouring under a misapprehension, madam,' he said.

Mrs Beattie blinked. 'I'm what?'

'Labouring— You've made a mistake,' said James.

'The Fancy likes all them breakteeth words,' put in the old man between slurps.

Both James and Mrs Beattie ignored him.

'A mistake, eh?' Mrs Beattie looked suspicious. ''Bout what?'

There was no delicate way of putting it and James didn't waste time looking for one.

'Miss Hensleigh is *not* my mistress.' Yet.

Mrs Beattie let out a derisive snort. 'Look, yer honour, it ain't no never mind of mine if you got a little something going. Do it out in the yard for all I care, but if she uses the rooms for business, then it's three shillin' extra an' lucky it ain't more.' She crossed her arms and glared at him.

James looked her up and down and she shifted her weight. 'Madam,' he said coldly, 'if I were to conduct a liaison with Miss Hensleigh, I would be prepared to pay a great deal more than three shillings extra for her comfort and it would be in far more pleasant surroundings.'

'Eh?'

'He means,' the old man said, with a leer, 'that he'd prefer to poke the wench on a featherbed.' He belched. 'Can't say as I blame him, not but what she'd be a tasty piece either way.'

Mrs Beattie glared. 'Well, why don't he say so?'

She scowled at James. 'You sayin' you ain't had Miss Lucy?'

'Correct,' he said through gritted teeth, reminding himself that the old man had to be over seventy and knocking his remaining teeth down his throat was out of the question. Not that he had many left to judge by the slurping.

'Reckon he's on the level about not tupping the girl up there, Mrs B.,' said the old man. 'Leastways, I ain't heard nothing like that.' He favoured James with a wink. 'Mr Albert Wynn, *at* your service.'

Mrs Beattie looked less than pleased. Her scowl deepened as she turned to James. 'Right. You reckon if you was going to do the nasty with Miss Lucy, it ud be in a featherbed?'

James bit back a savage suggestion that the woman mind her own business. To be perfectly fair, as far as Mrs Beattie was concerned, she *was* minding her own business.

'When is the rent, the *proper* rent, paid up to?' he demanded.

'Tomorrow,' she said. 'Month in advance for the cap'n.' Her mouth flattened. 'Know his sort, don't I? If it ain't paid, out they goes.'

Damn. What if Hensleigh wasn't back? He knew the answer—Lucy out in all weathers trying to earn the money, going hungry, risking another beating if she annoyed a shopkeeper, and after tonight, when that wretched boy Fitch had tried to pick his pocket, there was an added danger; she would be known as the associate of a pickpocket.

You offered her an alternative.

An alternative she hadn't accepted. But being thrown out on the streets might be enough to force her hand...

His stomach pitched and the question was out before he knew it was there. 'How much is it for the month?' Seeing the calculation in the woman's eye, James added, 'Don't pad it, madam. This is not about Miss Hensleigh being my mistress.'

'A crown.'

James nodded. 'Very well.' He took out his purse. Under the stunned gaze of the landlady and Mr Wynn, he produced two crowns and laid them on the table.

For an instant neither did more than stare as if they had never seen such a thing. Then Mr Wynn snatched them up.

'Why, you old buzzard!' Mrs Beattie grabbed a heavy pot, advancing on him.

Mr Wynn bit each coin and squinted at the results.

'Oh.' Mrs Beattie lowered her weapon.

Mr Wynn bounced the coins on the table in turn and passed them to her. 'Reckon they're good.'

With those teeth, James wasn't sure how he could possibly know.

'That's two months,' Mrs Beattie said, as the coins vanished into some fastness beneath her apron.

'Coal,' he said. 'For that I expect you to provide coal for Miss Hensleigh.'

Mrs Beattie's eyes narrowed. 'Coal, is it?'

He held her gaze. 'Coal. Yes.'

She snorted. 'Playin' the long game, ain't you?' She shrugged. 'Don't think I ain't up to yer tricks even if *she's* not. Buy her coal, visit her an' try some sweet talk, a bauble like as not. Fall like a ripe plum, she will.'

Chapter Seven

Lucy gazed into the fire. This was insanity. She should have kicked Lord Cambourne out. Men always expected something in return. Even Grandpapa. He had expected her to be a good and docile companion for Grandmama in return for house room. It had been very clear that she could expect nothing further from the family. That in taking herself and Mama in after Papa abandoned them, and keeping her after Mama's death, their duty was done.

When Grandmama died Uncle Bertram had informed Lucy that Aunt Caroline had no use for her. Aunt Caroline had written a reference for her as a teacher at a school in Bath, but Papa had arrived for Grandmama's funeral. Twenty-four hours after the will had been read, she had been on the London stage with him. Uncle Bertram had decided that forcing his brother to *take responsibility for his get* would produce an immediate result and cause no gossip.

To think she had been relieved. Four years ago Mrs Potter's Academy had seemed a prison. In hindsight it looked like a blessed sanctuary.

She shivered although the fire had banished much of the room's chill. Four years. Four years in which she had never known if she might find herself on the streets and her father in a debtors' prison. So far he had remained a step ahead of that and despite his initial annoyance at being lumbered with her, Papa had soon realised that clean lodgings were far more pleasant than dirty lodgings, especially since he didn't have to pay the landlady extra for it. In short, she had been useful.

They all wanted something. And if they didn't, then they had no use for her.

Even Lord Cambourne wanted to use her to get to Papa. And although he was prepared to help her, even that had a price. She swallowed, trying to forget the gentleness of his fingers on her shoulder. A featherlight touch and it had made her head spin. And he smelled good…of leather and clean linen and himself.

She clenched her hands against the surge of longing. Foolishness to think of him like that. She knew what he wanted from her. He wanted a mistress.

Is that such a disaster? Who would care? You'd

be better off with him, even briefly. You could get out of this mess, be safe. And he'd be kind to you. You know that...

Fool!

Common sense flung reason at the whisper of temptation.

You'll care all right when you're pregnant and in a worse situation than this!

The stairs creaked and heavy footsteps came across the landing. A very perfunctory knock heralded her landlady with a bucket of coal.

'Mrs Beattie. Good evening.' She blinked at the coal. 'Um, I haven't paid the rent yet.' And didn't know how she was going to find the money anyway.

Mrs Beattie came over and put the bucket down by the fire. 'Your man did that.'

'What?' Lucy's stomach knotted. Every feminine instinct screamed a warning.

'Coal, too, he said.'

How could she refuse him if he'd paid the rent?

Mrs Beattie set her hands on her hips. 'Thought I'd bring some up while he was out.' The lady's mouth was a flat line. 'Got something to say that he don' need to hear. Ain't my business, but I'm going to say it.'

Realising she'd have more chance of stopping a runaway coach, Lucy nodded dazedly.

'Mr Wynn's got the right of it...' Mrs Beattie began.

'Mr Wynn?'

'Aye. Took one look at your fancy man just now and said you'd done right well for yourself.' Mrs Beattie looked around. 'Can't blame him for not wantin' to do it here. Dessay it ain't quite what he's used to. Dine off gold plate, that sort.'

Didn't want to do what here? Lucy had no idea what that was about, although she thought gold plate an exaggeration, but Mrs Beattie hadn't finished.

'Thing is, I reckon you don't know what's what,' she said. 'Maybe you believe he's just lookin' for yer pa, maybe you don't—'

'Mrs Beattie—'

'No.' She waved Lucy to silence. 'I'll say me piece. Thing is, he reckons he ain't out to take you for a ride. Dunno who he's trying to fool. Me, you, maybe himself, but take it from me, a man don't pay a girl's rent less he wants something, and you—' she pointed at Lucy '—need to know what's what, or you *will* get took for a ride.'

Lucy swallowed. If Lord Cambourne had paid the rent she wouldn't be on the street tomorrow, but she knew what he expected in return.

Mrs Beattie continued. 'Lord knows men don't worry about these things.' Her lip curled. 'Sweet as pie, when they're getting what they want from a girl, but God help her once he's got it an' she's got his brat planted in her belly.'

Lucy blushed and Mrs Beattie nodded. 'That's right. Now, you know what happens, what goes where? All very well to worry about the chicken an' the egg, but it's what goes on with the rooster gettin' the egg into the chicken you got to think about now.'

Wondering if she could actually be any more embarrassed, Lucy nodded weakly. She had grown up in the country and knew how the fields got populated with lambs and calves each year, but speech was beyond her.

'Right. What you won't know is that there's ways of not catching.' Mrs Beattie drew a canister from a pocket in her apron and opened it. 'These here is Queen Anne's Lace seeds. You chew a spoonful, with water, straight after, or as straight after as you can.'

'Straight after—? Oh.'

Understanding crashed over Lucy and with it, shame. All this time she had thought of Mrs Beattie as the foe, even disliked her. And here she was, offering practical advice and help in the best way she could. Maybe she did have a fairy godmother...

She stared at the seeds. 'Mrs Beattie, you're very kind, but—'

'Don't say you don't need 'em, missy.' Mrs Beattie's scowl was thunderous. 'Maybe you will, maybe you won't. But it's better to have 'em when you *don't* need 'em, than not have 'em when you *do*.' She put the lid back on and smacked the jar down on the table. 'No need for anyone else to know what they are. Just a tonic for when you're feeling poorly is all a man needs to know. Don't like it when a girl takes precautions, do they?' She snorted. 'Like *they're* the one as has to birth the brat an' nurse it, an' have everyone lookin' sideways at 'em like you ain't good enough to sweep a dirty crossing!'

She crossed her arms and glared at Lucy as if challenging her to dispute this blistering view of the world's hypocrisy.

'Do they really work?'

Mrs Beattie nodded. 'Like a charm. I near died when the baby came. Me neighbour told me about these.' She lowered her voice. 'Reckoned it was just an old wives' tale, I did. But I tried 'em, an' I never caught again. Never told my man, neither. What a man don't know can't hurt you.'

Lucy took a very deep breath. 'Thank you, Mrs Beattie.' She got up. Whether she ever used the seeds or not, the advice had been kindly meant. Walking to Mrs Beattie, she put her arms around the woman and hugged her. After a surprised moment the woman returned the hug briefly and patted her shoulder.

'Well.' Mrs Beattie looked flustered. 'You just remember—a spoonful as soon after as ever you can.'

She moved away to the door, turned and fixed Lucy with a glare. 'An' you chew 'em good.' She banged the door behind her and was gone.

Lucy was left staring at the jar of seeds. Mrs Beattie's story had a ring of truth. She'd used them herself...*I never caught again.*

She caught herself up on the thought. Why did it matter? She wasn't going to become Lord Cambourne's mistress...was she? Surely if she said no... She hadn't *asked* him to pay the rent!

Would it really be a fate worse than death?

Of course it would!

Really? Worse than ending up on the streets with no choice?

She swallowed. Apparently part of her wasn't at all convinced of the fate-worse-than-death theory. If she could be sure of not getting pregnant, not bringing an innocent child into the mess that was her life, should she refuse the opportunity to escape?

She stared around the shabby firelit apartment. Fitch and Cambourne would be back soon. The least she could do was set the table. And if his lordship had gone out to buy dinner for herself and Fitch, then she would have to invite him to share it.

Ten minutes later she choked back a bitter laugh at the sight of her table. Three mismatched earthenware platters, a jumbled assortment of cutlery and three mugs. A jug of rainwater and a candlestick with an unlit tallow candle completed the ensemble.

'And me in my second-best gown.' Lucy gritted her teeth as she dragged the settle around to the table. With that and the single chair, at least it looked as if she were prepared for guests. And the table was polished and the crockery and cutlery washed.

Memory slid back. To Lord Cambourne sitting with her the other afternoon…playing chess…he had kissed her. Heat curled through her at the memory.

Take it from me, a man don't pay a girl's rent less he wants something… She didn't need Mrs Beattie to tell her that, but—she rubbed her hands over her face. Not only paying her rent, but buying her dinner. And Fitch's dinner. And he could have had Fitch arrested. He had relented because she had asked it. She had begged. Her own words came back to her. *I'll do anything.*

She shut her eyes. She was indebted right up to her neck and a kiss wasn't going to get her out of it this time. If Cambourne hadn't had a change of heart, Fitch would be in prison by now. And he was still in trouble. Those men clamouring for his arrest would be watching for him, setting traps. Fear tasted coppery in her mouth. More than ever she had to get Fitch off the streets… *Anything. I'll do anything.*

* * *

Fitch stopped at the passage leading into French-man's Yard. 'Tell Lu I'll see her later.'

James, his arms full, stared down at the boy. They had summoned the apothecary from his rooms over the shop and waited while he put up a pot of salve, then stopped at the Maid and Magpie for food. 'Where the hell do you think you're going? She'll think I had you arrested!'

The boy scowled. 'Got somewhere to be, haven't I? Only come this far to see as you didn't get bobbled.'

'Damn it,' said James. 'Thieving.'

A defiant shrug. 'Ain't all of us gets born with a silver spoon up our—' He broke off. 'Anyway, I got orders. Tell her to leave the window open.'

James stared. 'She's three floors up!'

Another shrug. 'Yeah. Easy from the roof, an' the old woman none the wiser.'

'You sleep there?'

Fitch looked a bit uncomfortable. 'Sometimes. Reckon she don't much like being alone. Ain't used to it.'

'And you are?'

'More than she is.' The boy scowled up at him. 'You might stay a bit. Keep her comp'ny.'

And he was gone, a small shadow slipping away to be swallowed up by deeper shadows. James let out a curse. What the hell was the point of not having the wretched guttersnipe arrested if he was just going to breeze off and court death anyway?

He knocked, heard the quiet 'Come in', and opened the door. Somehow the shabby room was transformed. It was no less shabby, but the table had been shifted closer to the fire, the single chair and settle drawn up to it. Earthenware plates were set out, with cutlery and pewter tankards. A single tallow candle, unlit, stood upon the table; the room was lit only by the dance and flicker of the fire. Somehow it looked welcoming. He had seen tables set with the finest Meissen porcelain, cut glass and silver, groaning with delicacies and felt less moved. Lucy, despite the trouble he had caused her, had taken the effort to set out what she had, even hauling the settle around with her bad shoulder.

Lucy rose from the settle, the blanket falling from her shoulders. The firelight burnished her curls to copper.

'Where's Fitch?'

The fear in her voice sliced through him. 'He wouldn't come up. Said he had somewhere else to be. I swear—'

'Oh, God.'

It was a whisper, no more, and even in the dim light he could see that she had paled as she sank back on to the settle. Two strides and he was beside her, the food dumped on the table as he sat down, took her hands. 'Lucy, I didn't—'

'A job. They've sent him on a job.'

She knew. 'Yes.' Her hands shook in his clasp, and something twisted inside him. He wanted to comfort her, reassure her. But what could he say? *Don't worry? He'll be fine?*

'Why didn't you *stop* him?'

'How?' Did she think he wouldn't have stopped the boy if he could?

She swallowed. 'I don't know. I'm sorry. It's not your fault.'

His fingers tightened on hers and her breath jerked in; she looked up, her eyes meeting his, wary and uncertain. With a mental curse, James became savagely aware of just how close they were, of her slender form that had fitted so sweetly in his arms the other day. He took a breath, reaching for control, and her soft fragrance stabbed deep. Not perfume, not expensive soaps and creams. Just her. Lucy. Herself. Desire raked him. A kiss. Just a kiss…

'My lord?'

She had not tried to pull away, but he forced himself to release her. He eased back and rose from the settle, his body fiercely aware of hers. 'If it's any consolation, I think the boy was not entirely happy about his evening's employment.' With a little distance, some of his control returned. Not much, but enough that he could breathe without the ache in his groin doubling.

She swallowed. 'I've been trying to keep him off the streets, but—' The soft mouth flattened. 'Someone has a hold on him. The other day he said they weren't happy about his earnings.'

A self-respecting cynic would see through that as something the boy used to justify himself to Lucy. But James couldn't forget that when it would have been safer for the boy to run, he'd stood buff.

'Well, his supper is here when he returns,' he said. 'He...er...told me to ask you to leave the window open.'

Lucy went a little pink. 'Oh. Thank you.'

James's memory stirred. 'Was *he* the cat on the roof the other night?'

Pink turned to crimson. 'Yes. Mrs Beattie would have a fit if she knew. But I hate the thought of him out there on the streets at night.'

James opened his mouth to suggest that she was being a fool and shut it again.

Reckon she don't much like being alone. Ain't used to it.

He could understand Lucy being soft-hearted about the boy. She was a woman after all. But what were the odds that a street thief had the instincts of chivalry?

'Would you care to stay for supper, my lord?'

He hesitated. 'Are you inviting me because you feel obliged to do so?'

She regarded him with raised brows. 'Apparently you paid my rent, bought coal—' she gestured to the full pail by the fire '—and you have provided dinner. What do you think?'

'That your manners are beyond reproach,' James said quietly. 'None of that matters a damn if you'd prefer I left.'

Those wary green eyes watched him for a moment. 'Do my preferences matter to you?'

'Yes,' he said simply. He didn't think what Lucy wanted had mattered much to anyone in a very long time.

She looked surprised. 'Then stay.'

He opened his mouth and shut it again. She trusted him. And somehow, telling her that he was the last man in London that she should trust felt like taking something from her.

He unpacked the food, setting it out on the battered table. A beef-and-kidney pie, a loaf of bread and a hunk of cheese, and a jar of ale. At the bottom of the basket he found the little pot of salve. He handed it to her. 'For your shoulder.'

Her fingers closed on it, brushed against his, trembling. 'Thank you. My shoulder is much better, though. I'll be able to play again in a couple of days and—'

'Not on the street.' His fingers closed over hers. 'Promise me.'

'My lord—'

He tightened his grip as she tried to draw back. 'Promise me.' The thought of some damned shop-keeper taking a stick to her had bile in his throat.

'You'd rather I starved in ladylike resignation?' she demanded.

Lucy shut her eyes and cursed her unruly tongue. She'd as good as admitted her destitution—*you think he hadn't realised it already?* But admitting it was like begging for help. Help he'd already given.

'I'm sorry,' she said. 'Forget I said that.'

'Not likely,' he said. 'Shall I light the candle?'

She blinked at the quick change of subject. 'Thank you, my lord.'

His hand hovered over the tallow candle. She didn't suppose he'd ever seen, let alone used, a tallow candle in his life. In his world candles were made of sweet-smelling beeswax, not sheep fat.

'Just call me Cambourne, Lucy.'

She stiffened. 'I have not given you permission to use my name.' And how ridiculous was that, to speak of giving him permission when already he'd used her name several times? Besides, anything he wanted, he could take. Anything he cared to do, he could do.

And yet he said he would leave if you wished it. That your wishes mattered.

He said nothing, just took the candle and bent, touching it to the dance of the fire. The wick flared, flickered and caught, burning steadily as he replaced it in the holder.

'Reminds me of my childhood.' He sat down.

'Lighting a candle?'

He smiled. 'The smell of sheep fat. There were always tallow candles in the nursery and schoolroom.'

'Oh.' Without thinking, she said, 'Grandmama only used beeswax in the drawing room and dining room, but Grandpapa always complained about the bill for wax candles.'

He grinned. 'So did my father. Used to ask Mama if she was burning them in the servants' hall. Did you live with them for long?'

Her hands tightened in her lap. She could tell him that it was none of his business, but what harm could it do?

'Ten years. Until I was sixteen.'

'Your mother?'

She shivered. 'She died when I was seven. Not very long after we went to live with my grandparents.'

'And you stayed.'

'Yes. They didn't know where Papa was.'

They'd gone to Grandmama and Grandpapa for

a visit because Mama was already ill. Her stomach churned, remembering the morning they had discovered Papa gone. He'd taken a horse very early. At first they had assumed he'd gone for an early ride. After all, that's what he'd told the groom who'd saddled up for him. Then Mama had found the note…

'Lucy?'

She came back to the present and realised that her nails were cutting into her palms. 'I'm sorry. I was wool-gathering.'

'Who is your grandfather?'

She swallowed. 'He died when I was ten.'

'Very well. Who *was* he?'

'Why does it matter?' Surely he wasn't going to try to get his money out of Uncle Bertram?

'Because I thought you might have relatives who could help you.' His voice was clipped.

That surprised a bitter laugh from her. 'No. My uncle would have sent me away when Grandpapa died, but Grandmama said I was useful.'

'Useful?' There was a queer, harsh note in his voice as he sliced into the pie.

'Yes. I could hold wool for her to wind, sort embroidery silks, run errands, read aloud to her.'

'You were *ten*.'

'I could read very well,' she said, deliberately misunderstanding. It hurt to recall Uncle Bertram's opinion.

If the girl is useful, Mama, then she may stay and save the salary of a companion.

There was nothing wrong with being useful. But it would have been nice to have been wanted, as well.

'And your grandmother is dead now?'

'Yes. She died when I was sixteen.'

'So you weren't useful any more.' The slice of pie landed heavily on the plate.

'No.' More like a liability.

'A loving family, in fact.' A slice of bread was cut and landed beside the pie. He handed her the plate. 'Your supper, Lucy.'

She flushed. 'Thank you.' She reached for the water jug. 'My aunt was going to find me a situation in a girls' school, but…Papa came and…and took me away.'

Uncle Bertram had lured Papa back, telling Papa that he'd been left something in Grandmama's will. Which, in fact, he had. Just not very much.

She waited politely while he cut a slice of pie for himself, poured a mug of ale. He raised it.

'Your health.'

He didn't think much of her relatives. And he hadn't got the name out of her. Although if they'd tossed a sixteen-year-old girl out with her wastrel of a father, it was unlikely they'd do anything for her now.

He watched her eat. Clearly her family was well bred. She ate neatly, despite the fact that she must be starving. Her manners were those of a lady and she had stopped well short of complaining about how her uncle had treated her. There was a dignity about her. The closest she'd come to criticism was when she'd said her uncle wouldn't help.

'Is your offer still open?'

His ale nearly went down the wrong way.

'What?'

'The other day—you asked me to be your mistress.' Her cheeks were flaming. 'Is that offer still open?'

Be careful what you wish for. Having asked Lucy Hensleigh to be his mistress, his conscience, conspicuous in its absence two days ago, chose now to make its presence felt. All the reasons why gentlemen worthy of the name did *not* make dishonourable proposals to innocents reared their heads.

He ought to say no. That he'd decided she wouldn't suit. 'Why?'

She sipped at her water. 'Because I've changed my mind.'

He'd got that much, but why had she changed her mind? 'Because I paid your rent?'

She scowled. 'No.'

'You're sure about that?' Because that wasn't why he'd paid the blasted rent, damn it.

Firelight danced in the soft curls as she shook her head. 'No, I mean, yes.' She rubbed her forehead with a frustrated sigh. 'That is, I'm quite sure.'

'Because I was out buying you dinner? Lucy, I don't want you to feel obligated.'

She stared at him in obvious confusion. 'Are you usually this fussy? What does it matter why I've changed my mind?'

Because his conscience, having developed a damned puritanical streak, was muttering unpleasant words—like *coercion*, and *blackmail*, and *unwilling*.

He held her gaze. 'If you come to me, it will involve a great deal more than a few kisses.' He had to make sure she understood. 'I want you in bed, your body mine, willing and naked.'

Mute, she nodded and scarlet mantled her cheeks. 'Are you a virgin?'

She nodded again. 'Does that matter?' Her voice sounded as constricted as his breeches felt.

'No.' It should matter. And it did. Just not in the way it was supposed to. 'You know what happens?'

'I know how babies are made!' This sounded like it came out through clenched teeth.

He let out a breath. 'I'll do my best to protect you from that.' It was far from certain, but if he avoided finishing inside her there was a lessened risk. He knew there were precautions women could take, but an innocent would know nothing of that.

'You'll take me, then?'

He wanted to. Wanted it like hell burning.

His conscience made one last, feeble stand.

'A week.'

Her face fell. 'You want me for a week?'

A ragged laugh escaped him. 'No. I'm giving you a week to think.' It was the best he could do. 'A few days in which nothing is decided, but in which I can court you. Afterwards, if you're still of the same mind, I'll take you.'

'Court me?'

She deserved that much. 'Take you out. Perhaps you won't like me.'

'Why does that matter?'

'Because it's better if we like each other. Will you tell me why you changed your mind?'

She looked at him, her chin high, and something in the proud, level gaze tore at him. 'What else is there for me, except to starve in respectable virtue, or end up on the streets? This way I have a choice, some control over what happens to me.'

'Your father—'

Her bitter laugh silenced him. 'I'll take my chance with you, my lord.'

His previous lovers—and there weren't that many—had come from the ranks of society widows, wives with complaisant husbands and a couple of experienced, highly skilled courtesans, all of whom knew exactly how this game was played. Never before had a woman told him that she'd rather take her chance with him than trust her father. Never before had someone depended on him. And never had he taken an innocent.

'A week,' he said. Anything could happen in a week. In the meantime his presence would suffice to keep her safe and he could ensure she ate enough for a change.

Chapter Eight

James stared at the note, which he had been handed as soon as he arrived home after his day out with Lucy. The week was nearly up. Tomorrow he had intended to ask Lucy for her final decision.

He'd never enjoyed a week more. Kensington Gardens, Richmond Park for a picnic, the Tower Menagerie, even the Pantheon Bazaar where he persuaded her to accept a simple straw bonnet—he'd taken his prospective mistress anywhere he thought they could avoid people who knew him.

She delighted him. Foolish little things were joys, like teaching her to skip a stone on a pond and deliberately having his quietest horse harnessed to a gig to teach her to drive. He'd forgotten the simple pleasure of being surrounded by a paddling of apparently half-starved ducks eager for the remains of a sandwich. Sitting on a rug under an oak in Richmond Park, watching while she sketched the view in a small journal he'd given her. She had been embarrassed when he gave her the journal and pencil, and he had suggested that she could sketch something for him in return. The little drawing of a swan on the river at Chelsea, somehow full of the light of a spring day, now sat safely on his desk under his desk blotter.

And day after day he knew more surely that he wanted her in ways he'd never thought to want a woman. She made no effort to amuse him, but he had never enjoyed himself with a woman more. She was simply herself and as the week wore on, he saw more and more of that self. This was not, he realised, going to be a short-term affair. He thought of Fox and Elizabeth. Was this how Fox had felt at the beginning?

Desire was a low burn in his gut. He wanted her, but scarcely dared let himself touch her. He'd promised her a week to think and she was going to have it without him trying to seduce her.

He read the note again. He had intended to take Lucy out to Richmond Park again tomorrow, but the note from Fox changed that. Elizabeth had information for him. Could they meet? His dearest Liz was missing St Anne's Hill—would James mind very much if they invited themselves out to his house at Chiswick? The following day? Perhaps a stroll in the park there and a light repast would revive Liz's spirits.

His own enquiries had netted nothing further about Lucy's father or his connection with Kilby. In fact, nothing solid had come to light about Kilby. He'd promised Hunt. He owed it to him to do his very best to find something. So he would have to see Elizabeth. And it was not as though that was a hardship. Elizabeth, along with Fox, was one of his dearest friends.

Carefully he drew out the little sketch Lucy had given him. The swan sailed on the river in a pool of light, somehow captured with the pencil, bringing back the soft breeze and the smell and dance of the river.

He'd always had good friends, people to advise him after his father had died, and then his mother. Friends like Fox and Elizabeth. Even his cousin William, who had stood as a trustee until he was twenty-five. Lucy had no one. No one to advise her. Perhaps that was something he could give her? Someone who could advise and help her. He set the sketch on the desk where he could see it and reached for pen and ink to reply to Fox.

Lucy stared up at the house as James handed her down from the curricle, and gulped. Somehow in the week of driving out with him she'd managed to forget that he was an earl, a member of the aristocracy and probably extremely wealthy. The elegant, Palladian mansion brought that knowledge crashing down around her with all the force of tumbling masonry.

She followed him inside, smiling at the hovering house steward, whom Cambourne presented to her with careless good manners. 'This is Field, Lucy. Miss Hensleigh, Field.'

Hensleigh. It didn't matter. Couldn't be allowed to matter, but she hated that she was lying to him in this way.

'Has Mr Fox arrived?'

'Yes, my lord. I believe Mr Fox is strolling in the gardens behind the house.'

'Thank you. A meal on the terrace in an hour, please.'

'Certainly, my lord.'

Numbly, Lucy followed Cambourne through the marble entrance hall and out into a corridor.

He turned to her with a smile as he opened a door leading outside. 'Mr Fox is my godfather. He is a member of the House of Commons and will be looking forward to meeting you. Ah!' He caught her hand and drew her forward across a terrace and down on to the softest green lawn. 'There he is.'

She had heard of Mr Fox. Grandpapa had been a member of the House of Commons, but not, of course, a Whig. He had been an admirer of Mr Pitt. And he had loathed Charles James Fox. Loathed him and thought him a fool. Many a time he had returned from a parliamentary sitting, and fumed to Grandmama about *that scoundrel Fox.*

She drew a deep breath. This was hardly the moment to make her grandfather's political views known. Not when Mr Fox was smiling at her kindly and bowing over her hand.

'Miss Hensleigh. How do you do?'

'How do you do, sir?'

He patted her hand and released it. 'James, you young dog. Are you presenting Miss Hensleigh for my approval? You won't get it, you know. She's far too charming and pretty for you.'

Lucy's cheeks burned.

'Thank you, sir. I had already realised that.' Cambourne took her hand and set it in the crook of his arm. She fought the betraying quiver at his touch, the shortness of breath.

He seemed not to notice, but said, 'Is Elizabeth not with you, after all?'

'Oh, yes.' Fox looked about. 'She stepped into the house for a moment. I am sure she will be back direct— Ah!' He hurried towards the house, hands outstretched.

A tall woman stood on the terrace. Elegantly dressed, her face was shaded by a silk-trimmed straw bonnet.

Mr Fox reached the lady and took her hands, drawing one through his arm in a gesture at once familiar and tender. He brought her forward.

Cambourne greeted her, pleasure and affection in his smile. 'Elizabeth.' He held out both hands and kissed her cheek. 'Thank you for coming. I hope I have not dragged you away from something in town?'

'Oh, nonsense.' The lady's smile lit her face. 'Indeed, I am growing homesick for fresh air and was never more pleased when Fox said we were coming here today.'

'Liz, dear.' Mr Fox touched her arm. 'Do let James present Miss Hensleigh.'

Liz. Elizabeth. The name tugged at Lucy's memory. Something Grandpapa had said…

Those smiling, expressive eyes turned to Lucy. Then she tilted her head to one side as a puzzled frown creased her brow.

Cambourne took Lucy's hand, drew her forward.

'James—' the lady's low, musical voice was uncertain '—are you—?'

'Elizabeth, may I present Miss Hensleigh? Lucy—' he squeezed her hand '—this is my dear friend, Mrs Armistead.'

Lucy's breath jerked in.

Elizabeth Armistead. Grandpapa had spoken of her as well as Fox. He had taken so little notice of Lucy that he'd never bothered to watch what he said in her hearing. He hadn't noticed her presence any more than he would that of a servant.

The Armistead harpy's still got her claws in Fox. Might have been a tolerable fellow but for that. Dare say she gives him all his rubbishing ideas about the common man. God knows but she's common enough!

Nothing against a man setting up a mistress and visiting her discreetly. But he lives with the woman! How can you trust a fellow with no discretion or private judgement with matters of state?

Lucy's world shook and the bright morning dimmed around her. For the first time she fully understood the social consequences of the step she was taking. If she became Cambourne's mistress she would be cut off from the world she had known for ever. From her family.

From that step there could be no going back. She would become part of Elizabeth Armistead's world—a world where a woman was bought and paid for. For a single, blinding instant hurt rose up and swamped her.

And then she saw Cambourne's face. Saw the understanding and silent acceptance in his grey eyes. He'd done it deliberately.

You have to come willingly, knowing exactly what you are doing...

She looked back at Mrs Armistead and those quizzical, gentle eyes held resignation. 'James, dear—' Mrs Armistead spoke very quietly '—I think Miss Hensleigh would be more comfortable if I waited in—'

'How do you do, Mrs Armistead?' Lucy dropped the curtsy a young lady made to an older matron.

Surprised warmth leapt to Mrs Armistead's eyes and a smile curved her lips. 'How do you do, Miss Hensleigh?'

Lucy managed a smile. The sun still shone, the earth had not opened in fire and brimstone. And yet as she met Cambourne's gaze, saw the smile in his eyes, she knew her world had altered. In acknowledging his introduction to one of the most notorious women in the kingdom, she had tacitly accepted his suit.

'James, you fool!' Elizabeth spoke under her breath as he escorted her along one of the garden paths. 'Is that child your mistress?'

He hesitated. 'Not exactly. Why do you ask?'

Elizabeth favoured him with a look that could cut steel. 'Because she's the sort of girl a man like you usually cuts his right hand off for rather than seduce. She's a lady, James! Even I can see that.'

'Even you?' he parried. 'And what are you if not a lady, Elizabeth?'

Her mouth flattened. 'A whore. Before I settled

down with Fox I'd had more men than you will have women in your entire life if you live to be a vigorous ninety!' James spluttered, but she went on. 'I don't forget that, James, and nor does anyone else. Pretending otherwise butters no parsnips.' For an instant the accents of the streets she had escaped broke through.

'And Fox?' James shot her a glance. 'I think he'd have something to say about that.'

'Perhaps,' Elizabeth admitted. 'But he loves me with his eyes open. And whatever I am, that girl is a lady. Why is she *not exactly* your mistress?'

James let out a breath. His gaze strayed ahead to where Lucy walked with Fox, her hand resting on his arm.

'Because she has not yet accepted my offer of protection.'

She acknowledged the introduction to Elizabeth. She is going to accept.

He should be feeling elated. Instead he was conscious of a deep unease. What Fox, if he were a conventional sort of godfather, might have called his conscience.

'I hope my godson is taking good care of you, my dear.'

Lucy gulped. 'Er…no.' Then, as Fox's eyebrows rose, she said, 'That is, yes, he is, but…I'm not, we're not— It's not what you think. Exactly.'

The bushy brows rose even higher over the kindly eyes. 'And what, exactly, do I think?'

She took a deep breath. 'That I'm his mistress.'

He nodded. 'Still negotiating, eh? Who were you with?'

Her mind blanked. 'Who—? Oh! No. I wasn't... I'm not...I've never—' Whatever she was or wasn't, or had never, she sounded like an idiot, so she shut up.

Fox's brows snapped together. 'Never?' His head cocked and he subjected her to a piercing examination. 'No. What the deuce is the boy thinking? Who is your family?'

'My family?' She stiffened, tried to withdraw her hand, but his tightened over it with startling firmness. 'My family has nothing to do with this.'

He scowled. 'Nonsense. No point trying to convince me you're not well born and James must know it as well as I do.'

She gave him as much of the truth as she dared. 'My father is a gamester. His family cast him off and me, as well.'

Fox nodded slowly, his eyes on her face. 'Gamester, eh? Hensleigh's not your real name, of course. Chances are I'd recognise it. Spent enough time in the hells myself once.' He cleared his throat. 'Well, I dare say it's none of my business, except as it touches James.'

* * *

'James?'

Elizabeth's gentle voice recalled him. He looked at her. 'Her father is connected to this business I'm trying to ferret out,' he said. 'I need to keep her out of it.'

Elizabeth's hand tightened on his arm. 'Kilby.'

'Yes.'

She was silent for a moment, her eyes distant, as though she saw things long past and buried, a shadow on her face. At last she spoke. 'Fox told me why you want Kilby.' She let out a sigh. 'Very well. I know your cousin by sight, at least.' A wistful smile came to her lips. 'And I remember Huntercombe. Although that was before he inherited the title. A nice boy. Kind.'

James digested that. 'You…er…knew him?'

Her smile curved wickedly. 'James, dear, he was the well-heeled, handsome heir to a great title with an appreciation of an attractive woman. And it was before Fox. Of course I knew him!'

She brushed a gloved finger at her eyes. 'Perhaps you might remember me to him? Tell him how very sorry I am for his loss.'

She glanced at James. 'So at first you just bailed your cousin out.'

He nodded. 'Yes. It seemed the right thing.' His cheeks heated and he cast her a glance, saw the tilt at the corner of her mouth. 'Somebody once extracted me from a mess of my own making, as I recall.'

She laughed. 'If you're thinking I did anything very much you're sadly mistaken. I merely told Harriet you'd be a dreadful husband and started a rumour that you'd gambled away your fortune—Fox's influence, you know.'

That explained why his then mistress, in possession of his written proposal of marriage, dashed off in an inebriated flight of fancy, had returned the missive for a paltry thousand and a pair of diamond earrings, and promptly taken another lover.

'A dreadful husband?'

'Autocratic to the last degree,' she assured him. 'And a shocking bully!'

He grinned. 'I still owe you for that.'

'Nonsense,' she said. 'She never intended to marry you, but you would have paid through the nose for the privilege. All I did was persuade her that she'd better take what she could quickly before the creditors descended.'

They walked on slowly in the gentle spring sunshine, the gravel path scrunching underfoot. Flowers crowded the garden beds and were aflutter with bees. On the ornamental lake ahead a duck led a flotilla of ducklings. Fox and Lucy had stopped to watch.

'He likes her,' Elizabeth said.

James could see that. His godfather still had Lucy's hand tucked into the crook of his arm, his head inclined towards her. Fox's fruity chuckle drifted back to them and the unease deepened. James glanced at Elizabeth, wondering if Fox would also take him to task about Lucy.

She can still say no. She could always say no. She has a choice.

But an uncompromising voice kept asking: *What's her other choice?*

Fox had walked on a little way with her and Lucy breathed a sigh of relief that the catechism was apparently over.

'D'you want him?'

The blunt question robbed Lucy of breath and thought. Memory poured through her. The heat that sparked along every nerve when he touched her, the shivery, melting sensation when he lifted her down from the curricle, the sense of utter rightness when he held her... Her breath shuddered out. And his kiss—deep, possessive, igniting feelings that she had never known existed, an aching wildness, a yearning. Oh, yes. She wanted him and she ought not to. Against every precept she had been brought up to accept, she wanted him in a way that ought to be repugnant, at least according to Aunt Caroline...

Her cousin Henrietta had married when Lucy was

fourteen. The night before the wedding Aunt Caroline had explained the marriage bed to Henrietta, not bothering to send Lucy from the room. It had sounded awful. Painful, humiliating… Aunt's final words had been daunting in the extreme.

A lady does her duty quietly. She does not betray unbecoming interest, merely obeys her husband's requests, and endeavours to submit. Gentlemen are different. They have Urges and may seek to relieve them in the arms of Another. A sensible lady will see this as an indirect sign of respect—that her husband does not view her *as a suitable object for his baser needs.*

At fourteen, Lucy had thought that marriage sounded dreadful and she forgave Aunt Caroline all her bad temper and peevishness if she had to put up with *that* all the time. Especially with Uncle Bertram.

Now, she wasn't so sure. At least, she was still perfectly sure about Uncle Bertram—Aunt Caroline had her sympathy. But the way Cambourne had kissed her—

She faced his godfather with her chin up. 'Yes. I want him.'

Fox let out a rich chuckle and patted her hand. 'You've a deal of courage about you. Not one girl in a hundred would have admitted that. Well, never mind,' he said in a comforting voice. 'Dare say he'll come to his senses sooner or later.'

'Kilby, then.' Elizabeth's voice became clipped. 'He's dangerous, James. Brothels, gaming hells, thieving. He's not particular.'

'He's had no trouble with the magistrates that I could find,' James said.

Elizabeth snorted. 'Don't be naive. You know a blind eye is turned when it suits. How many gentlemen enjoy brothels and gaming hells?'

'And being beaten to death when they can't pay?'

Elizabeth frowned. 'That's not common knowledge,' she said. 'But I did get a whisper of it. Only a whisper, and only because I already knew and asked the right questions.' She laid her hand on his arm. 'He's feared, James. If you want him, you'll have to take one of his forcers and get him to turn King's evidence.'

Immunity for the men who'd beaten Nick and murdered Huntercombe's brother? It tasted sour in his mouth.

Elizabeth's gaze was uncompromising. 'It depends on how much you want Kilby.' Her mouth tightened. 'And remember this, he doesn't tolerate betrayal. That's why he's lasted so long—those who cross him disappear. Are you using Miss Hensleigh to get to him?' Anger edged her voice.

* * *

'Come to his senses?' Lucy stared at Fox. That made no sense at all. She could understand Fox worrying about Cambourne's lack of sense had he been offering marriage, but he wasn't. To him, she was *Another*. Not a wife.

Fox laughed, his expression rueful. 'Yes. It takes some of us longer than others.' He glanced back to where Cambourne and Mrs Armistead were speaking quietly. Lucy blinked. It looked very like Mrs Armistead were scolding Cambourne. If a man so self-assured could be said to hang his head, Cambourne was doing it.

'My Liz is a woman in a million,' Fox said softly. 'I don't deserve her, either. But at least I know it.'

It seemed an odd thing for a man to say of his mistress.

'You have been together a long time, have you not, sir?'

His tender smile shook Lucy's heart. Some day would Cambourne smile like that at or about her? 'Twenty years. Never wanted anyone else after Liz. She's the only one for me.'

Knowledge came to Lucy in a lightning rush. 'You love her.'

The smile deepened 'Yes, of course.'

There was no *of course* about it. But now she had seen it, Fox's love was so obvious she wondered that she hadn't seen it at once. Grandpapa's mutterings about harpy's claws were nonsense. Only love could have held Fox with Elizabeth Armistead all these years.

'Cambourne is not offering love, Mr Fox,' she said very quietly as they strolled on. He had been very careful *not* to offer love. He had been almost brutally honest with her. It was not his fault that his honesty had had quite the opposite of its intended effect.

Fox nodded. 'Perhaps not. But love grows over time. Grows and changes.'

'Only if it is there to start with.'

He stopped beside a clump of purple-and-yellow violas. 'Johnny Jump-ups, my Liz calls them. No doubt I'm an old fool, but I call them Heartsease. Before they came up a few weeks ago I dare say it looked as though there was nothing there at all. And if you'd dug in the bed you'd have been hard-pressed to spot the seed. But it was there all along.' He smiled down at her. 'And who knows what hand planted the first seed?'

Elizabeth's words stung.

'Damn it! It's not like that!' Only…as James looked at Lucy, walking ahead with Fox, he admitted his guilt; it had started like that. He was using Lucy. Oh, not with any intent of harming her. He hadn't stooped that low. But even so, his carelessness had put her in danger. And now it was different. Now Lucy mattered. Even the boy, Fitch, mattered. A chill slid through him at the thought of Kilby going after Hensleigh through Lucy. Kilby, from the sounds of it, would use and discard any tool he could.

He clenched his fists. 'I want her safe, away from her father.'

'Tell me, Miss Lucy—' Fox's voice was very kind '—do you *wish* to become a man's mistress?'

She hesitated, unsure of the answer to that, or even if there was an answer. A man's mistress? Any man? 'No, but—just Lord Cambourne's mistress.'

Fox cocked his head. 'Ah. A distinction, then, in your mind. Very well. Do you know, I think it is high time we found out what James has arranged for luncheon.' He raised his voice. 'James! Surely you were brought up better than to keep visitors wandering around with their stomachs growling?'

James had arranged for a meal to be served al fresco on the terrace in a sheltered, sunny corner. He found himself enjoying the meal enormously. He always enjoyed the company of Fox and Elizabeth, but Lucy's presence brightened everything. Of course it was odd to eat with Fox and Elizabeth with another woman present. No lady of any social standing would consent to be seen with the notorious Mrs Armistead. To do so would spell utter ruin. It was different for a man. A man could associate with as many notorious women as he liked and be hailed as a devil of a fine fellow. The hypocrisy irked him.

'Liz, my dear?' Fox wiped his mouth. 'Should you care to visit Vauxhall tomorrow night? I thought we might invite these two youngsters.'

James set his wine glass down carefully and gave his godfather a very hard look which Fox ignored.

A faint smile curled Elizabeth's mouth as she considered her lover. 'Vauxhall? What a splendid notion, sir.' She glanced at James. 'Will you and Miss Hensleigh join us?'

Lucy's fork clattered on her plate. 'I don't think— that is, I don't have—'

James stared at her and she stopped, cheeks crimson. Her hands twitched at her gown and understanding crashed over him.

The faded, old-fashioned gown was probably her best. It wasn't patched like the other gown he'd seen her wear, but it was worn, ill-fitting. It was not something a woman would want to wear out at all, let alone to a fashionable venue like Vauxhall.

'Lucy, I can—'

'No. Please. You have already done a great deal for me, sir.'

Her chin was up, her mouth set in a firm line. He

let out a frustrated breath as the colour in her cheeks deepened. Damn it! He'd done so little for her. A bonnet and a sketchbook, some music and the books he'd lent her. Did she think he would let her dress like a scarecrow when she was his?

But she wasn't his. Not yet. And accepting a gown now would put her under a further obligation. His fists clenched. That was the last thing he wanted—Lucy to feel obliged to accept his offer.

'Perhaps I can help.' Elizabeth broke the awkward silence. 'I am sure I have a gown that would suit.'

James opened his mouth, and shut it again as a booted foot collided with his shin under the table. Fox cleared his throat.

Elizabeth continued. 'My maid is much your size and height. If it is altered to fit Lucy, it will do well enough.'

Why, James wondered, did Elizabeth, now in her fifties, have in her armoire a gown suitable for a girl of twenty?

Lucy looked uncertain. 'It is too much trouble. You scarcely know me, ma'am.'

'No trouble at all, my dear,' Elizabeth said. 'James can collect it tomorrow and bring it to you.'

James sat back. So *that* was the strategy. He would buy a gown after all and Lucy would think—

'You are very kind, ma'am, but—'

'My dear—' Elizabeth's voice was wistful '—will

you not permit me this pleasure? I will never have the joy of dressing a daughter.'

James stilled as Elizabeth's eyes met Fox's gaze and a smile passed between them. A tender smile with a hint of regret. Had they wanted children? Not been able to have them?

'Liz, dearest Liz.' Fox held out his hand.

'It was the choice we made, Charles.' Elizabeth placed her hand in his and Fox's fingers closed tightly. She turned back to Lucy. 'Altering a gown and seeing you wear it will be the greatest of pleasures for me.'

'And for me,' Fox said. 'I'm a sentimental old fool, as James will tell you.'

'The deuce I will, sir.' James gave Elizabeth a level look which she returned calmly. 'What time should I collect the gown?'

She smiled gently. 'I shall send a note around.'

'Elizabeth—'

She waved further discussion away. 'It is all settled. You may busy yourself tomorrow choosing a pretty trifle for Miss Hensleigh. A fan or some such unexceptionable thing.'

Lucy's troubled gaze flickered to him. 'I don't need—'

'Of course you do, dear.' Elizabeth said. 'Fans are very useful. One may express all the things one is not permitted to *say*. Annoyance, admiration, dislike.' She glanced at James. 'In extreme cases one may rap an annoyance over the knuckles. All the more satisfying if he actually bought it for you.'

After luncheon Fox and Elizabeth made their fare-wells.

James handed Elizabeth up into their carriage. 'Are you really going to alter a gown?' he asked very quietly.

Her smile glimmered. 'Let us say that I am going to provide a gown.' She settled her skirts elegantly. 'And all she requires—chemise, stays, stockings, shoes, a cloak.'

'But—'

'No, James.' She laid gentle fingers on his wrist. 'I think if she had the choice—'

'She has a choice!' He could barely keep his voice down. 'Elizabeth, you can't imagine—?'

'That you might constrain her?' Her smile was a little lopsided. 'I know you would not. But circum-stances might and I think she would rather give her-self for love—'

'Love?' Something in his chest grew tight. 'Eliza-beth, I swear I did not seduce her with tales…er… offers of love.'

'I know that, too.' Her tones became clipped. 'And I can assure you that for a girl in her situation to fancy herself in love is the greatest folly imaginable.'

'Folly?' For some obscure reason that hurt.

'Yes. Folly. A woman in love is vulnerable, James. She makes decisions based on sensibility, not sense. And men—' her lip curled '—*gentlemen* are so quick to take advantage.'

Fox, seated beside her, patted her hand. 'Liz, dear, I believe we may trust James to behave just as he ought.'

Could they? He was damned if he knew any longer how he was supposed to be behaving.

But the fire in Elizabeth's eyes died down and she sighed. 'Yes. I know. I apologise, James. But, please, allow the child her pride. Let me dress her for tomorrow night.'

She was right. 'A fan.'

'Yes. A pretty one in ivory. That will go with anything.'

Lucy's breath caught as Cambourne came back into the entrance hall from farewelling Mr Fox and Mrs Armistead. Would it always be like this? Her heart leaping at the sight of his tall, lean figure? The aching pleasure of his slightly crooked smile? The way his grey eyes crinkled at the corners when he laughed, and the stray lock of hair that fell over his brow, making her long to push it back? And he had laughed this week and smiled. As though he were happy just to be with her. As though they were friends, lovers even. Not prospective mistress and protector. Cold slid through her. The day was nearly over, the sun slipping into the west beyond the river.

'Is it time to go?'

He nodded. 'Yes.'

Something was bothering him. Had been bothering him since they'd sat down to eat. His gaze lingered on her for a moment and then he turned, spoke quietly to the footman at the door.

'Very good, my lord.'

'Thank you.'

She liked that about him. He never took his servants for granted, always remembering to thank them for a service. And yet there was never the least question that he was in command, expected to be obeyed at all times. So different from her father, grandfather and uncle, who had all treated the servants as so much lumber. Surely if a man were considerate to his servants, he might be expected to look after his mistress well.

He smiled. 'Will you walk with me? There is something I should like you to see.'

She rose and he held out his hand. His fingers closed over hers and she fought down the leap of pleasure at the simple touch, at the way he tucked her hand into the crook of his elbow and held it there. As if he planned to keep it there always.

Not always. Don't think about always.

Always was a dangerous, slippery beast, not to be relied on. Now had to be enough. And now, when they were alone, she had to tell Cambourne her decision.

He led her down the steps under the great portico and around one side of the house. How did one say something like that? On the lawn a peacock strutted, tail spread. Desperate for something, anything to say, she exclaimed, 'Oh! He's beautiful!'

James snorted. 'That's what my mother said. Stupid things, really.'

She drew a deep breath. 'My lord?' At his quizzical sideways glance, she flushed. 'Very well. Cambourne. I accept your offer.'

Although he kept walking, she had the impression that something within him had stilled utterly. They walked on towards the wall that enclosed the park, half-hidden by shrubbery. Cambourne said nothing, and if it hadn't been for the sudden tightening of his fingers on hers, she would have wondered if he'd even heard her.

Behind a mass of shrubs a small wooden door was set into the wall. Cambourne drew a key from his pocket, unlocked the door and opened it, gesturing her through. Puzzled, Lucy stepped through the door and into another world.

Gone were the ordered, sweeping vistas of the park. This was a garden where shady trees seemed to have simply grown where they felt like it. Not far away a great oak towered, a swing moving lazily in the breeze attached to one of its lower branches. Further away a small grove of cherry trees reached up to the sun, their fruit already set. Beyond them were roses, a dancing riot of colour closer to the house.

'Won't the owner mind us just walking in?'

'No. He doesn't mind.'

The laughter in his voice had her looking up at him. Sure enough the corners of his eyes were crinkled up. 'You own it?' Of course he did. He had a key for the garden gate. The gate that led into his own park.

'Yes. The carriage will meet us on the other side.'

'But doesn't someone live here?' The house, a good-sized cottage, did not have that sad, abandoned look of houses that were not lived in.

'There's a caretaker. The last tenant, an artist friend of my father's, died a few months ago. The house needed repairs so it hasn't been let again.'

'Oh.' She looked about. It was exactly the sort of house she had once allowed herself to dream about. Large enough to be comfortable with a garden where a dog would not be a nuisance. Where even a cat might be welcome… And she was dreaming again. 'It's very pretty. Did your father's friend like it?'

'Very much. He lived here for thirty years. My father liked his work, so he kept the rent low.' Amusement curved his mouth. 'And bought a great many paintings. A convenient arrangement for both of them.'

They walked on. Closer to the house there were flower beds, where colour leaped and rambled. Nasturtiums, blazing orange, sweetpeas clambering over an old gate and everywhere the roses, drowning the air in fragrance. And still he had said nothing about her acceptance of his offer. She swallowed. Perhaps he had tired of her without ever having her. This week had supposedly been to give her a chance to know her own mind. It was just as likely that he had had a change of—well, not heart; hearts were not supposed to be involved—but a change of mind. She wouldn't find out by remaining mute.

'Sir. Cambourne. If you have changed your mind—'

'Changed my mind?'

'About...' About what? 'About our affair.' That was the right word. *Affair.* Businesslike.

He stopped, brought her around to face him and his mouth was on hers in searing possession. Shock rippled through her. Shock at the heat of the kiss, at the fierce strength in his arms about her. She yielded on a gasp, giving him her mouth, and instantly the kiss gentled. Tender, beguiling, he sought entry, and she gave it, opening her mouth to the press of his tongue. Gentle hands caressed and moulded her body to his. Fire shimmered through her, melting her, opening an ache inside that demanded relief.

Shaking, James forced himself to release her, eased back to rest his cheek on her hair. His breath came raggedly and his heart hammered. 'No. I haven't changed my mind.' And if he didn't get her into the curricle and safely home, he was going to be consummating the relationship right here and now. Somehow, although he was supposed to be the one in control, with all the answers and power, she constantly tipped the balance, shredding his control and putting the conventional, expected answers in doubt. He was no longer even sure of the right questions. He had set this particular wheel in motion, not thinking where it might stop.

Lucy had come to him. Freely. Willingly.

He raised her hand to his lips. 'I'll make the arrangements and tell you tomorrow.' Her fingers trembled as he kissed them and something tightened in his chest. He vowed silently that she would never regret trusting him.

'He took her out for the day, guv.'

Kilby scowled. 'Out *again*? Where?'

Jig shrugged. 'What? I got wings now, 'ave I? Used 'is carriage, he did.'

'And he's still taking her back to her lodgings?'
Jig nodded. 'Yeah. Didn' stay long, never does.'
He flexed his fingers. 'We could still grab her, guv.
Easy as pie. No one ain't going to—'

'No.' Kilby's voice rapped it out. 'Too dangerous. If
a man like that gets wind of it, we could bring hell's
own kitchen down around our ears. If he's leaving
her there, just taking her out, he's courting her.'

'Courting?' Jig didn't quite believe that. 'Like,
getting a leg-shackle?'

'A wife?' Kilby laughed. 'Not damned likely. He'll
be after her as a mistress, but that doesn't mean he
won't cut up rough if we snatch the prize out from
under him. We wait. When her loving papa shows
up, just knowing we're on to the wench might be
enough to make him cough up if he's holding out on
me. And if it isn't—' Kilby's smile turned unpleasant '—his daughter will regret it very much, but I'm
not going to risk it without Hensleigh back in town.'

Jig scratched his ear. 'What difference does that
make?'

Kilby's smile was predatory. 'Because his lordship
will think Hensleigh is responsible for the girl's dis-
appearance. He'll go after him, not me.'

It was the choice we made.
Mrs Armistead's wistful voice refused to be banished.

Lucy stared at the jar of seeds on the shelf above the flickering fire. James had made sure she had enough coal.

A spoonful as soon after as ever you can... Chew 'em good.

And yet Cambourne had promised to provide for a child. Men didn't always keep their promises, but she thought he would. Just as Mr Fox would have done. And it sounded as though he and Mrs Armistead, while not regretting their decision, wished they could have decided otherwise. So if there really was a way to protect herself...at least at first.

And how will you protect your heart?

She shut her eyes. Only by never imagining that he returned her feelings, by remembering that love was not part of the transaction, and that anything she felt for him must remain hidden within the walls of her own heart. Only how was she supposed to do that when the man insisted on skipping stones with her? When he gave her a journal to sketch her dreams in? When he kissed her in a garden golden with the late afternoon and brimming with roses?

Chapter Nine

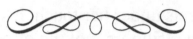

The gown, shimmering pale-green silk, and its attendant undergarments lay on the neatly made bed, a fantasy in the candlelight. Lucy could only stare, her breath uncertain. Even Henrietta, when she married Mr Bentinck, had not had such a gown as this. Silk stockings, whisper-fine, lay on the faded, patched counterpane. Dancing slippers to match the gown stood beside the bed. The faint fragrance of lavender drifted from little sachets that had nestled in the folds of the garments.

Tears burned behind her eyes as she read the accompanying note again.

My dear,
I confess I lied when I said I had a gown that could be made over. But I trust you will forgive the deception and think only of the joy this gave me.
You may believe me that Cambourne, in this,

has been no more than my courier, although I
hope his taste in fans is acceptable.
Your affectionate friend,
Elizabeth Armistead

Lucy's fingers slid, wondering, over the silk. It whispered secrets under her touch. It seemed that the silk caressed her fingers, not the other way around, that it was alive with dreams and possibilities.

Or did it whisper temptation? Lies to ensnare a fool.

Cambourne was waiting for her out in the other room. He had carried all the boxes and parcels in here, placed them on the bed and then shut the door behind himself, his face a mask. Doubt reared, hissing.

He doesn't really want you. Why would he?

But if he did…

She took a deep breath. Apparently she was her father's daughter after all, because she was about to risk everything on the biggest gamble of her life. If it worked, when Cambourne tired of her, she would have a nest egg, enough to buy an annuity to live on quietly and peacefully for the rest of her days.

A shiver went through her at the thought of Cambourne tiring of her. Would he tell her himself? Send a note? How did a gentleman dismiss a mistress? And how did the mistress manage when, in addition to virtue and reputation—unavoidable losses in the circumstances—she had been foolish enough to risk her heart?

Glancing once at the closed door, she stripped out of her old gown and washed with the bucket of water she had hauled up earlier. Quickly she towelled dry and slipped on the chemise and petticoat. They drifted against her skin, nearly weightless after the coarse, hard-wearing garments she was accustomed to. Soft, fine, exquisitely stitched and not a patch or darn to be seen.

She picked up the stays, wriggled into them back to front and tightened the laces as much as she could before squirming and wriggling them around into place. They hung far too loosely and she reached for the stay strings, now behind her.

She could barely reach the strings, let alone tighten or tie them. She had forgotten. Not since she left her uncle's house had she worn stays, or any clothing, that required assistance to fasten. And the undergarment she usually wore would show above the neckline of the silk gown.

The door opened and James braced for the sight of Lucy in—well, he'd no idea what Elizabeth had chosen, she'd made him promise not to look—but he expected to be—

He'd expected to be able to breathe. But all the air

in the room disappeared as if sucked out by a raging inferno. Everything in him turned to iron as he called on every scrap of self-control and restraint, every heartbeat a hammer blow.

He tried to speak and wondered if he'd swallowed his tongue. Reminding himself to breathe, he tried again. 'Lucy?' His voice sounded odd, distant, thick.

Utterly delectable, she stood, clutching her stays to her with both hands. The fine, nearly transparent petticoat drifted around slender legs, reaching only to mid-calf. She had put on the stockings and the daintiest green silk slippers and the sight nearly felled him. Somehow it was more erotic than if she had left legs and feet bare, his imagination was more than compensating. With a savage effort he forced his gaze upwards and wondered if he'd survive the evening. The cream peach-skin curves of her upper breasts invited him to caress, to love, to taste... She'd taste like— Lord, he had no idea how she'd taste, but he doubted that he'd ever get enough of it.

'I...I can't tighten my stays.'

He was only marginally aware of what she had said. Her soft voice lured his senses as he understood that, in this case, knowing what a woman was wearing under her gown meant his mind leapt straight to imagining taking it all off her later on.

He heard a strangled voice, his own, say, 'Ah, tighten,' as if he'd never heard the word before.

Slowly his brain won control from body and instincts. Tighten...doing them up. Helping her dress, not undress. Not easing the stays from her fingers and removing them, not slipping the translucent lawn from her body while he kissed her insensible...

'Cambourne?'

The trembling uncertainty in her voice brought him back to reality. And reality was a cold, shabby room and a girl crimson with mortification, whose eyes held his gaze steadily. On a rush of shame he saw what an unthinking fool he'd been. He hadn't fully explained Lucy's circumstances to Elizabeth. Elizabeth, given her limited approval of his pursuit, would have sent her own maid rather than put Lucy in this position.

He took a slow, careful breath, reaching for the last crumbling shreds of honour, and rose, thanking God he'd left his evening cloak on against the room's chill. He had an erection that would have startled an experienced woman, let alone an innocent.

'Of course, sweetheart. Turn around.' His voice was husky and his hands shook.

She obeyed. 'You...you have to tighten them from the top down, sort of bit by bit.'

He swallowed. She sounded terrified. As though she knew exactly how fragile was his grip on honour and restraint.

'I kn—' He choked that off. She might suspect,

but she didn't need to hear that he was perfectly familiar, at least in theory, with how to lace a pair of stays. Not that he'd ever done it. But he supposed that if he reversed the process of *un*lacing them, that would work.

His fingers awkward, he began, trying not to breathe the sweet feminine scent that rose from her. His mind whirled, lungs tight as he tried to breathe as shallowly as possible. She smelled of sweet, delicious woman. *His* woman.

He wanted to bend over, breathe her in, nibble on her creamy vulnerable nape, nip at the tender, sensitive curve between neck and shoulder, hear her soft cries as he discovered all the secrets of her body. In the candlelit shadows, her hair glowed copper fire, braided and tucked up under itself. Errant curls drifted around her face and he longed to release the whole fiery mass to tumble over her shoulders, to lose his hands in it.

Desperately he forced his gaze back to the regimented laces marching down her slender back. He fought not to notice, or at least not to let his hands settle on, the gently female curve of waist and hips, the enticing globes of her bottom.

'Is…is that tight enough?'

God knew his breeches were.

She gave an experimental wriggle that nearly had him bent double in an agony of need.

'I… Yes. Thank you.'

'Not at all.' Amazing that the manners drilled into him as a child acted as an anchor now, holding him to a semblance of honour.

'I might need help with the gown, too. Um, it fastens at the back.'

Of course it did.

'When you are ready.' Ready? God help him, *he* sure as hell was.

The door closed, and he shut his eyes, praying for strength, wondering if this was proof that God, a capricious Fate, or both, had a sense of humour.

She deserved better. Better than a hasty, furtive coupling in these shabby rooms. She deserved his time, his care, his…tenderness. He frowned, looking carefully at that last word. Tenderness? Where had that come from? Care, gentleness, certainly. But tenderness?

Would she agree to come with him tonight? Unsure if everything could be done in time, he'd not mentioned the possibility yesterday, but everything was ready at Chiswick. His servants knew to expect him and everything was prepared for her.

Had he read her wrongly? She had liked it out by the river, liked Hawthorne Lodge. True, the house was small, but it was comfortably furnished and she would be safe there. Safe and close to him. He'd arranged to be at Chiswick for the rest of the Season and part of the summer. Not as convenient for him as London, but he didn't want Lucy in town.

In the past when he'd had a mistress he'd set her up in St James's, paraded her in the Park, at the opera. The affair had been public and that had been a great deal of the fun, apart from the sex, of course. Amusing to see the envy on other men's faces, as they speculated on what it was costing him and how inventive his *inamorata* might be in bed.

That wasn't Lucy. She was different, and... The voice that had whispered of tenderness murmured again: *You're different. Different with her.*

Lucy was picnics, walks by the river, driving lessons, maybe a puppy. Oh, he wanted her in bed right enough, but if anyone was fool enough to speculate on Lucy and bed in the same breath, he'd have to cough his teeth back up to carry them home.

'Cambourne?'

He turned and could say nothing. It wasn't lust that silenced him, that scattered his wits, although that was certainly there. It was—he didn't want to think about what it was, because, without even knowing what it was, it squeezed his guts to a jelly.

'Is something wrong?' She had that soft, lush lower lip between her teeth in the way she had when she was nervous that made him want to nip it himself. And then soothe it with his tongue. 'The gown... Is it—?'

'The gown is—it looks very well.' He sounded like a dazed schoolboy. 'It... You look—' Was there even a word? 'Very pretty.'

Pretty? She looked like a wood nymph. Soft green silk loosely skimmed the creamy curves of her upper breasts and his fingers itched to trace the sweet forbidden boundary of silk and skin—and he'd swear her skin would be the softer—slide beneath and ease her right back out of the gown and into bed.

'I can't reach the fastenings.'

He nodded, still lost for coherent thought, let alone speech. How the hell could a gown be even more inviting than her undergarments?

'Turn for me.'

She did so and his reluctant fingers dealt with the hooks and tapes.

'There are flowers,' she said, as he slipped the last hook. 'Silk flowers. I wasn't sure if they were to go somewhere on the gown.'

He took a careful breath. 'Show me.'

He followed her back into the bedroom and tried not to notice the bed.

She held out the flowers, tiny cream-silk rosebuds on silk-wrapped wire stems.

'For—' What was wrong with his voice? He cleared his throat and tried again. 'For your hair.' He took the flowers, turned her and, one by one, slid them between the strands of her braid, twisting the stems to anchor them in the soft, fragrant fire.

Carefully he set the last one in place and brought her around to face him. 'There.'

'Will I do?'

He swallowed. 'You're beautiful.' She was a goddess. A sylvan goddess to tempt mortals to destruction. Slowly, he slid his hands down her arms to clasp her hands. Her eyes widened as he raised her hands, feathered his lips over one wrist. Skin softer than silk, tissue-fine. And her breath, trembling in over-parted lips.

'My lord?'

That slashed at him. 'No. Not that, sweetheart.'

'Cambourne, then.'

Other lovers had called him that, women he had liked, even been fond of, but—

'James. Call me James.' He kissed her. The lightest brush of lips at first, lingering, tasting, then deepening. He kissed her open-mouthed until her lips parted on a sigh and his tongue slid within.

Spicy-sweet. He kept the kiss gentle, stroking slowly, tenderly into the haven of her mouth. The shy response of her tongue against his ripped a shuddering groan from him. He wanted more, so much more, and yet he thought he could kiss her, just kiss her, for ever and it would not be long enough. Her arms had slipped about him and he drew her closer, one hand sliding into her hair, holding her captive for his hungry mouth, the other on the supple curve of her waist. She came willingly and he eased her against the insistent ache of his body.

*A few more kisses, a few more caresses...*the sly little voice urged him on...*she'll agree to anything you want...*

With a muttered curse he broke the kiss and stepped back, feeling as though part of himself had been ripped away. She gazed at him, her expression dazed, clouded, her lips swollen from his kisses. He wanted to pull her back into his arms and finish it.

'Lucy.' His ragged breath roughened his voice. 'We're not going to do this. Not here. Not now.'

She flinched. 'I wasn't—' She took a shaken breath. 'I didn't mean—'

'No. I know you didn't.' He risked reaching for her hands again, needing the connection. He was going to be honest with her if it killed him. 'But I did.'

And if I don't get you out of here, I will.

Lucy struggled for breath, for a mental footing. Cambourne's—she could not quite think of him as James, despite his request—Cambourne's eyes held a heat and hunger that threatened to consume her, and yet he had retained control and pulled back when she had not even recognised the danger.

'Lucy.' His gentle, diffident voice was at odds with that hunger and the contrast tore at her. 'You said that you had considered my offer, that you would accept it.'

'Yes.'

He seemed oddly hesitant. 'I have the house at Chiswick.'

Part of her recoiled. Cambourne Hall was beautiful, but it seemed so cold, so grand. Could she live there? Perhaps with him she could, but she knew better than that. He could not live with her. He would visit. When he wanted her. The rest of the time she would drift around that enormous, coldly elegant house like a ghost in a marble tomb.

'The Chiswick house?' She tried to sound happy.

'Yes. I've made arrangements to be there for the next couple of months at least.'

She stared. Did he mean he would leave her in town, while—

'Hawthorne Lodge is prepared for you. It's not big, but it's comfortable, and you would be close to me.'

'Oh.' The little house in its rambling garden, by the river where swans sailed in regal disdain and ducks scrambled for bread.

'Lucy—' his hands tightened on hers '—you would be safe there.'

'Safe?'

A queer expression flashed over his face. 'Safer than you are here without anyone.'

She stiffened her spine. 'I'm all right.'

Except you have no money, not even enough for food. But she didn't want to give herself like that— in exchange for a roof that didn't leak and a meal in her belly. She wanted…what she wanted had no place here.

She braced herself. 'And you would visit me there.' What a wonder the English language was in its flexibility—*visit* had a whole new meaning.

He nodded. 'Yes. And I swear I'd take good care of you.'

She had known this moment was coming, this final decision. But it had not been *now.* And now it was *now. This* now. *This* moment. And she understood that even now she could step back. But she didn't want to step back. She wanted to step forward. To him.

Such a small step. But once taken her life would break into the past and whatever her future held. And that break would widen into an unbridgeable chasm; it would be impossible to go back.

On this side lay respectability with its attendant fears and virtue its own dubious reward. She could try to contact Uncle Bertram and Aunt Caroline. They were likely up for Parliament. They might help her find a position, but even so, what surety would she have against sickness, or old age? A governess earned twenty pounds a year if she was lucky.

If she went to James...

D'you want him?

She had not lied to Fox yesterday. She would not lie to herself today, pretending that the only reason she was going to accept James was fear of the future. She was going to him because she wanted him and this was the only way she could have him. She did not know if she would have made this decision without the spur of poverty, but she would not pretend that was the only reason.

'Sweetheart?'

The endearment pierced her, lodged deep within.

'When shall I come?'

His fingers tightened. 'Tonight. I can take you there from Vauxhall. Everything is prepared.'

'Tonight?'

The gently bred, ladylike part of her that Grandmama had reared said she ought to be fainting, or at least having the vapours. The other part, the wild part she had not even suspected, leapt to life, to the unknown, to adventure. And something else, the lonely part of her that longed to belong, even in the smallest way, somewhere that she was wanted.

His fingers brushed her jaw, feathered fire over the skittering pulse in her throat.

'Sweetheart, *that* does not have to happen tonight. You'll be tired, I know. But—' again that queer flash of…relief? '—I'll have you safe. Nothing else has to happen until you're ready.'

A whole flight of butterflies had taken up residence in her stomach. Tonight, then. There was no point in putting off the inevitable, even though he was giving the choice, the final decision, to her. Her heart shook; he was considering *her* desires, *her* needs, before his own. She could not remember anyone doing that since her mother's death.

'I'll need to pack—'

He shook his head. 'No. You can—'

'But—' She gulped. Ridiculous to expect him to let her go in rags because she had missish scruples about accepting new clothes when she was prepared to be his mistress. However, until she did… 'I can't live in *this*.' She plucked at the silken gown. 'And I'll need my night—' She faltered, seeing the tender curve of his smile. Very well, perhaps she *wasn't* going to need her nightgown. 'I need my violin.'

His smile deepened. 'Definitely bring that. Do you play the piano?'

'Yes, but—'

'I'll have one moved from the main house. There are two there.' He frowned. 'Actually, it might be three.'

He wasn't sure how many pianos he owned? 'There's no—'

A swift kiss stole her wits and breath. 'We can argue about that later,' he said. 'Let's get you packed for now.'

Chapter Ten

Ten minutes later, James vowed that the next time Lucy moved house it would take her a great deal longer to pack. Even with the books he'd lent her and the little chess set, her possessions took up rather less room than the new gown and its accessories had. And yet the closet had held two spare sets of gentleman's clothing, admittedly somewhat worn, but nevertheless Hensleigh possessed more than the clothes he stood up in. And one assumed he'd taken more away with him.

Selfish bastard.

'That's everything,' said Lucy. 'Oh!' She hurried across to the fireplace and took down a small jar. 'I'd better not forget this.'

'What is it?'

She went very red. 'Er…just a tonic. For ladies.'

Ah. Well, that explained the blush. He knew women often felt poorly at a certain time of the month, but it was not the sort of thing that a woman wished to explain to her lover.

His gaze fell on one last parcel lying on the table. He'd nearly forgotten something, too.

He picked it up and handed it to her. 'For you.'

'You didn't have to—'

'Oh, yes, I did,' he told her. 'Or face Elizabeth's wrath.'

She smiled. 'The fan?'

'Open it and see.'

He watched as she undid the string and pulled the paper away.

'Ohhh!'

The little ivory-silk reticule tumbled into her hands. She stared at it, stroked it with a careful finger. 'It's beautiful. Just beautiful.' She looked up and the shimmer of tears in her eyes shocked him. 'Thank you. It's perfect.'

'Elizabeth wouldn't tell me anything about your gown, but she said an ivory fan, so I thought— The fan's inside.'

He thought her fingers shook as she opened the clasp and drew out the carved ivory fan. The palest pink-satin ribbon wove between the delicate leaves of the fan. He waited, but she said nothing. Did she like it, hate it?

'Thank you.'

It was no more than a whisper and a single tear

slid down her cheek. His throat tightened. 'There is something else.' He prayed for the right words. 'I hope you will wear it for me.'

He pulled the jeweller's box from his pocket, opened it and took out the little amethyst ring. She stared at him, her cheeks pale. 'Give me your hand.' When she didn't move, he took her right hand and slid the ring on to her finger. It shone there in the candlelight, right and perfect on her small hand.

'You don't have to give me jewellery.'

With any other woman he would have known that for a piece of disingenuous nonsense. Would have made some flippant reply about it being more than his reputation was worth to let his mistress go forth before being appropriately adorned.

'When I saw it, I thought it would suit you.' He had seen the ring and wanted to give it to her. To Lucy.

'Thank you. I will wear it always.'

He smiled. 'I might give you another one.'

She looked up. 'I know you spoke about jewels, but there is something I would rather have. If…if you do not mind?'

What the devil could she possibly want that she thought he would mind? Her own carriage? He had every intention of giving her one. A riding horse? Naturally, she would have—

'I want Fitch.'

'What?'

'Instead of more jewels, I'd rather give Fitch an education, have him trained for a profession, or a trade if he prefers.'

'Instead of jewels.' These, then, were the terms of her surrender?

'Yes. I know it would be terribly expensive—'

'Not so much.'

'—especially if he went to school, but—'

'Lucy, he might not wish it.' The boy might well refuse to leave the life he knew. Even if he agreed, he might be impossible to reform. An image flashed into his head of the boy, throwing away his chance to run, standing skinny and protective at Lucy's side. He sighed. 'But we can try. Do you know where he is?'

She shook her head. 'I've scarcely seen him this week. But I could come back to find him, couldn't I?'

Not damned likely. Once he had her safe, she was never coming back here. 'No. But I'll find him and bring him to you.'

'You will? You don't mind?'

Mind? That she was loyal to a fault? That she would not desert a friend? 'No, I don't mind.' He was going to educate and reform a street thief to please his mistress. If anyone found out about the deal he had struck they would think he had slipped his moorings. He wasn't sure that he hadn't. And now was not the time to tell her that helping Fitch did *not* get her out of accepting the occasional jewel from him.

Jig swore under his breath from the cover of an alley as his nibs and the wench emerged from the passage down to the yard. Even in the weak light of Lord Tom Noddy's carriage lamps he could see the wench was dressed finer than fivepence. He could *hear* the rustle of silk, damn it! All prettied up for him, she was. An' all them boxes, and the damned fiddle it looked like. Not to mention the way the wench was leaning against his lordship, all sweet and cosy. Didn't need no one to tell him *she'd* found a softer bed.

His lordship's voice carried easily, telling the coachman to drive them to the boat landing at Westminster Steps...*right, boat up to Vauxhall, that was*...then...yes, meet later at Vauxhall and on to Chiswick. Jig eased back with a curse. He'd been inside more than one of the nobs' fancy places out at Chiswick as a boy, slidin' through a window you wouldn't have thought a cat could get through.

He cast a disgusted glance after the departing carriage. Well, this was one piece of prime goods Kilby wouldn't be getting his hands on. And he still had an evening of waiting for Hensleigh.

* * *

Lights blazed in the elm groves, glimmering on silks and satins, glinting off jewels.

James kept Lucy close, guiding her through the laughing, chattering crowd, ignoring curious glances from various friends, pretending not to see them at all. 'Elizabeth's note said they have a supper box near the intersection of the Grand Walk and the Central Cross Walk.'

Elizabeth's voice came back to censure him: *I think she would rather have given herself for love.* And then she had called it folly. Folly for a woman to love, because it made her vulnerable…*and she would know exactly the knife edge a woman in Lucy's situation must walk.*

And now he was guiding her through the gossip and speculation of Vauxhall, past the Grove, along the northern range of supper boxes, where he was recognised and she was assessed. Some of the supper boxes held clearly respectable family parties, others rather more lively groups of men and their fancies.

He hurried her past. He wanted nothing more than to reach the far end of the range and have her safe with Elizabeth.

'Cousin James! Cousin James!'

'Are you joining us?'

He froze at the familiar voices, cursing silently,

and turned slowly. There, in a supper box, sat his cousin William with his wife, Susan, and their two young daughters. The girls were waving delightedly. William, on the other hand, looked as though he had bitten into a lemon and Susan had leaned across the table to whisper to the girls. Their eyes widened, crimson flooded their cheeks and they subsided, averting their gazes.

Under almost any other circumstances their blunder would have amused him. Amelia, at sixteen, was not quite out, and Jane was—he racked his brain—younger.

William cleared his throat. 'Good evening, James.'

'Good evening, William.'

'A very fine evening,' William observed, not so much as the flicker of an eyelash indicating that he had seen Lucy.

James's fists clenched. 'Indeed. You will excuse me? I am joining Fox and…a companion.' It sickened him that he had to refer to Elizabeth so dismissively, pretend she didn't exist, just as his cousins were pretending that Lucy didn't exist.

'Fox?' William frowned. 'Of course, he is your godfather, but—' He coughed. 'Well, you had best be on your way.'

William loathed Fox. 'Yes. Good evening, William.' He didn't speak to Susan, or acknowledge the girls. He couldn't. Not with Lucy on his arm. And

he could see Fox and Elizabeth in a box on the opposite side of the walk, not twenty yards away.

Oh, hell! Why in God's name had William chosen
tonight of all nights for a family visit to Vauxhall?

'Is that Mr Fox waving to you?'

Lucy's voice was very quiet and he glanced down.
'Yes.'

Her face showed nothing, certainly not that her
new status had just been rubbed in it.

'How did they know?'

'Know what?' That was a parry. He was playing
for time.

'Your cousins—at least your Cousin William—
how did he know—' her voice faltered now '—what
I am?'

*He didn't. Not until I deliberately didn't present
you to his wife and daughters.*

By that single, deliberate omission he had labelled
her: *whore*.

He couldn't tell her that. 'He assumed. Because
you are alone with me, unchaperoned.' That wasn't
entirely untrue, although a betrothed couple could
walk here unchaperoned. Or a trusted family friend
might escort a young lady. But in that case William
would have known the girl. And all the avid looks
Lucy had been receiving from men who knew him
were based on the same logic. He didn't have to try
hard to imagine the ribaldry foaming in their wake.

Have you seen Cambourne's little redhead?
Cambourne's here. He's got a new filly.

Followed by salacious speculation on said filly's staying power and performance, or whether or not she was yet broken to saddle.

Beside him, Lucy lifted her chin. 'It doesn't matter.'

The hell it didn't! But they were at the box and Fox had risen, beaming.

'Miss Lucy.' He bowed over her hand. 'You fairly take my breath away. Not a word would my Liz say about the gown—why, you look like spring herself.' He took both her hands, leaned forward and kissed her cheek.

Elizabeth met James's gaze with a level look. He grimaced. She had seen his family's reaction, then. And if she had seen, so had Fox. He bowed over her hand.

'The world, James,' she said very softly, 'is not always fair. Especially to women.'

Lucy tried not to care that his family had cut her dead. It was to be expected. Really, they hadn't even needed to cut her. Cambourne—she couldn't yet think of him comfortably as *James*—had not so much as acknowledged her presence during that brief conversation.

'Don't let it bother you, my dear.' Mrs Armistead reached across the table and patted her hand.

There was no point pretending not to understand. 'I suppose I had not thought of how it must work in practice.' She summoned a smile. 'Of course I know that no gentleman would present his…his mistress—'

'Are you?'

Lucy drew a deep breath. 'I have agreed. He is taking me to Chiswick tonight.'

Elizabeth nodded. 'Are you sure there is no other choice?' Lucy stared and Elizabeth smiled. 'You are wondering why, of all the women in London, I would warn you against such a course.'

'Yes.'

Elizabeth's hand gripped hers. 'Because I know the risks. All of them.' Her mouth flattened. 'Insult, abandonment, destitution.' She let out a breath. 'Pregnancy. Although James would provide generously for a child and its mother, remember that most gentlemen consider a mistress expendable. Once they tire of one, or perceive the bloom to be gone—' She shrugged. 'The nature of the beast.'

'And Mr Fox?'

'Is the exception, not the rule, child.' Elizabeth's gaze strayed to where Fox stood with James not far away in a small group of men, chatting comfortably of politics.

As if he felt Elizabeth's glance, Fox looked her way and a smile passed between them, so tender and intimate that Lucy felt as though she had intruded on something very private.

'I committed what should have been the greatest folly of my life by falling in love with Fox,' Elizabeth said, her eyes still on him.

'But he loves you,' Lucy said.

'Yes. Fox loves me.' Elizabeth looked back at Lucy. 'But you should not chart your course based on my luck.'

'Do as I say, not as I did?' Lucy asked.

Elizabeth sipped her champagne. 'Good advice is often that way.' Her smile was wry. 'It has the benefit of experience.'

Lucy steeled herself. 'May I ask for another piece of advice?'

Elizabeth was silent a moment. Then, 'Are you going to ask if he loves you?'

Pain coursed through Lucy. 'No. I don't need to ask that.'

Elizabeth looked at her closely. Whatever she saw seemed to reassure her, but her smile was sad. 'He will never lie to you.' She frowned. 'Well, not about that. If he ever does tell you that he loves you—' She sighed. 'Never mind. I'm weaving fairy tales. What do you wish to know?'

'Yesterday, you implied that you and Mr Fox decided not to have children.'

Elizabeth became very still. 'Yes.'

'It can be prevented? Someone told me about Queen Anne's Lace—'

'Chew the seeds well,' Elizabeth said. 'As soon as ever you can after he has been with you.' She leaned forward. 'And there are other ways.'

James's mind kept drifting from politics to Elizabeth and Lucy. What the devil were they talking about so earnestly? Or rather, what was Elizabeth talking about? She seemed to be doing most of the talking, with Lucy putting the occasional question.

'Eh, Cambourne?'

With difficulty he dragged his attention back from the supper box. 'No, I cannot agree that this is good for Europe—this revolution in France has plunged everyone into war. Surely more could have been achieved by moderate reform?'

One of Fox's cronies snorted. 'And when would that have happened under Louis? Fellow was still convinced of the Divine Right of Kings, for pity's sake! No, Fox has the right of it. A shake-up was needed and—'

Lucy had reached over the table and Elizabeth was holding her hand.

'Worried about what advice the Armistead might

be giving your new filly, Cambourne?' Mr Hawksburn slid assessing eyes over Lucy. 'Still got the bloom on her, eh?'

James hung on to the reins of his temper. 'You said something, sir?'

Oblivious, Hawksburn rattled on. 'How to hold on to a man past her time, very likely.' He shook his head. 'Fox is a fine fellow, but Lord! He's a fool about that woman! Past her prime when he took her! You know, we had it all sewn up for him a few years back. Could have married the Coutts chit. A banking fortune. But he whistled it down the wind, if you please. All he had to do was break it off with the Armistead, but blow me if she didn't somehow get her hooks deeper!'

'Hooks?' James asked silkily, his fists clenched.

Hawksburn realised his danger, edging back. 'Ah, figure of speech, don't you know.'

'Then I suggest that you be very careful of your speech to and about Mrs Armistead,' James said in lethal tones. 'I account her a dear friend and will tolerate no disrespect.'

'Of course not.' Hawksburn stepped back further.

'Nor,' James continued, 'would it be wise to speak disrespectfully to or of her companion. Are my figures of speech clear enough, sir?'

'Er...yes.' Hawksburn's Adam's apple bobbed. 'Quite clear, my lord. In fact, extremely clear. You'll excuse me? Chap I simply must speak to! Good evening!'

James gave him a frigid nod. Breaking Hawksburn's nose, although satisfying, would embarrass Elizabeth—who had always ridden above such insults—and upset Lucy.

She is the sort of girl a man like you usually cuts his right hand off for before seducing...

Thank God he was taking Lucy out of town. She would not be exposed to so much insult and hypocrisy out at Chiswick—

And how long could he keep her hidden? How long before she was lonely and longed for more than his company? Oh, she would have the boy, but women—*people*—needed more than the company of a lover, and—he took a flying guess—a twelve-year-old boy. Women needed other women. Who would Lucy's friends be? Beyond Elizabeth, miles away at Chertsey on this side of the river, what other women friends could she have?

His male friends would be more than happy to acknowledge her—while ensuring that their wives, daughters and sisters were kept safe from her contaminating influence. Oh, those women would know of her existence, but when they spoke of her—and they would—it would be with pitying scorn or outright disgust.

Even the men, with very few exceptions, would

view her as a commodity, an amusement he'd bought and could discard when it ceased to amuse or became inconvenient. Hawksburn had merely expressed society's opinion.

'Well!' Fox clapped him on the back. 'I think Cambourne and I have ignored the ladies quite long enough, gentlemen. You will excuse us?'

The group drifted off, after exchanging polite farewells with Elizabeth. A couple cast speculative glances at Lucy, caught James's eye and backed off.

She would be safe with him. Safe from everything, insult, her father's folly...*safe from you?*

Because he was using her, too. When Hensleigh returned he would be after his daughter in a heartbeat, not to wrest her from ruin, James suspected, but to demand his cut. It hardly mattered which. James would have him precisely where he wanted him. He would forgive the debt, tear up the vowels, in return for useful information on Kilby.

Other ways, indeed. Lucy's head was spinning with all she had taken in. Elizabeth was an absolute fount of practical advice on how to avoid pregnancy.

Close by, Fox and James still talked politics. They didn't seem to agree terribly often, but somehow managed to argue their points without becoming angry with each other. Passionate, yes, but not angry.

Unlike Grandpapa, who had not tolerated anyone who disagreed with his views.

A couple of gentlemen had greeted Elizabeth, attempting to draw her into the conversation, but she had demurred with a smile, saying that she was enjoying a private chat with Miss Hensleigh.

Hensleigh. The name grated. It felt like living a lie, but even now when she was leaving her father, she would have to keep her real name secret. If it came out and got back to Uncle Bertram and Aunt Caroline, they would be mortified. And her younger cousin, Anne, was only sixteen. Scandal could ruin her chances of a decent marriage.

But would she even exist if the only people who knew her true name pretended she didn't exist? Or would she simply fade away and be forgotten, along with her name?

She managed a smile as Fox seated himself beside Elizabeth with a comfortable sigh. 'I believe the orchestra is tuning up for a dance.' His dark eyes twinkled at Elizabeth. 'A pity my dancing days are past. But yours aren't, James. Are you going to lead Miss Lucy out?'

'I can't dance.' She said it quite casually, as though it were not something every young lady was supposed to be able to do.

Elizabeth looked surprised. 'You really can't dance?'

'I never learned.' Officially she had shared her cousins' dancing lessons, but it was amazing how often during a dancing lesson she had been required to run an errand, or sit with Grandmama reading aloud or winding wool. The dance lessons she had attended had been when she was needed to play the piano.

She stole a glance at James. Would he be disappointed? It was obvious, after meeting Elizabeth, that a man could want more in a mistress than a gauche girl who couldn't even dance.

He was watching her. 'Did your cousins not have a dancing master?'

'They did, yes.' Wasn't it even safe to *think* around him?

He nodded. 'I see.' He reached across the table and possessed himself of her hand and her heart skipped several beats as his fingers closed gently on hers.

'Then I shall have the delight of teaching you,' he said softly, his smile just for her. 'But not here. Will you walk with me instead?'

If he kept smiling at her like that she would forget Elizabeth's good advice—the part about keeping her heart intact, or if not intact, private. Also according to Elizabeth it was quite normal for a gentleman to parade a mistress before his peers.

It gives one an advantage when finding a new protector if the candidates have already been primed.

At the thought of James tiring of her, her heart ached. But she stiffened her spine. There might be no new protector, but if she was to be his mistress she must be seen with him. She summoned a smile and every scrap of pride. 'Yes, please.'

If she was going to do this then she would do it properly and hold her head up as Elizabeth did.

Chapter Eleven

James escorted Lucy north along the Central Cross Walk. He ignored most of the friends who greeted him, only favouring them with a brief nod. Curious glances were cast at Lucy, but if he hadn't felt her hand tense on his arm each time a man looked her up and down, he would have said she hadn't noticed. Thousands of lanterns glimmered in the trees, turning night to day beneath the leafy branches. They turned right into another illuminated path.

'At the far end is the Dark Walk.' James kept his voice neutral. 'We can go right around, or turn back.'

An odd little smile trembled on her lips. 'Can we ever go back?'

She had understood, then. 'So, we go on?'

She looked puzzled. 'Yes.'

He didn't blame her for being puzzled. She had consented. At the end of the evening she would go with him. And yet he kept asking if she was sure. Could it be that *he* wasn't sure?

No. He wanted her. Wanted her to be with him. Every nerve and sinew ached to hold her, keep her safe and happy. He had no doubts on his own account, only hers. Elizabeth's warning haunted him. S*he would give herself for love...*

A small group strolled towards them from the end of the walk. James stiffened. Hawksburn and some of his cronies with their wives. James gritted his teeth as the gentlemen favoured him with friendly nods, while their ladies appeared blind. Hawksburn, his smile malicious, murmured to Lord Fanshawe, whose brows rose as he grinned, subjecting Lucy to a slow assessment, his gaze insolent.

He turned back to Hawksburn. 'Very tasty.' His voice carried easily and Hawksburn paled a little, pulling him along.

James discovered that his fists had clenched themselves and forcibly relaxed them.

'That gentleman,' Lucy said. 'Mr Hawksburn? Elizabeth said he annoyed you.'

'He usually does.' James tried to let the rage just blow through and away, but it snarled on the jagged edges of his own self-disgust. Elizabeth saw, and knew, entirely too much. 'Don't waste a thought on him,' he said.

They turned the corner into the Dark Walk and left the crowds behind. There were a few couples strolling, but most kept to the light. No respectable woman was brought here by a man who cared for her reputation. And yet he had brought Lucy. He'd already sunk her reputation and here in the dark there was the illusion of privacy. The chatter drifted behind them, the voices outside their sphere.

'It's still bothering you.'

That struck straight and true to the heart.

He parried. 'What makes you think that?' Her hand trembled on his arm.

'Because you look at me differently.' She gestured. 'As if you're, I don't know, angry. But not with me. About me.'

She stopped and faced him in the shadows. 'Elizabeth said he disliked her connection with Mr Fox.'

Trust Elizabeth to know that. Had she known about Hawksburn's role in the Coutts fiasco? They had approached James for support, but he had refused to be a party to it.

'If you have changed your mind, sir,' she said quietly, 'I would rather you told me now.'

Sometimes turning back wasn't possible. The time for explanations was past and at some point in the last week Lucy had become too important for him to risk losing her. Somewhere, hidden in the trees, a nightingale wove its shimmering spell of liquid song.

He bent and brushed his mouth over hers, felt the swift indrawn breath, the quiver of response. 'I haven't changed my mind.'

'I'm glad.' A mere whisper, breathed against his lips as she stood on tiptoe to reach. With a groan he stepped off the path, into the deeper shadows beneath the trees, where the nightingale's enchantment reigned and drew her into his arms.

Restraint. Lucy felt the heat and tension searing him as she surrendered her mouth to the dark promise of his kiss. A small part of her mind warned that a man who took her from the path, from safety, was not to be trusted. But a deeper, surer instinct reassured her, recognised the leashed strength cradling her, the tenderness of his mouth possessing hers. The hot, male taste of him seduced utterly. Slow, deep strokes of his tongue that sent heat surging through her to coil aching within. Every part of her softened against him, responding to the rhythm and answering, her own tongue dancing with his.

His arms tightened on a low groan and in a heartbeat the kiss flashed from gentle to fierce, his mouth on hers all hot demand. She had not known that strength could be gentle, could seduce, that restraint and hunger had a taste. Nor had she known that her body could feel so much and still want so much more.

He had to stop.

He knew that. He even knew there was a reason

for it. A damn good reason. But lost in their kiss he'd forgotten what it was. But the last feeble commands of honour held their ground.

Aching, James broke the kiss and raised his head. Lucy's face was a pale oval in the consuming shadows, enough that he could see her eyes, wide and dazed, her lips softly parted and trembling. She felt right in his arms. Every slender curve nestled against him, her cheek now resting on his chest, one small hand over his heart. Even the drifting fragrance of her hair twined through him with the quiet scents of the grove and the nightingale's promise.

Out on the path other couples strolled by, close together, somehow outside the dark enchantment of the song-rimed shadows that enfolded them. Here they were apart, untouched.

'We can't stay here.'

Her soft words lifted the spell. Truth tended to do that. He couldn't keep her apart, in the shadows, hidden.

'No.' After a quick glance to check that no one was close enough to recognise them, he led her back to the path. The last thing he wanted was a tale that Cambourne had tupped his new filly in the shadows beside the Dark Walk. Apart from anything else, Elizabeth would kill him while Fox held her evening cloak.

Tucking Lucy's hand into the crook of his elbow, he held it there as they walked towards the brightly lit South Walk to join the throng of merrymakers. James ignored the knowing glances tossed their way and forged a path through the chattering crowd.

He swerved around a group of giggling young ladies and came face to face with Nick. Nemesis, the goddess of retribution, he realised in a blinding flash, could take on any form she liked to achieve her ends.

'Evening, James.'

Nick's blue eyes brimmed with laughter. 'Fox said I'd find you somewhere around the walks. The pater is practically frothing at the jaws.' He chuckled. 'Lord! I thought he was going to have apoplexy when he told me what happened. Amelia and Jane are in utter disgrace, poor girls!'

Nick sketched a graceful bow to Lucy. 'Beg pardon, ma'am. I don't believe we've met.'

Even the polite good humour of his tones didn't disguise the amused, frankly envious gaze. He held out his hand to Lucy, with a smile. 'Nick Remington at your service, ma'am. Cambourne's my cousin.'

James resisted the urge to slap Nick's hand away. Lucy was already extending her hand. 'Lucy Hensleigh, sir.'

Nick, bowing over her hand, snapped upright.

'Hensleigh?' He stared at James. 'What the devil?' He dropped Lucy's hand as though it were an adder.

James swore mentally. 'Nick, you are decidedly *de trop.'*

Lucy had paled, but her chin was up. 'I collect you have an acquaintance with my father, sir.'

James wanted to applaud. She sounded for all the world like the haughtiest of well-bred young ladies.

'Father?' Nick shot another glance at James. 'Yes. That is, if your father is Captain Ned Hensleigh?'

He saw Lucy swallow. 'Yes.'

'James.' Nick's voice was tight, furious. 'I need a private word with you.'

'Not here.' There was no way in hell that he would step away from Lucy in this crowd. 'I'll escort Miss Hensleigh back to Fox and Mrs Armistead, then I can give you a moment.'

For a second he thought Nick would argue. He'd not known that Nick's eyes *could* harden like that. The boy was growing up, although he'd picked a damnably inconvenient time to do it.

'Very well.' Nick cut a savage glance at Lucy. 'I dare say my father won't actually have apoplexy when he sees us.'

'James, have you lost your mind?' demanded Nick in an undertone. They stood a few yards from the supper box where Lucy sat with Fox and Elizabeth. 'What are you doing with that girl?'

'Having supper,' James said. 'Nick, this is none of your concern, so—'

'The hell it isn't!' Nick's hard-eyed stare bored into him. 'She's probably a—'

'Enough. You'll speak of her with respect.'

Nick's jaw dropped. 'Damn it, James! If she's Hensleigh's get, she's hardly as pure as—'

'I said enough!' This time he let the naked steel show. 'She's nothing to do with that.'

'Where's Hensleigh?'

'Still out of town.'

Nick swore. 'And you've stolen his *daughter*?' His voice rose. 'To cover a debt of a thousand pounds? For God's sake! What happens when he finds out and the bully boys come after *you*? Is the money he owes you worth a beating?'

A short, strangled cry had James whipping around to meet Lucy's shattered gaze. Faced with a choice between seeing that look on her face or a flogging, he would have chosen the flogging. He deserved it while she didn't deserve what he'd done to her. Elizabeth's arm had gone around her shoulder protectively.

'Lucy.' He took a step towards her.

Her face bone-white, she faced him. 'I think, sir, that you owe me an explanation.'

* * *

Lucy's fingernails bit into her palms as Cambourne explained how he'd used her. Nausea churning, she stared at her uneaten supper, the transparent slices of ham, the green peas. A thousand pounds. Not one hundred. One *thousand*. She did not dare ask if he had been taking her in payment for the debt, or in revenge for the beating his cousin had received. She didn't want to know, although he'd probably tell her.

So when he fell silent, she took a careful breath, blanking everything from her mind except the words she must say. 'I should like to go home now, my lord.'

Silence followed, brittle enough to shatter. Or perhaps that was her heart. How odd not to realise how completely she had given that foolish organ until he broke it.

'Lucy—'

'To Frenchman's Yard.' Important that she be utterly clear.

'My dear.' Elizabeth's voice was gentle. 'Come with Fox and myself. At least for tonight. Tomorrow—'

'Thank you, ma'am.' Lucy summoned a smile. 'You are very kind, but I must not. Lord Cambourne will take me home. Safely.' She dared a glance at Cambourne. 'I suppose I can trust him to do that.'

He flinched, as if for all the world she had hurt him. Well, his pride, perhaps. And maybe not even that. He probably just didn't like that she'd hinted he couldn't be trusted. She knew him well enough to be certain that the implied insult would ensure he did exactly as she had asked.

If anyone was staring at them as they walked out to the coach field, James didn't notice. He was aware only of the woman beside him, her whole being encased in sheet ice.

When he would have handed her up into the carriage she ignored him, barely giving the footman time to put the steps down and get out of the way before she got in unaided.

'Back to town. To Frenchman's Yard.' The order felt like a death knell.

Digby blinked. 'Aye, m'lord.'

James got into the coach and shame sliced deeper as he saw she sat, spear-straight, with her back to the horses as if she were a maidservant.

'Lucy—'

'Did you think I was part of it?'

'What? No!' Horror stabbed him.

'That's something. Then I was just a way to get to my father and this…Kilby.'

The fragile sound of her voice twisted the knife

deeper inside him. 'I'm sorry.' Useless words if ever there were any.

Digby's whip cracked and the coach moved forward.

'A thousand pounds.' He heard her gulp, take a breath. 'You lied to me all along.'

Shame scored him. 'It wasn't the money, Lucy. Or at least that wasn't very important.'

'Not important?' He could have bitten his own tongue out. His eyes had adjusted to the darkness in the carriage and he could see her staring.

'It must be nice to be rich.'

He deserved that and she deserved the rest of the explanation he hadn't wanted to give where there was a chance anyone could have overheard him. 'Lucy, when your father sold Nick's vowels to Kilby, it wasn't the first time he'd done that sort of thing. Nick's beating was probably a warning. But there was another boy. And he died.'

'*What?* Papa wouldn't—' She fell silent and the only sound within the carriage, jolting over the rough grass of the field, was her suddenly ragged breathing. It hurt James more than he would have believed.

'I'm sorry, sweetheart.' She flinched at the endearment and that hurt even more. He went on. 'Do you remember telling me about the young man who followed your father home? And your father told him Kilby held his vowels?'

'Yes.' It was the merest thread of sound.

'Did you ever hear his name?'

A moment's silence.

'Moreby—something like that.'

'Moresby?'

'Yes, it could have been.'

He braced himself to strike the final blow. 'Gerald Moresby was beaten to death soon after. It was put down to footpads, but his brother told me Gerald had come to him after an earlier beating, desperate for money to pay a gambling debt, saying it was a matter of life and death.'

Silence stretched between them again, measured only by the depth of his shame. He thought nothing could be as terrible as that silence until she spoke.

'I'm sorry I said that about…being rich.' His breath caught on the jagged edges of pain. She went on, 'Of course the money didn't matter beside—' she took a shuddering breath '—but Papa couldn't have—' Her voice broke. 'You think he knew? Knew what would happen?'

Not even to spare her pain would he lie to her again. 'Kilby has a reputation, Lucy. Certainly if your father didn't know before Gerald Moresby died, he knew Kilby would be merciless when he sold Nick's vowels.' He was silent, remembering

Hunt's grief and guilt. 'Gerald's brother, Huntercombe, didn't realise, didn't believe him when he spoke of life and death. So he refused to give the boy the money.'

'But your cousin, he didn't die, so maybe—'

'He survived what would have been the warning. He came to me and I paid the debt for him.'

'One thousand pounds that of course you wished to recoup.'

'No!' He had to make her see. 'I wanted to teach your father a lesson. That was all. But then, after I'd met you, Huntercombe told me about his brother—'

'You wanted justice.'

That had been part of it. 'I wanted to make sure other young idiots didn't die. We're all idiots at that age, but—'

'How old was he?'

He shrugged. 'About the same age as Nick. Nineteen? Twenty?'

'As you say—we're idiots.'

A half laugh ripped from him. 'I meant men— *boys*—are idiots at that age. We think we know everything, that we're immortal. Hopefully we grow up.'

He dragged in a breath. 'Lucy, I didn't lie about wanting you. Won't you come to me, sweetheart?'

This silence was even worse, as she seemed to shrink back into the opposite corner, as far away from him as she could get. At last she spoke, her voice very low and tired. 'No. I won't lie to myself any more.'

Something inside him shattered. 'Lucy?'

'I thought you cared for me a little.' Her voice was no more than a wisp of sound. 'Because you were kind. Even to Fitch. And I thought you were honest with me. Because...because you cared about me, just a little.'

Her voice wobbled and, unable to bear it any longer, James reached for her.

'No!' She jerked back. 'Even when you insisted I take the time to think about the step I would be taking—I thought you were being honest, making sure I understood. But it was to spin things out. So you didn't have the nuisance or expense of setting me up as your mistress if you didn't—'

'Lucy! You *can't* think that!'

Her chin lifted and in the weak light of the lamps he caught the flash of fury.

'Don't tell me what I can or cannot think, my lord!'

He had lost her. Except she had never been his. He set his jaw. Just because he had lost her didn't mean he would let her walk back into the mess of her father's life.

'Lucy, please, come with me. Just for tonight and—'

'*What?*'

He realised how that sounded. 'Not like that. I swear I won't touch you, won't come near you—'

'You really must think I'm an idiot, if you think I'll fall for—'

'Go to Elizabeth, then.' He reached forward and gripped her hands, holding on despite her efforts to break free. 'Not to your lodgings.'

'I suppose you think I'll warn my father and Kilby!'

'*What?* No!' Lucy wrenched free as he struggled for words. 'I want you safe, damn it!'

She snorted. 'Safely out of the way, more like. Go to hell, my lord. I can find my own way without you.'

Lucy sat as far back in the corner of the rocking carriage as she could, keeping her breathing even, quiet. She could do nothing about the tears sliding down her cheeks, but she'd be damned before she'd let Cambourne know she was crying.

In the opposite corner Cambourne sat quietly. He had not spoken again after she'd told him to go to hell. She didn't know if she had convinced him that she wouldn't go with him, or if he was biding his time. She kept track of the turns the carriage made and knew they were headed back to town, that he wasn't going to trick her out to Chiswick.

She needed to blow her nose and there was a handkerchief in her reticule, but that would tell him as plain as day that—

'Here.' He leaned forward and a handkerchief was pressed into her hand. She swallowed. He'd known she was crying anyway. So she blew her nose and wiped her eyes. So much for pride. Surreptitiously she slipped the little amethyst ring from her finger and put it in the reticule with the fan.

Knowing that she was crying silently in the dark had shredded every last scrap of his pride and scraped his conscience raw. He ached to hold her, comfort her…and that was the very last thing she wanted. Although if she were forced to choose the noble Earl of Cambourne as comforter or lover, he didn't think the lover had a cat's chance in hell. With a shock he realised that if *he* were given the choice, he'd choose to comfort her. But it was more than a little difficult for a man who had used and deliberately deceived a woman to figure as her comforter.

There was a slight chance, rather less than the cat's, that by the time the carriage reached Fleet Street she might reconsider. He could only ask.

Chapter Twelve

She refused.

Not passionately. Not in fury.

She refused politely. That was worse.

James followed Lucy's hurried footsteps up the inky-dark, creaking stairwell to her lodgings. He couldn't see a damned thing and the bandboxes he'd grabbed from her bumped against the banisters, slowing him down even more. Ahead, he was aware of Lucy's ragged breathing. With the steep climb or more suppressed tears, he didn't know.

Above a door crashed open. 'Where the hell have you been, you stupid girl?'

A swift, feminine gasp. 'I went out for supper. Why should you care?'

James froze, then took the last flight two at a time. He surged on to the landing and nearly crashed into Lucy before he saw her in the light spilling from the open door of her lodgings.

Hensleigh stood in the doorway, holding a candle.

'Care? Where the hell is my supper?' He sounded positively aggrieved. 'Damn it! The old harridan downstairs said you were gone for good! Where had you that gown?'

'A friend gave it—'

'A friend—? *Who the hell is that?*'

Hensleigh was peering, trying to see past the pool of light into the shadows where James stood.

'The person I had supper with. Excuse me, sir. I'm tired.'

Lucy tried to slip past, but Hensleigh grabbed her wrist. 'Supper with a man? In a new gown?' He almost spat the words. 'Why, you little trollop!'

James dropped the bandboxes and crossed the landing in a heartbeat. He caught the raised hand before it could descend and spun Hensleigh around, pushing the man into the lodgings ahead of himself.

'Touch her, Hensleigh, or whatever your real name is, and I'll knock your teeth down your throat.'

Rage poured through him and his grip tightened on Hensleigh's wrist as he forced him further into the firelit room. A bottle stood on the table and James caught the reek of gin on Hensleigh's breath.

'You!' Hensleigh's face turned pasty as his eyes widened in recognition.

'I see you remember me.' James gave the man a shove that sent him staggering backwards. 'Did you also finally remember your daughter?'

Behind him, Lucy made an odd little sound.

Hensleigh's gaze flickered between them cagily. 'Well, I must say, it's a fine thing when a fellow comes home, to the bosom of his family, and finds that his only child has been debauched!'

'He didn't touch me!' Lucy's voice cracked like a whip.

Hensleigh ignored her. 'I trust, Cambourne—' he drew himself up in a sickening parody of sorrowing fatherhood '—that as a *gentleman*—' the word held just a soupçon of doubt '—you are prepared to make generous restitution?'

A humourless crack of laughter escaped James. 'Restitution? Not satisfaction, Hensleigh? Does that mean you're willing to sell her rather than protect her?' He was bitterly aware of Lucy, hearing her father barter the price of her virtue.

'Why, you damned hypocrite!' Hensleigh blustered. 'You think to ruin my little girl and not—'

'If I had, Hensleigh, then I'd meet you gladly over pistols.' The man flinched and James smiled coldly. 'But I'm damned if I'll pay her father to pimp her!'

He turned to Lucy and steel bands contracted about his chest at the redness around her eyes, the waxen quality of her expression. 'You can still come with me. Be free of this mess, and—'

'Are you claiming that you *haven't* seduced her?' Hensleigh's disbelief was palpable.

'No.' Lucy looked straight at James.

Desperation clawed at him. 'Think! Think what he is! He ought to be trying to beat me to a pulp! Not angling for *restitution*.'

'I meant, of course,' Hensleigh said, 'the only restitution one gentleman can offer another in such a—'

The oath James let fly silenced Hensleigh and shocked James himself.

'Really?' he continued, ice flooding every vein. He wanted to choke the man, but spoke with savage control. 'And what if I offered your note of hand for your daughter's innocence?'

'My…my note of hand?' Hensleigh's voice shook and he licked his lips. 'You'd give it back for—' He broke off and cast a furtive glance past James to Lucy.

'Or should I sell it elsewhere, Hensleigh?' James asked. 'To Kilby? As you did with other notes?'

'No!' Hensleigh's face was grey, his hands shaking. He looked at Lucy, standing by the door. 'Now, my dear—' his ingratiating tone sickened James '—it's plain enough you like Cambourne here. We'll say nothing about your foolishness in letting him, well, mum for that. No point being missish. If you had a tiff, least said, soonest mended. 'Twill be a deal better if you go with him now.'

'Better than what?' Lucy's voice cracked like

shards of ice. 'Better than selling myself on the street?'

Hensleigh flinched.

She turned to James. 'Should I be flattered you set so high a value on me?' Her voice shook. 'Or should I say, on my favours?'

Pain slashed at James. 'Lucy, come with me. You can see what he is, surely.'

Her mouth threatened to turn upside down. 'I never had any illusions about him.' Each low, trembling word landed like a blow. 'But I was fool enough to have illusions about you.'

Something silver shone on her cheek. 'What does a thousand pounds buy, my lord? And for how long?'

'My lord?'

James ignored Hensleigh's yelp. Her question stabbed deep. As deep as the silent tear rolling down her cheek.

'A thousand pounds?' He didn't recognise his own voice, harsh and low. 'Nothing of any true value.'

He turned away. He had to *show* her, make her understand that he would never force her. Deliberately he took Hensleigh's note of hand from his pocket and handed it to him.

Hensleigh's jaw dropped as he examined the note. 'What? But—' His gaze flashed to Lucy. 'But you aren't taking— Now see here, girl—'

He shut up as James took one step towards him.

'If Lucy comes with me now, or comes to me later, that is *her* choice.' Cold warning rang in his voice. 'And if I so much as suspect that you've raised your hand to her your life won't be worth a groat.'

He turned to Lucy, taking one last look at her, memorising every sweet, lost inch of her. The shattered eyes, the soft mouth that had surrendered to his, the proud, defiant set of her chin.

'You're leaving?' She sounded dazed, disbelieving 'You aren't going to make me go with you?'

'Yes.' His heart ached. 'I'll call again in a day or so. But if you change your mind in the meantime, send me a message.'

'But, the note—'

'Has nothing to do with you, sweetheart.' He couldn't help it, the endearment just slipped out. Because that was how he thought of her—as his sweetheart. 'Goodnight, Lucy.'

'Goodbye, my lord.'

The finality of that chilled him to the core.

'Hi! Wait up, Cam—my lord!' Heavy footsteps followed him down the inky stairwell.

Hensleigh caught up at the bottom, breathing hard and clutching a taper. Grotesque shadows leapt on the walls.

James shrugged off his clutching hand. 'I've nothing to say to you, Hensleigh, but if any harm comes to her, you'll answer to me.'

Hensleigh pushed past him, blocking the way to the door. 'Now see here, my lord, she's a little skittish now, but no doubt you could bring her around—'

'Go to hell!' James shoved past, opened the door and strode through.

'Wait!' Hensleigh charged after James. 'Listen, my lord. Better if you take her now.' He cleared his throat. 'After all, I've got my note and—'

James grabbed Hensleigh's cravat, lifting him to his toes.

'Hensleigh, you've got that note because I don't want anything of yours soiling me, including money.'

Realising that Hensleigh was wheezing for breath and had dropped the taper to scrabble at his throat, James released him and turned away.

'You don't…want her?' Hensleigh struggled for breath. 'You…just used her to get to me?'

It was all James could do not to plant his fist in the man's face.

'Go to hell, Hensleigh.'

A small, dark shadow confronted him just as he stepped into the passage.

'Messed that up right an' proper, didn' yeh? What'd yeh bring Lu back 'ere for?'

James took his hand off the carriage pistol in

his right-hand pocket, but kept his left hand on his purse. 'Fitch. What are you doing?'

The boy shrugged. 'Looking for a doorway now.'

Understanding dawned. 'You were going to slip into Lucy's lodgings.'

'Yeah. But her dad come back. Spittin' mad she weren't there, but Mrs B. telled him she had a fancy man.'

He kept walking and the boy kept pace. 'So now you're going to sleep in a doorway.'

'Keeps the rain off.'

The boy's voice was matter of fact. No doubt sleeping in a doorway was perfectly normal for him. Stepping out of the reeking passage, James turned to look at the boy properly. How old was he? Ten? Twelve? The carriage stood a few yards away and in the yellow glow of the lamps the boy's thin, grubby face was truculent.

'Thought you was going to look after her.'

So had he. 'You can come home with me if you wish.' And why the hell he was making that offer, he couldn't begin to imagine.

Fitch's face took on a careful blankness. 'No, thanks, guv.' He took a step back. 'That ain't my trade.'

'What?' Then James took in the fact that the boy was edging back further, one stealthy step at a time.

'Hell! I'm not going to—' He wasn't going to say

it. Not to a child. Not even this one who had probably seen more of the world's vices than James could
comprehend. 'You're perfectly safe with me. I'm offering you a safe place to sleep and a meal. Not—
not *that.*'

Fitch stopped, but kept his distance. He gave all
the appearance of a wild creature, ready to flee at
the first sign of danger.

'Why?'

'Why did Lucy do it?'

The boy shrugged. 'Dunno. First I thought she
were a fool. But—'

'But she's not,' James finished for him.

'M'lord?' His coachman sounded nervous.

'Yes, Digby. A moment.' He looked back at Fitch.
'I, on the other hand, probably am a fool. But you
can have a meal and a bed for the night. We'll talk
about your future in the morning.'

'Future?'

James took a deep breath. 'Lucy asked me this
evening about you coming with her. She didn't want
to leave you. So she asked me if I'd help you.'

'With a job?'

'If you like. Or school.'

'School? *Me?*'

Fitch sounded as though the sky had crashed
down around them. James wasn't sure it wouldn't
do just that.

'It's what she preferred, I think.'

'Yeah, but she ain't goin' with you now.'

'No. But that doesn't make a difference to what I promised her.'

'You reckon it'll change her mind.'

'No.' But, oh, if it did… 'I don't know, Fitch. And it makes no difference.' It couldn't. It was the only thing Lucy had ever asked of him—Fitch's life in one guise or another. He shrugged. 'It's little enough. Now, are you coming?'

After a moment's consideration Fitch nodded. 'Yeah, s'pose. For tonight at least. But I'd just as soon not ride inside if it's all the same.'

James's mouth tightened. 'For God's sake! I'm not going to—'

'Feels funny, thought of me ridin' in one of them fancies.' Fitch scratched his privates and James made a mental note to speak to him about the niceties of life.

'Right. Come along, then.' James escorted Fitch to the front of the carriage. 'Digby, this is Fitch. Have you got room up there for him?'

The coachman gaped down at them. 'My lord?'

'Keep a guard on your pockets. Our young friend here is a pickpocket. We're going to do something about that.'

Digby's eyes looked as if they might actually pop out. 'My lord?'

Fitch sneered. 'Can't he say nothin' else?'

James cuffed his shoulder lightly. 'You keep a respectful tongue in your head.' He tried not to grin at the outrage on Digby's face. 'Steal anything from Digby, or—' he glanced at the footman by the door '—Roger, and you won't sit comfortably for a week.'

Fitch scowled. At Digby, and at the offended-looking Roger. 'Yours, ain't they?'

'In a manner of speaking.'

'Right. I don't steal from me mates. Reckon I can stretch that to cover them. Sides, I don't guess Lu would like it.'

And there was the key to handling the boy; if Lucy wouldn't like it, then he'd at least try not to do it. Angels, and Fitch was no angel, couldn't do more.

'You're right, she wouldn't. Up with you, then.'

He was prepared to help the boy, but Fitch scrambled up like a monkey, leading James to wonder just how many upper-storey windows his protégé had slithered through.

Fitch, having gained the seat beside Digby, touched his forelock. 'I'm Fitch, guv. Pleased ter meet yeh.'

Digby slanted him a look. 'That's Mr Digby to you. And if you do lift me watch, the missus'll be after you with a broom, so she will.'

James grinned. 'Advice to be heeded, Fitch. Mrs Digby was my nanny. She's a force to be reckoned with. Wielding a broom or not.' He smiled up at

Digby. 'Can you find the lad a comfortable spot for the night?'

Digby looked back resignedly. 'Aye, m'lord. And after that?'

'We'll work it out.'

James stepped into the carriage and sat back against the squabs as Roger put up the steps and closed the door. He shut his eyes briefly to contemplate the disaster of his evening. He'd no one to blame but himself. From start to finish he'd behaved like a complete bounder to Lucy. It didn't matter that he'd wanted to avenge Nick and gain justice for Gerald Moresby. None of that had been Lucy's fault. He'd known that and used her regardless.

In the shadows of the carriage something pale glimmered on the opposite seat. He reached out, picked it up and his heart turned over. Lucy's reticule and, judging by its weight, it wasn't empty. His hands unsteady, he opened it. The fan…his fingers probed…a very small handkerchief and, nearly lost in the bottom, a ring. He sat back, holding the ring, his throat raw.

Chapter Thirteen

'You're sure, Jig?' Kilby's eyes had narrowed, giving Jig a nasty shiver in his belly. 'You think there's no danger from this lord if we take the girl?'

'I'm a-tellin' of yeh, guv,' said Jig. 'He took the wench out for the evenin'. All dollied up she were an' luggage in the boot. Everything all sweet between them. So I hung around, watchin' for Hensleigh an' he come back. Then I'm blowed if his lordship don't bring the girl back. Didn't he, Wat?'

'That's right, Mr Kilby, sir,' Wat said. 'Not long after I follered Hensleigh up from the Bolt.'

'Interesting.'

'Yeah.' Jig continued. 'I slipped in the front door. Hensleigh accusing Lord Tom Noddy of seducing the girl and 'im swearing he'd not touched her and refusing to take her.'

'So he refused to buy the girl?' Kilby straightened.

'Yep.'

'Right.' Kilby stood up. 'Take her at the first opportunity and get her safely stowed at Maud's.'

'Aye, guv.'

Wat nodded.

Kilby fixed them both with a piercing look. 'I've had a look at the girl. Prime goods. She'll bring a high price, especially unspoiled. There's to be *no damage whatsoever* to the merchandise. I've already told Maud about the girl. She'll examine her soon as she gets her.'

Both men nodded.

'Aye, guv.'

'That's right, Mr Kilby, sir.'

The pair of them left the room.

'Reckon it ain't fair we get all the risk grabbin' the bitch an' don't even get a taste,' Wat grumbled. 'Who's to say they ain't both lyin' an' Lord Tom Noddy already done the job on her. Coulda done 'er in the carriage. So who's to know if we 'as a bit o' fun?'

Jig shrugged. 'It's your throat, mate.'

Wat shifted uncomfortably. 'Just a bit o' sport, like!'

Jig nodded. 'Yeah. Tell yeh what. Since it's sport, I'll have a little wager with the boys on what he cuts off afore he kills yeh.' When Wat swallowed, Jig said, 'There's plenty of morts out there without gettin' yerself sliced over this one.'

* * *

James sent for Fitch the next morning as soon as he'd consumed a fortifying pot of coffee. Digby had assured him that 'the lad' would be comfortable enough in the grooms' quarters and he had every faith in the man. Digby had put James on his first pony, bound up numerous youthful injuries and put him over his knee and thrashed him for overfacing a pony at a fence.

His butler, Penfold, escorted Fitch, unnaturally clean and clad in someone's oversized breeches and shirt, into the library, a pained expression on his face. 'The, er, boy, my lord.'

Fitch slung him an offended look. 'Got a name, don't I?'

James choked back a laugh. 'Thank you, Penfold. Is there some cake or fruit available for Master Fitch?'

From Penfold's expression it was clear that if the world as he knew it hadn't already ended, it was about to do so in fire and brimstone. 'Certainly, my lord. Ah—' he cast a defeated glance at Fitch '—milk, as well?'

'*Milk?*' Fitch blanched. 'Ale's fine. Or gin.'

Penfold frowned. 'Milk,' he pronounced, on firmer ground now. 'More coffee, my lord?'

'Definitely. Oh, leave the door open, Penfold. If

Master Fitch yells for help you are to ward me off with a pitchfork.'

'My lord?'

'That's an order.'

'Very good, my lord.'

Penfold departed, leaving the door wide open, and James gestured to a chair. 'Sit down, Fitch.'

Fitch stared at the fatly upholstered chair as if it were a device of torture. 'Reckon I'll stand, guv, if that's all right.'

His gaze flickered everywhere and James understood. The boy was uncomfortable. According to James's elder sister the library was so shabby as to be a disgrace, but James liked it. Shabbiness aside, it was *his* room, where he received family or his closest friends. However, to Fitch it would seem like a royal palace.

Fitch pointed at the marble busts of various Roman and Greek poets, philosophers and playwrights lining the top of the bookshelves. 'They your family, guv?'

James grinned. 'No. The wisdom of the ages up there. My great-grandfather brought them back from the Continent.' He rose, walked over to a small table and picked up the plain, wooden chair beside it. 'Here. Try this.' He placed it by the fire.

Gingerly, as if the chair might bite, Fitch sat. 'No need to leave the door open on my account.'

'Oh?' James sat down again. 'What brought you to that conclusion?'

Fitch rolled his eyes. 'Asked yer stable boys, didn' I? An' the boot boy. Ain't none of 'em bigger'n me, an' they all said you was all right like that. Never had nothin' worse from you than a penny for holdin' a prad. So—' he shrugged '—I figured you was all right.'

While James digested this and prayed for more coffee, Fitch continued, 'Mr Digby says as how you might give me a place in the stables. He let me help with the prads afore breakfast.'

James nodded. 'Is that what you want?' It wasn't what Lucy wanted for the boy. She had wanted him schooled, taught a trade, or even a profession.

'Dunno. Mr Digby wouldn' let me go in with the prad as he said bites, so I reckon it wouldn' be so bad.'

'What about school?'

Fitch shifted on what James knew was a damned uncomfortable seat. 'Can't read or write, so what use ud school be to me?'

'Teaching you to read and write?'

'Yeah, that's what Lu says, but I dunno why you'd do that.'

'Because she asked it of me.'

Fitch scowled. 'Right. Well, I thought about it an'

I reckon you think it'll change her mind. So, no thanks.' He made to slide off the chair.

'I told you last night, it won't make a difference,' James said. 'At least stay and eat your cake.'

Fitch slid back on to the chair. 'All right.' He crossed his arms.

James stared at him. How the hell did he convince the understandably suspicious guttersnipe to trust him? Somehow he had to do it. Instead of jewels, a carriage and a house in the most fashionable part of town—all things a prospective mistress had every right to expect—Lucy had asked for a child's life. He'd used her to get to her father, nearly got her evicted and been indirectly responsible for the beating she'd received from a shopkeeper. He owed her.

'It won't make a difference,' he repeated. 'She asked it of me and I agreed. It has nothing to do with anything else. You have my word on it.'

Fitch stared at him for a long moment. James had the uncomfortable sensation of being judged.

'Like, a bargain?' Fitch asked. 'What's in it for you?'

God! 'Nothing. She asked it of me.'

Another lengthy silence followed, during which James wondered if there were points for trying.

'Right.' Fitch spat in his palm and held it out.

James blinked. When in Rome…

The door opened to admit Penfold just as James

spat in his own palm. The porcelain on the tray rattled alarmingly.

Undeterred, James and Fitch shook on it.

'Penfold,' James said, 'how timely. Thank you.' He tried to look as though he sealed bargains like this every day. God, he needed that coffee!

Fitch craned his neck for a better look at the contents of the tray as Penfold set it down. 'Blimey! Didn' you have breakfast, guv?'

'I did. That's for you.' James reached for the coffee.

'Oh.' Fitch's eyes widened. He reached for the cake, and stopped, his hand hovering over a large slice. Scowling, he looked at Penfold. 'Thanks. Very good of you, I'm sure.'

Penfold's brows shot up and he made a peculiar sound. 'You're most welcome, Master Fitch.' He bowed to James. 'Is that all, my lord?'

James grinned. 'For now. Thank you, Penfold.'

The butler withdrew, his back rigid.

'I say something wrong?' Fitch demanded.

'Never mind.' James tried not to laugh.

'Lu taught me to say thank you.' Fitch was positively aggrieved. 'She's got real pretty manners.'

'She does and she taught you well,' James said. 'You're a credit to her. Help yourself to cake and have some milk.'

Fitch took a slice of cake and sank his teeth into it,

munching cheerfully. He watched warily as James leaned forward and poured a glass of milk. Swallowing the cake, he picked up the glass and took a gulp. And another. He eyed the glass in patent surprise.

'Not quite what you're used to?' James asked.

'Nah. Ale's more my thing of a morning.' Fitch took another gulp. 'But this ain't bad.' He wolfed down the rest of the slice of cake and washed it down with milk. 'Lot of cake there,' he said questioningly.

James gestured to it. 'Help yourself.' He sipped his coffee.

'Can I take a bit to Lu?'

The coffee cup rattled into the saucer. 'Are you going to see her?'

Fitch swallowed more milk and wiped away a creamy moustache with his shirtsleeve. 'Yeah. Reckon she'd like to know.'

James's gaze went to the silk reticule lying on his desk. It still held the amethyst ring, the fan and a tiny lace-edged handkerchief. His chest felt constricted. 'Yes. I think she would. One thing.'

'What?' Fitch asked around a mouthful of cake.

'Make sure she knows I'm not doing it to change her mind.'

Fitch looked at him and nodded slowly as he swallowed. 'Right. Any message?'

Message? He floundered. 'Just…just tell her that I'll keep the ring for her.' Always.

Fitch took another huge mouthful. 'S'good,' he said. 'Shoul' ha' some.' He gestured to the plate.

'Why not?' James took a slice and watched in fascination as Fitch wolfed down his third slice. 'No need to rush,' he said drily. 'There's plenty of it.'

Chapter Fourteen

Lucy looked at the address on the card Elizabeth had slipped into her hand the previous night. Drawing a deep breath, she took her old cloak off its hook and swung it over her shoulders. She would ask Elizabeth to send a servant for the rest—assuming her father didn't sell everything the moment she was out the door.

She pushed aside the curtain and stepped out into the room. Her father looked up immediately from his chair by the fire.

His eyes widened. 'Where are you going?'

Lucy barely glanced at him. 'I'm leaving. I'll send a servant for my things.' She'd had time to think last night. Ample time to stare into the dark and consider her future. It stretched out, bleak and terrifying whichever way she looked, but she was leaving her father.

He scowled. 'No. Better if you don't. If you want to go to Cambourne, I'll take you.'

She opened her mouth to tell him that she wasn't going to Cambourne and shut it again. If he thought she was going to James, he'd be less likely to take her belongings straight down to Mr Jessup's shop. Besides, she didn't want him to know where she was. 'If you think I'll take you to haggle over the price, think again!'

He actually managed to look wounded. 'I'm your father!'

'You tried to sell me!'

Outrage flooded his face. 'You're selling yourself! Or are you persuaded that he can be brought to offer marriage, you stupid girl!'

She swallowed, heat pricking at her eyes. In the end James hadn't been offering anything, but— 'He asked me to be his mistress. I accepted. It seemed safer than being your daughter.'

'*Lucy!*'

Slamming the door, Lucy fled down the stairs. She wasn't, she absolutely wasn't, going to cry again. She had cried enough last night for a lifetime.

What had she been thinking even to consider becoming a man's mistress when she had already fallen in love with him?

Freedom. Safety. She still wanted them and she was still an idiot. Oh, she'd known that James was not offering marriage, but short of that folly she'd fallen prey to every romantic illusion under the sun.

Believing that he cared for her, would look after her and provide for a child if she couldn't prevent it.

He would still have taken you with him last night. You *decided not to go.*

He used me! Lied to me!

He fed you. Looked after you. He didn't take you when he could easily have done just that. He made you think about it. Understand what you were doing. He didn't offer you lies about love—just his protection.

She had refused. So now she would do the only thing that was left—she would go to Elizabeth and ask for help finding a position, even a protector if she had to. Her stomach roiled and her heart cracked a little further, but she gritted her teeth. If she had to be a mistress, then she wouldn't make the mistake of falling in love again. She needed someone she wouldn't weave dreams around. Dreams led only to heartbreak and disillusion.

Automatically she searched the street and pavement for Fitch. Probably he knew Papa was back and there was no need to warn him not to come. James had been kind there, too. Not having him arrested… buying enough food for both of them…

He used you!

Heat stung her eyes again. Had even his desire been feigned? The problem was that she didn't *want* to believe that it had all been lies. She had wanted to be *wanted*. Even like that.

Oh, God! What a little fool he must have thought her!

He still wanted you to leave with him last night...

What was the use of remembering that? Or remembering the gentleness in his voice—*You can still come with me, sweetheart. Nothing has changed. I still want you...*

She pushed the memory down. He'd gone to the expense of preparing that house for her, so of course he'd want to gain some use from it. And he'd certainly desired her last night...

'Yeh're not goin' ter scream, bitch.' Something sharp bit into her side. 'Come quiet now an' yeh won't get hurt. Nor yeh don't want summink ter 'appen ter yer pa, or that varmint Fitch.'

'Please—'

'I'm sure yeh beg real nice, missy.' The knife jabbed and fear choked her, along with the man's rancid breath. 'But there ain't no use wastin' it on me. Now, see that there carriage?'

She nodded, a coppery taste in her mouth. The shabby vehicle just ahead had slowed to a crawl by the curb.

'Yer goin' to get in without no silly carry on. Ain't no one goin' ter hurt yeh. Just a bloke wants a message give ter yer pa.'

She tensed, ready to scream, to fight.

The knife jabbed again. 'Just think of yer pa, missy. An' Fitch. Seen 'im today, 'ave yer?'

Fear was sour in her mouth as she took another step. The carriage was right beside her, its door opening... She might risk the knife for herself, but Fitch— The knife prodded and she stepped into the carriage.

Her assailant swung in behind her and she found herself sandwiched between two of them. The thick, foetid reek of unwashed humanity and foul breath closed her throat. The man already in the carriage banged on the roof and the vehicle lurched forward. 'That were quick.'

Fury, laced with terror, seized her. 'Where's Fitch?' she demanded. 'What have you done with him?'

The second man roared with laughter. 'Fitch?' He looked past her at his companion. 'You got her in that easy acos she was worried about *him*?' He grinned at Lucy, his breath sickening. 'Ain't seen Fitch. Dessay he's out pickin' pockets if he knows what's good fer 'im.'

She dragged in a breath, and lashed out, fingers clawed. He jerked backward, swearing as she raked him, and powerful arms grabbed her from behind, followed by swift pressure on her throat. She spun into swirling blackness as something sickly sweet was crammed over her nose and mouth.

* * *

Fear crawled from Fitch's belly to his mouth. He eased back into the shadows, shame licking at the fear.

You didn' help her! She's your friend an' you let them take her. You know what they'll do to her, an' you didn' help!

His stomach churned. Kilby had sent Jig after her, so likely the man in the carriage had been Wat. They'd have killed him for trying.

He dragged in a shuddering breath and something slid down his cheek. Annoyed, he wiped at it. His fingers came away wet. Dazed, he stared at the wetness. Years it was since he'd cried. And he weren't going to start now. He needed to think.

Shoving his hands in his pockets, he encountered the cake he'd brought for Lu. The sour choking lodged high in his throat with the urge to find Kilby and tell him…tell him he was done. Done and—

Get your throat cut, doin' that.

He took another ragged breath, realised he was still crying. He scrubbed at his face. First thing he had to do was lighten a few pockets. Make his day's take an' then hand it over. He fingered the napkin-wrapped cake in his pocket. It had to be business as usual.

The world had gone mad. It spun darkly around Lucy in slow, sickening swoops. She couldn't move, couldn't even open her eyes. Close by someone was moaning. Rough female voices sounded in a whirling darkness.

'Get her clothes off. She won't be needin' them.'

There was coarse laughter as swift hands stripped her while others held her still.

'Ooh! Got a bauble, she does. Won't need that neither!'

She struggled feebly as the ribbon holding her locket was torn away.

'The awd bitch is countin' the coin already. Word's out round the gents' clubs that she's puttin' up a real virgin tonight.'

'Virgin, eh? Won't be fer long, if that's true. They checked she's the goods, all right?'

'Kilby had Maud check straight off. She's the real deal… Word is Kilby had her grabbed deliberate… 'Ere, she's comin' round—gimme that rag. Another whiff an' she goes down the cellar till they're ready for 'er.'

Again the sickly rag was clamped over her mouth and nose and the world dissolved again.

The boy hadn't returned. James poked a burning log in the grate and tried to shrug off disappointment. It had been a long shot at best. Even if Fitch had been willing to try, what was the likelihood that a boy bred to the streets, a pickpocket and likely worse, could change?

Somewhere between zero and zero.

He'd been a fool even to think of trying. Probably the boy would have used the opportunity to steal God only knew what. Setting the poker down, he stared around at the library. The boy must have seen it as a thieves' paradise.

Then why hasn't he returned?

Probably realised how closely he'd be watched, by the staff as well as James himself, and calculated the odds of getting away with it or finishing on the business end of a noose.

Unbidden his hand slipped into his pocket. He fingered the amethyst ring. He was doubly a fool. He'd known the odds and he'd been prepared to try.

And now you're giving up? Just let him slide back without making the least push to change his mind? What if he encountered some of his old colleagues?

He clenched his fist. Perhaps Lucy had been right to walk away from him if he could consider giving up this easily. Tomorrow morning, he would call at Hensleigh's lodgings. Not to pressure Lucy over her own decision, but he could ask her to tell Fitch the offer remained open. Hopefully he could find the boy himself.

Some of the churning restlessness eased. But he still had to tell Hunt that the search for Gerald's killers had stalled. He couldn't risk Lucy, and if he went after her father for information there was too great a chance she'd be caught in any crossfire. Hunt had been out when he'd called earlier.

The mantel clock chimed six. He had a dinner and at least two balls he'd been invited to attend. No doubt his valet, Marsham, was already laying out his evening clothes, since he was in town after all.

Deep in the house, the doorbell clanged. He didn't move. He'd given instructions that he was not at home and he was seriously considering sending up a message to put the evening clothes away.

He'd got as far as mentally framing a polite apology for dinner, when a light tap on the door made him frown.

Which bit of 'I'm not at home to anyone' had Penfold failed to comprehend?

The door opened. 'Lord Huntercombe, my lord.'

James sighed. This was why he paid Penfold so generously, for knowing when to ignore instructions and use his brain.

Hunt looked tired. Deep shadows around his eyes and a strain about the mouth suggested he slept as badly as James. Yet he summoned a smile. 'Cambourne. Good of you to call earlier. Is there news?'

James waved him to a chair. 'Brandy?' He gestured to the decanter and glasses on his desk.

Hunt sat by the fire. 'Thank you.'

James poured two glasses and walked over to give one to Hunt. He sat in the other chair beside the fire and they sipped in silence.

'Good brandy.' Hunt swirled the amber liquid.

'My father laid this down. Getting a little low now.' How was he to tell the man that he knew who was responsible for Gerald's death? Knew, but could go no further. What damn irony that Lucy herself had given him the final snippet last night.

'So? There's progress?'

James set his glass down. 'Of a sort.'

Hunt did him the courtesy of listening in silence until he'd finished. Somehow that made it worse.

'An innocent,' he said at last. 'You're saying you'll go no further because of this man, this Hensleigh's daughter.'

James swallowed. 'I'm sorry, Hunt. Without being able to ensure her safety—'

'And you think she's an innocent?' Disbelief tinged Hunt's voice as he leaned forward. 'Cambourne, is this the filly you displayed at Vauxhall last night? The girl who supped with you, Fox and Elizabeth Armistead? And you think she's an *innocent*?'

'How the hell—?' James answered his own question. 'I dare say it's all over the clubs.'

Hunt laughed. A sound totally devoid of amusement. 'Major topic of conversation. For God's sake!

She's played you, Cambourne! I mean, what are the odds?' Hunt shook his head. 'If she's your mistress, that should keep her safe enough.' His mouth hardened. 'And give you time to recover from your infatuation.'

It sounded cold, ruthless and calculating. And it was exactly what he'd intended. Only he'd complicated it by falling… He shied away from that. He'd complicated things, anyway, and—

'She refused to become my mistress.'

Hunt raised cynical brows. 'What? You didn't offer enough for—?'

Hunt broke off and James realised that he'd surged to his feet, fists clenched. Slowly, breathing carefully, he sank back.

Hunt gave him a considering look and sipped his brandy. 'If you think she's that sort of girl, why introduce her to Elizabeth?' Then, at James's cold look, he sighed. 'Very well. Elizabeth is hardly your average, common tart.'

James nodded. 'She asked me to convey her sympathy about Gerald.'

Hunt let out a breath. 'Yes. She would. Tell her— no. I'll do it myself. Tell me—' he fixed James with a curious look '—what did Elizabeth think of the girl?'

The doorbell clanged and James frowned.

'You're expecting someone?' Hunt half rose. 'I should be getting along if—'

'I'm not expecting anyone.' James waved him back. 'Penfold will deal with it. At least finish your brandy.'

The doorbell executed a jangling cannonade.

Hunt raised his brows. 'Someone's impatient.'

Hurried footsteps sounded on the marble tiles of the entrance hall and then Penfold's voice rose indignantly. 'Now, see here, you young limb! That's no way to treat his lordship's—'

'To hell with that! I got to see him urgent!'

James was already on his feet and halfway across the room.

'His lordship is occupied! You come along with me and—'

James flung the door open.

'Leave go! Jus' tell me where—'

'Fitch. I'm here.'

The boy broke free of Penfold's restraint and ran, skidded, across the tiles. Sweat dripped from his flushed face, his shirt clung damply and his skinny chest heaved.

'Guv! It's Lu!' His breath shuddered in. 'Kilby's men grabbed her. Word is he's goin' to sell her for her pa's debts.'

Everything in James condensed to solid, icy fear.

'When? When did they grab her?' His voice

seemed to come from a long way off, almost to belong to someone else.

''Bout two. Heard the bells.'

'Two?' It was nearly seven o'clock. His hand shot out, gripped Fitch's shoulder. 'And you're telling me *now*?'

The boy flinched, but he squared up at once. 'Had to find out where she was, didn' I? Where they're selling her. More'n one knock shop that'll sell a girl for Kilby. Then I had to get here!' His grubby fingers manacled James's wrist. 'I know where she is, guv. But we got to hurry. Kilby's put the word out.'

Seven o'clock. James's stomach roiled. 'We'll never make it.' He'd be in time to kill anyone who'd touched her, hurt her, yes; but not in time to save her. The knowledge was razor-sharp.

But Fitch shook his head. 'We might. He wants top price. Auction's fixed for late this evening. Gotta give folks time to finish their fancy dinners, don't he?' He met James's eye. 'Gents. Your sort.'

James forced his mind to work. Kilby would never get the price he wanted from the dregs of the stews. So he'd got word to the dissolute of the *haut ton*. Men with real money who'd pay for a terrified girl and not give a damn that she was unwilling as long as they got their money's worth.

'Cambourne?'

Hunt had come to the door and stared at Fitch. 'What the hell is *that*?'

James looked at Fitch. The boy glared at Hunt, but didn't answer. Once, James could have answered the question unequivocally: a street thief, a gallows bird. Now— 'He's mine.'

Fitch turned a startled gaze on him. 'Right. We going?'

James nodded. 'Yes. Penfold—have the carriage brought around. Digby on the box, a man beside him. Two men on the back. All armed. Loaded carriage pistols in the inside holsters.'

'For God's sake!' Hunt exploded. 'You're going God only knows where on the say so of—'

'Dunno 'bout God,' Fitch said. 'Reckon He ain't got too much to do with Kilby, but I know where. An' it ain't right in the rookeries. Fancy gents with money won't go there.'

The doorbell jangled again and Nick walked in. 'Why is the door—? Good lord!' He stared at Fitch, revolted. 'Have you caught a burglar, James?'

Fitch returned the look with interest. 'Ain't none of yer friends got no manners, guv?'

'My cousin, Nicholas. Nick, this is Fitch. He brought me a message. You'll have to excuse me.'

'Ah, right.' Nick cleared his throat. 'Just wanted to apologise if I queered your pitch with the Hensleigh wench last night and—'

He took a startled step back as Fitch squared up, fists raised. 'She ain't no wench!' he spat. 'An' if you're the one made her decide not to go with the guv las' night, then it's your fault she's in trouble now!'

Nick stared. 'What? James, what the hell is he—?'

'Remington.' Hunt glared at Fitch. 'Try if you can talk some sense into Cambourne. This…urchin… is intent on taking him into the stews after the girl! It's probably a trap!'

Fitch looked at James. 'Guv?'

James returned the look. 'It's not a trap, Hunt. There's no time to convince you with the real reasons I know that, but think! Why bait a trap in a way sure to bring me in heavily armed? There are better ways to do it.' He saw Penfold, still hovering. 'Go!' he snapped. 'Nick!' James caught his shoulder. 'Go up to my room and tell Marsham I need my duelling pistols. Both pairs and everything needed to load them.'

Nick's eyes widened. 'Duelling pistols?'

'Yes. Hurry!' James laid his hand on Huntercombe's shoulder, as Nick darted off up the stairs. 'Hunt, Kilby had your brother beaten to death over unpaid debts. He's had Lucy delivered to a brothel.' He gritted his teeth. Lucy, alone, terrified and helpless. Kilby was a dead man walking. 'Even if I suspected a trap, I wouldn't take the risk.'

Huntercombe swore. 'Very well. I'll go with you.'

* * *

She had no idea how much time had passed from when they slammed the door on her, sick and fainting, to the point where she regained full consciousness in the dark. Cold struck up at her and she realised that she was lying on the ground. Her mind cleared slowly and memory slid back. The two men…the sickly-smelling rag…two women pulling at her clothes… Her throat felt raw and scratchy and her stomach roiled.

Please, God, let this be a bad dream.

The utter darkness did not abate and she pushed herself to a sitting position against what felt like a stone wall. She struggled to her feet and leaned, shaky and sweating, against the wall. Somewhere close by water dripped intermittently. She shivered. The wall was damp and cold through her clothes… *her clothes…* On a jolt of horror, she realised the truth; she was wearing only her chemise. The women had stripped her.

Sick terror uncoiled, ate at her. Shaking, her hand went to her throat. Yes, the locket was gone. Perhaps it was just a robbery and they'd locked her up to make sure they escaped safely.

The awd bitch is countin' the coin already. Word's out round the gents' clubs that she's puttin' up a real virgin tonight.

It wasn't a robbery. She leaned against the wall,

fighting the panic that rose up to choke her, forcing herself to breathe deeply, to *think*.

If she could escape and get to James…he would help her. It wouldn't matter that she had refused him, that she had told him she never wished to see him again.

Exploring by feel, she found only a chair and it didn't take long to ascertain that her prison was tiny. No more than nine feet square with the one heavy, wooden door. A door whose latch refused to rise and which didn't even shudder when she slammed her shoulder against it.

Panic surged anew and she drew breath to scream for help.

She didn't. Common sense prevailed. If they'd stripped her of her clothes and thrown her in here, then it was unlikely that anyone would let her out just because she screamed.

Feeling her way, she found the chair again. Something skittered across the floor. She swung the chair in that direction and shuddered at the startled squealing.

Chapter Fifteen

They left the carriage on Millbank Street and followed Fitch towards the river. The lantern Fitch carried only heightened the darkness lapping at them, but it was as nothing to the darkness of fear consuming James. Not for himself—for Lucy. All he could think was that his own stupidity had put her in danger. And not just Lucy. Nick had insisted on coming as well. He'd agreed, but had sent notes to Bow Street and Fox requesting reinforcements.

'There 'tis,' muttered Fitch, pointing across the street at a shop that appeared to trade in used clothes. To the left of the building was a solid double gate, wide enough to take a carriage, with a closed hatch at face height.

Nick stared. 'That's a carriage gate. What do they need with—?'

'Ain't you got no brain in yer noggin?' Fitch muttered. 'That way they can get the merchandise in without no one the wiser. 'Cause sometimes it ain't so willing. An' some of your lot pay extra to drive in. All nice and private-like.'

Nick gaped at him and Fitch continued. 'I'll knock on the hatch an' tell the doorman you're all here to bid at Madam's special sale.' He spoke directly to James. 'You'll need to grease his fist, but he'll let you in all right with me to say it's all bowman.'

Hunt snorted. 'I dare say.'

Fitch spared him a glance. 'Money talks an' they know me.'

'You'll stay outside, Fitch,' James said. Damned if he'd take the boy in.

Fitch rolled his eyes. 'Like I've never been in a knock shop before,' he said. 'Good pickin's in there. But I'll wait. If the Runners come with your mate, I'll show 'em which house. You get Lu.'

He'd get her out or die. He glanced at Nick and Hunt.

Hunt's mouth tightened. 'I'm in.'

'Don't waste your breath,' Nick muttered. 'I'm going in.'

If William and Susan ever heard about this... 'Pistols ready?'

'Yes. You?'

'Yes. No shooting unless there's no choice.' Six pistols between them. If Lucy had been harmed he'd empty all of them into the bastards responsible. But once fired, a pistol was useless. Fear for her clawed at his throat. He forced it down, below the icy veneer of control, below the killing rage. 'Let's go.'

At the shriek of the bolt being dragged back, Lucy scrambled up, crouching to the side of the door, heart pounding, the chair ready in her hands.

The door opened and a sickly light showed the dirt floor and dank walls.

'Where the—?'

She sprang, swung the chair hard, cracking the man over the head, so that the chair broke as he dropped with a groan. Leaping over him, she made a dash for the passageway, still clutching a splintered chair leg. A second man made a grab and she dodged, twisting away, stabbing the broken leg at his belly. He fell back, cursing. She hesitated, trying to get her bearings, and a powerful arm snaked around her waist from behind, lifting her right off her feet. The chair leg was wrenched from her. She screamed, kicking and scratching, but the third man held her effortlessly. The man she'd jabbed with the chair leg was coming towards them, his face savage.

'Hold the bitch, Jig!'

His fist slammed into her midriff and her vision exploded in white-hot pain. Wheezing, dazed, she collapsed in her captor's grip.

The man who had hit her caught her hair, jerking her head up. Sobbing for breath, Lucy saw the clenched fist through a fog of pain, knew he was going to hit her in the face.

'No!' The man holding her swung her aside so the blow went wide. 'Mark the goods, the price goes down. Kilby'll carve the difference outta us, if she don't cover her pa's debts. An' it's better if she's got some fight, pushes the price higher.'

'She hit Case!' whined the other man she recognised as the second man in the carriage. 'Near gutted me with that chair leg, too!' But he let go of her hair.

'He'll live,' the other said. 'Come on, Wat. Let's get her upstairs.'

Terror fogged Lucy's brain as the two men dragged her, struggling, along the passage and through a door into an ill-lit stairwell. 'Please, no!' she begged. 'Let me go! *Please!*'

A rough laugh greeted this. 'Reckon not, Miss Dolly Mop!' Wat grabbed her breast and squeezed. Pain shot through her and she cried out, fighting to twist away.

Wat leered, digging his fingers in harder. 'Wriggle all yeh like, missy. Shows off the goods real nice. There's some mighty fine gents out there waitin' to slap down the ready for yeh. Pity it can't be me an' Jig here, but we ain't got the money for a virgin ride. Still, we might get a bit when they've done with yeh up there.'

Desperation lent Lucy strength, but they forced her up the stairs into another passage and through a curtained doorway. Light blazed and she shut her eyes, only to open them again at the roar.

Sick and shaking, she stared in horror at the crowd of men, *gentlemen*, in the brightly lit, crimson-draped room. Most were drinking and all were watching as she was dragged, squirming and kicking, to a low dais. The men hauled her up and a heavily rouged woman carrying a riding crop, a scarlet gown barely covering her nipples, stepped on to the stage.

'There you are, gentlemen. One genuine, guaranteed virgin. Let them see her, boys.'

Whistles and cheers went up as the men forced Lucy to turn full circle. The madam caught the hem of her chemise with the riding crop and lifted it to further howls of appreciation. Fear sour in her mouth, Lucy kicked out, struck flesh and staggered as the man who had hit her before slapped her.

'Fifty!' came a yell, as she was brought around to face the crowd.

The madam scoffed. 'For a virgin? That's quality goods, that is.' Lucy shuddered as the woman used the riding crop to outline the curve of one breast. 'Untouched. And there's a reserve on this filly. Bidding starts at five hundred.'

Hope flared in Lucy at the sudden silence. *Five hundred?* No one would pay that!

Murmurs rose again and Lucy prayed. *Please God, let it be too much.*

A lazy voice drawled, 'For that price she'd better be untouched.'

Ice condensed in Lucy's stomach as the man looked her over. Older than her father, he was heavily built, powerful. Well dressed, a diamond glittered in his cravat. His gaze on her was cold, greedy. Merciless. Fear clogged her throat.

The abbess nodded. 'Checked meself. Five hundred an' she's yours, m'lord.'

'Very well. Five hundred.' Lucy's blood congealed as his gaze slithered over her, lingered on her breasts. 'And half back if she's not a virgin ride.'

The ice in Lucy's stomach burned as terror choked her.

The woman's eyes narrowed. 'Then you agree to a witness. Ain't havin' you breakin' choice goods, then pretendin' you didn't get your money's worth.'

'Done.' He moved forward and Lucy tensed to fight.

The abbess flung up a hand. 'Not so fast.' She looked at the crowd. 'Any other bids?'

'Five-fifty!' Three younger men near the back of the room shoved their way forward.

The original bidder swore. 'Six.'

'Six-fifty!' said another of the younger men.

Mother Atkinson cocked her head at the trio. 'Who's bidding?'

The first young man leered. 'Pooling our resources. Game of dice will settle who gets what first.'

Lucy's stomach roiled as a roar of lecherous laughter and lewd suggestions went up. Desperate, she scanned the crowd. Only lust stared back. She bit her lip, forcing back tears. Whatever else she couldn't control, she wouldn't cry in front of these brutes!

The first bidder scowled. 'Seven hundred.'

'Seven-fifty.'

The bidding rose and the murmuring grew, money exchanging hands as men bet on the outcome, and Lucy prayed. Prayed that the first bidder would win. She'd not stand a chance against three. Her mind had cleared and she stood quietly. If she fought now, she would be subdued. Better to save her strength. When they took her out of here, perhaps there would be a chance to escape… Even if there wasn't a chance, she was going to try…

'Twelve-fifty,' the original bidder snapped.

The trio of younger men conferred briefly. 'Fifteen hundred!'

The older man spread his hands. 'I'm out.'

Fear icing her veins, Lucy shut her eyes.

'Any further bids, gentlemen?' The tone of the madam's voice said she knew it was over. 'Right. Going, going—'

* * *

James sprinted down the corridor towards the red door, Nick and Hunt at his back, the porter's words pounding in his head.

Door at the end. Biddin's started. Tasty piece she is, too.

He crashed through the door, taking in the scene in one swift glance. Hunt cursed viciously. Lucy, clad in her chemise, face white, stood gripped by two bruisers on the stage. A red handprint marred her cheek as she stared at him. The abbess, Mother Atkinson, stood to the side, riding crop raised to slash down on a cloth-covered table.

'What's the bid?' he shouted.

'Here!' Fred Tavering protested. 'She's ours!' He gestured to Blydon and Riggs.

James took a step forward, his fists clenched. 'Is that so, Tavering?'

'Bid's accepted,' Riggs snapped, although Tavering fell back a step.

'Hammer ain't fallen.' Mother Atkinson brandished the crop, assessing James. 'You want her, my bucko?' she demanded over Riggs's protest. Her gaze flicked to Riggs and his friends. 'Well, so do they. Bid's fifteen hundred. What's yours?'

'Hell!' Nick sounded stunned.

The abbess smirked. 'Pace too hot? Nice little filly. Guaranteed unbroken.'

James clenched his fists, his gaze never leaving Lucy's white face. 'Two thousand.'

'For God's sake, James! It's a king's ransom!' Nick muttered under the uproar. 'The pistols...'

'Not yet.' Hunt kept his voice low.

James spared Nick a glance. 'All that matters is getting her out. We'll use the pistols if we have to.' If his bid wasn't accepted...

Nick let out a breath and nodded. 'All right.' He lowered his voice. 'The pair holding her are the ones who beat me up.'

James looked at the two thugs, memorising them. Wat and Jig, Fitch had told him. He'd get Lucy out first, but after that, there was no hole deep or dark enough to hide them. If Kilby had used them to kidnap Lucy and beat Nick, the chances were high they'd killed Hunt's brother.

He glanced at Hunt. 'Don't do anything rash.'

Hunt's eyes burned. 'Don't worry. Revenge is a dish best served on ice.'

Tavering and his cronies conferred hastily. Blydon shook his head, casting a nervous look at James. Tavering grabbed his arm, shaking him, but Blydon shrugged loose, speaking low and fast. Whatever he said had Tavering casting an edgy glance at James, too.

'We're out,' Tavering snarled.

The abbess looked around. 'No one else? Going...

going…*gone*!' Her riding crop slashed down on the table.

James glanced at Nick and Hunt. 'Cover me.' He strode forward, shouldering men and several whores aside.

Montgomery stepped into his path. 'Didn't think this was quite your thing, Cambourne.' He jerked his head towards Lucy. 'Pretty little wench. Tavering and his friends outbid me, but after you're done—'

James's fist shot out and Montgomery went down, blood spraying from his nose. 'Don't bother calling me out,' James snarled. 'I only meet gentlemen.'

The crowd scrambled out of his way.

Mother Atkinson met him as he stepped up on to the stage, blocking his path. 'Payment.'

His jaw hardened. He'd never hit a woman in his life, but by God he'd make an exception for this one.

He took a death grip on his temper. 'You'll get your money,' he said softly, and knew the edge of satisfaction as the abbess flinched. 'I'll give you a draft on my bank.'

The woman's eyes narrowed. 'Think I don't know your sort? Renege and skip town in a blink, you would!'

He let his contempt show. 'Do you think I carry that sort of money? Tavering and his friends know where to find me.'

The abbess cocked her head and nodded. 'Right. You do this draft and she's all yours.'

James reached into his pocket and brought out the draft he'd written up before leaving the house, along with a travelling inkpot and a pen. He scrawled in the amount, signed it, and handed the paper to the abbess. She squinted at it and nodded. 'Right. But you renege and we'll come looking for you. Remember that.'

He gave a short nod. He didn't doubt it. 'Step aside, then.'

She did so slowly, an insolent smile on her face. 'Long as I gets the money, I don't care who has her.'

He ignored her, his eyes on Lucy.

'Have they hurt you?'

'No,' she whispered. 'But, James, that money!' Her face was bone-white, her eyes huge, every limb trembling.

'Forget it.' His own hands shaking, he released the clasp on his cloak and swung it off his shoulders. His gaze whipped to the men who still held her. They dropped her wrists and backed away.

Lucy's breath jerked in as James wrapped the cloak about her. 'Don't faint, sweetheart,' he murmured. 'I may need a hand free. Let's get you out of here.' He felt her pull herself together and steady, and pride surged through him.

The abbess narrowed her eyes, suddenly suspicious. 'You aint taking her nowhere, cully.'

The two men who'd been holding Lucy moved forward at her signal. 'Reckon you ain't goin' nowhere, me lord,' said the larger, baring his teeth. 'Property of the house, she is.'

James tensed, ready to force Lucy down if there was any shooting.

'Your mistake, boys.' The double click as Hunt cocked his pistols stopped the men cold.

'She's coming with us.' Nick drew his pistols. 'Stand back.'

The double click of Nick's pistols fell into shocked silence. Hunt faced the dais, his pistols trained on the men, Nick stood back to back with him, covering the crowd. The abbess scowled as her men backed away. 'They won't shoot an' I got money on this—'

'Damn it, Maud,' one growled. '*You* ain't facing a gun.'

'An oversight.' Holding Lucy close, James reached into his right-hand pocket and brought out a pistol, cocked it and trained it straight on the abbess. 'Usually I'd hesitate to shoot a woman, but not you.'

She swore and stepped back. 'Fine. Take her.' Her eyes spat venom. 'But if she's that important to you, don't even think of reneging on the money. Some fine day someone will come for it an' for her.

Got that, cully? Less I gets that money, yer dead meat an'—'

The door to the front hall crashed open. 'Runners! That little gobshite Fitch ratted us out!' The man whirled and fled. There was an instant's stunned silence before the room exploded into panic.

James grabbed Lucy, dragging her back against the wall. 'Stay behind me!' He gave a cursory glance at the scrambling crowd of men, Montgomery among them, fighting their way to the door. They weren't a danger. Mother Atkinson on the other hand...he watched her, kept the pistol levelled.

Her mouth twisted in a snarl, she looked straight at James.

'Get out if you can.' He lowered the pistol slightly.

Behind him Lucy gasped. 'James—!'

'I won't risk you,' he said. 'Go on!' he snapped at the abbess.

The abbess stared for an instant, then fled through a small door near the dais. James watched her go. If Kilby wasn't taken, and the money didn't reach him, Lucy would never be safe.

The men who'd held Lucy made for the same door. James swore and fired. One went down screaming, clutching his knee, and brought his comrade down in a yelling tangle.

James dropped the now useless pistol and pulled

out another. 'Stay down!' He cocked the pistol. 'I won't shoot to wound next time.'

They stayed down, neither prepared to risk making a run for it.

James glanced at Nick and Hunt. They had followed his example, moving back against the wall, staying clear of the scrum. The room was half-clear as men jammed, struggling through the narrow door. A muffled crash, followed by another, settled to a rhythmic pounding. The men remaining in the room, including the three James had outbid, stared around wildly. Blydon grabbed his companions and pointed to the door by the dais.

Nick and Hunt stepped forward shoulder to shoulder, pistols raised, blocking their exit. 'Not you, lads,' Hunt said pleasantly.

Lucy dozed in the carriage, sliding in and out, always aware of James's presence, that she was safe, held close in his arms. Beyond all hope he'd come for her. His cloak enfolded her in the faint scent of cologne and *him*, musky and male. Eventually the coach stopped and she became aware of his cousin, Mr Remington, at the door.

They spoke quietly, James giving instructions. 'Take the boy now. I'll ask Fox and Elizabeth to escort Lucy down tomorrow.'

'Of course. Anything else?'

Elizabeth. Had he known she was going to Elizabeth? The one woman who wouldn't judge, who could help her.... The boy....

'Fitch.' Someone had yelled his name in the brothel...

James's arms tightened. 'Nick is taking him out to Chiswick. He's quite safe. You'll see him tomorrow.'

She relaxed into his warm strength. With him, she was safe. Somehow out of time and out of the suddenly dangerous world she walked. Vaguely she was aware when the clop of hooves and rumble of wheels halted again, but before she could force her eyes open, she was gathered into powerful arms and lifted effortlessly. She drifted again, feeling a gentle pressure on the top of her head. As if he'd kissed her hair. Better than any useless dream...

'Put a warming pan in my bed... What? Of course Miss Hensleigh will need a nightgown! One of my nightshirts will do for now. Bread and butter. Tea.' His quiet voice continued, giving orders. Dimly, she wondered where he was going to find such things as bread, butter and tea in her father's rooms. She doubted that Papa had bought any. And who was carrying out the instructions... *Put a warming pan in my bed... His bed? His nightshirt?*

Reality crashed down around her and she forced her eyes open. She was in an unfamiliar, book-lined room, lying on a sofa, still wrapped in his cloak and with a blanket tucked around her. A fire danced in the grate. A comfortable leather chair sat close by, its sagging seat and worn arms, along with several newspapers on a wine table beside it, suggesting that it was someone's preferred chair.

He'd brought her to his home. And he still didn't know her real name.

A moment later a door opened and closed. Footsteps, muffled by the Turkish carpet, rounded the sofa. Shame flooded her and she closed her eyes again, wondering how a dream became a nightmare. She opened her eyes as James sat down in the chair and reached forward to take her hand.

'Lucy. Sweetheart.' Her heart ached. Not just at the endearment but the sheer tenderness in his voice, in his eyes. 'You're safe here.'

'You bought me,' she whispered and pulled her hand away. She sat up carefully, clutching the cloak and blanket.

His face whitened and his mouth became a hard, flat line, as his hand balled to a fist. 'Lucy, it was the only way to get you out of there safely! Not because—' His voice shook. 'I ransomed you, Lucy. I didn't *buy* you. And I brought you here to keep you safe.' His hand reached for her, fell. 'Not to seduce you. I swear it.'

'Those other men—' The words, the knowledge,

caught in her throat. 'They weren't going to bother seducing me.'

'No.' His voice was flat, uncompromising.

'My father's debts—' Her voice broke and she swallowed, but she forced herself to meet his eyes. 'They said that was why. There was a reserve on me. Five hundred pounds.'

His eyes remained gentle. 'It's over, Lucy. Penfold is bringing you tea and something to eat. Then I'll see you settled for the night.'

She followed him upstairs, still wrapped in his cloak, dazed at the size and grandeur of the house. Soft carpet cushioned her feet, the panelled walls painted white and gilded. 'My room.' He opened a door and gestured her in. 'That's the dressing room.' He pointed out a small door. 'I'll be in there. Another door leads in to it from the hall.'

A nightshirt was laid out on the turned-down bed and a jug steamed on the washstand. 'You'll want to wash,' he said. 'I have a few things to do downstairs before coming up. Will you be all right?'

Mutely, she nodded. She wanted to beg him to hold her, to stay, but she held the words back.

'You're safe here,' he said. His mouth twisted. 'Even from me.'

The pain and guilt in his eyes tore at her. 'I know,' she whispered. Not knowing quite why, she reached up and placed her hand against his cheek, felt the warm rasp of the shadowed darkness of his jaw, felt the tension racking him.

He stared at her and slowly his hand rose to cover hers, hold it there. His head turned and he pressed a kiss into the palm of her hand. She trembled as he drew it away from his mouth and closed her fingers as if to hold the kiss safe.

'You shouldn't trust me,' he said roughly, still holding her hand between his. 'I asked you to be my mistress. That hasn't changed. I still want you.'

A quiver went through her, heat curling inside, ready to explode. 'Yes. But you won't force me.' She knew that as surely as she breathed. 'Armitage. My real name is Lucy Armitage.'

His hand tightened on hers. 'Is it? Thank you, sweetheart, but trust should be earned.' He held her hand a moment longer, then his mouth twisted into the travesty of a smile. 'Goodnight.'

Chapter Sixteen

James stared at his desk. It might as well not have been there. All he saw was Lucy, her green eyes on his, her palm the sweetest caress against his jaw. Had she the slightest notion just how much he had wanted to take her in his arms and make love to her? What it had cost him to step back and not betray her trust?

It didn't matter what it had cost him. His folly had cost her enough this night. From what Fitch had picked up in the tavern, it had been his poking about that had alerted Kilby's men to her existence. And even without knowing that, knowing her father had been willing to sell her innocence—to sell her to *him* the night before—should have alerted him to her danger. But he'd left her with Hensleigh, or Armitage. He had the connection now—Sir Bertram Armitage, MP, must be Lucy's uncle. Knowing he would have had no legal right to remove Lucy without her father's consent—could have been charged with kidnapping—didn't help. He could have dealt with Armitage. It wouldn't have meant taking Lucy as his mistress if she weren't willing. He could have placed her under his protection in the truest sense of the word. In short, he could have behaved like a gentleman. As he was going to do now.

He let out a breath. There were things he had to do before he got Lucy out of town tomorrow. He pulled paper towards him, dipped his pen in the inkpot and scrawled a note to his bank. He had to ensure that the two thousand pounds was paid on presentation of that draft. Not otherwise would Lucy be safe. His hand shook as he sprinkled sand on the instructions.

You were nearly too late.

The knowledge, the raw, lingering fear, ate at him, consumed him.

A fierce pounding on his front door had him spattering sealing wax on the bluntly worded missive to Child's Bank.

He stiffened. He doubted anyone was fool enough to come looking for Lucy. And if they were, not to hammer on the front door. But he reached for his pistols, loading swiftly.

'My lord?'

Penfold stood at the door. His eyes widened as he saw what his master was at. 'You think someone's looking for the young lady?'

James cocked a pistol, pointing it at the floor. 'If

they are, they'll regret it,' he said. He offered the other pistol to Penfold, who took it. In his youth Penfold had served as a footman. He knew how to handle a pistol.

'Ready, m'lord.'

James strode from the room and across the entrance hall. 'Stay back a little. If there is trouble, fire on anyone who gets past me.'

He reached the front door. 'Who is it?' he demanded, standing to the side of the door.

'Hensleigh! For God's sake, let me in!'

James stiffened. 'Are you alone?'

'What? Yes. Yes! Please, Cambourne! I beg of you!'

James threw the bolt, flipped the latch and backed away, the pistol trained on the door. 'Enter.'

The door burst open and Lucy's father almost fell inside, sweaty and breathless. 'She's gone,' he gasped. 'Lucy—they've taken her!'

'Shut the door, Armitage!' James snapped. 'Bolt and latch it. Now.' He gestured with the pistol.

Armitage froze, realising that he faced two armed men. 'M-my lord? You... Who gave you that name?'

'The door!'

Armitage fumbled to obey and James forced down rage, the savage instinct to throttle the man who'd flung Lucy to the wolves.

Armitage turned. 'Cambourne—they've taken her. Taken Lucy! And I can't find out where she is!'

James stared at him, disgust a bitter brew in his gut, and lowered the pistol slightly. 'In there.' He gestured to the library.

Armitage hurried past him as James took the second pistol from Penfold. 'Don't disturb us. I'll see him out and lock up.'

'Very good, my lord.'

James followed Armitage into the room and resisted the urge to vent his fury with a slammed door.

'Were you concerned for your daughter or yourself?' he asked, stalking over to his desk.

Armitage flinched. 'Cambourne, they took her and—'

'Sold her.' James set the pistols down in easy reach.

Armitage blanched. *'Please!* I was an idiot, but I never meant—'

'Lucy is mine.' James cut him off. 'Whatever name you use. Come near her again and, father or not, I swear I'll kill you. Make sure your other debtors know that she is no longer yours.'

Understanding and something that might have been relief flashed across Armitage's face. *'You* bought her? *She* told you her name?'

'She is mine,' James repeated.

Armitage's gaze darted to the ceiling. 'She's

here, then.' He started toward the door. 'If I could
see her—'

He stopped dead in his tracks as James levelled
a pistol.

'No further.' James held his shocked gaze. 'She's
no concern of yours. Now or ever.'

Armitage actually looked affronted. 'Now, see
here, Cambourne—she's my daughter, damn you!'

'No. Damn *you*,' James said. 'Your daughter?
Would that be the girl you tried to sell me last night
for a thousand pounds?' Bile rose in his throat at the
memory. 'Did *you* sell her to Kilby?'

Armitage's gaze fell. 'It wasn't like that! He was
threatening me—her! They were there when I came
off the stagecoach last night. Said I had twenty-four
hours to pay the five hundred I owed Kilby, or otherwise I had only one thing of value.' He was bab-
bling now, his voice a desperate whine. 'They didn't
say, but I knew they meant her! So I thought if you
took her, then she'd be safe. Even Kilby would never
dare touch her if she was under your protection!' He
recovered some of his bluster as James lowered the
pistol again. 'You wanted her! Don't pretend you
didn't! Bringing her presents. Taking her out to eat.'
He snorted. 'You even paid the damn rent!'

James could have pointed out that Lucy had been
hungry, that a pound of tea and lending her a few
books hardly qualified as aids to seduction, and that

he'd paid the rent to save her from eviction, but he didn't bother. He was guilty as charged. He'd asked her to be his mistress and he still wanted her more than his next breath.

'If you'd told me the truth, I'd have helped,' he said.

Armitage stared. 'You'd have given me the money?'

James laughed harshly. 'No. But I would have made sure Lucy was safe.' Even from himself. 'You were right—they'd never have dared touch her if she'd been under my protection. But you wanted the money, didn't you? So you gambled again, this time with her safety, and didn't tell me the danger she was in.'

Armitage's gaze fell. 'You don't understand—'

'How you could risk her?' James shook his head. 'No, I don't. You've forfeited the right to call yourself her father. Now get out.'

Armitage took a step back. 'Just tell me—is she safe? Did they—?' He broke off, his face white. 'For God's sake, Cambourne! Were you in time?'

James looked at the man, saw guilt and fear in the weak face, and relented. 'Yes. I was in time.'

Armitage's eyes closed. 'Thank you. Will you… will you tell her I was here?'

Silence lay between them.

At last, James said, 'You did not sell her?'

Armitage shook his head. 'No. I swear I did not.

I…I had decided to come to you. Tell you what danger she was in, but she left, and—'

'Then if she asks about you I will tell her you came.'

The man flinched, but he nodded. 'She…she will want her violin.'

'I'll send a servant.' He hesitated. 'Call again early afternoon.'

Armitage nodded. 'Thank you.' His voice broke on the whisper as he turned to go. He stopped. 'Your cousin, and the other boy—I'm sorry. If it helps, Kilby used Montgomery to lure them and others into the hells. It was how he paid off his own debts.'

James froze. 'I see. My thanks, then. Goodnight.'

Fear crept closer in the darkness, leering and unstoppable. It slid, faceless, merciless, crawled under her skin as she struggled to move, whispered threats as she forced a silent scream from her paralysed throat. Horror burst in her mind as the monster's claws tightened, held her helpless…

She came back to herself, sitting bolt upright in a strange bed on a surge of terror. Her breath came hard, ragged, as she fought off the nightmare.

A door slammed open and James was there, his face pale in the faint glow from the fire. She tried to speak, but only a shuddering gasp of relief came out. James's room. She was in James's room. In his bed.

'Lucy.'

He was beside her before she could draw the next breath, his arms about her, holding her safe. Shaking with reaction, she burrowed against him, feeling his heat and strength pour into her, banishing the clinging tendrils of fear.

'You're safe, sweetheart.' His arms, strong and sure, made it true. 'It was only a dream. A nightmare.'

Sometimes dreams could be real, for a little while. All it took was the courage to accept them.

'Stay with me,' she whispered.

His lips brushed her temple. 'Of course. For as long as you need. I'm here.'

'You said you still wanted me.'

He shuddered, holding firm against the urge to take her mouth, tumble her beneath him and show her just how much he still wanted her.

Instead, he took her hand, brought it to his lips and pressed a kiss into her palm. 'Yes.' He bit, not quite gently, at the base of her thumb, felt the answering tremor and fought for control. Surely he could kiss her without danger…

'Then…won't you take me?'

'Take you?' His brain couldn't quite comprehend what she was asking.

She wriggled a little, pulled back to meet his eyes. 'As your mistress—if you still want me.'

Somewhere at the back of his mind, a fierce little voice told him that this was his chance to behave like a gentleman, assure her that he would not take her as his mistress. That she—

He swallowed. 'Lucy, you don't have to—'

'I know. You've made it very clear that I don't have to. I want this. I want you.'

She reached out, trembling fingers traced his jaw, his cheek, a butterfly's caress, and it was all he could do not to turn his head and kiss them.

'You want me?' His voice was a barely recognisable croak.

'Yes.'

Such a little word to encompass and turn his entire world upside down.

She leaned forward and touched her lips to his, the briefest and probably the most chaste kiss he'd ever received. It cracked the edges of his control.

'Will you consent to be my lover, my lord?'

James shut his eyes. His consent. Somehow she had turned everything upside down again. 'With all my heart.'

Slowly, slowly, he drew her to him, every beat of his heart a hammer blow. Slender curves moulded to him, fitting perfectly. With an odd little sigh she raised her hands to his shoulders and pressed closer, the soft rise and fall of her breasts against his chest an agony of pleasure.

'Are you going to kiss me?'

'Oh, yes.' He was going to kiss her until their heads spun.

Eventually.

But instead of kissing her, he caught at the end of her braid where it hung over her shoulder and tugged the ribbon free. It floated away and he slid his fingers into the silky mass, unwinding the braid, until her hair tumbled around her shoulders. It curled around his fingers, cool fire that lured and seduced in a soft abandon only a lover would ever see.

'I've wanted to see it like that.' If he had his way no other man ever would.

Lucy's pulse leapt at the dark, velvet promise in his voice, the heat in his eyes, as his fingers speared into her hair, tilting her head back. Her breath caught as his mouth lowered to within an inch of hers.

'Now I can kiss you,' he murmured.

Please, oh, please.

She wanted his mouth on hers. Ached for it, burned for it. Her lips parted on a shuddering gasp, but his mouth brushed her temple, trailed teasing fire to her jaw and nipped gently.

More. She wanted more.

'I...I thought—'

'Don't think.' His breath was warm in her ear,

heat and tremors chasing through her as his tongue traced the curve. 'Just feel.'

She might never do anything else ever again. When had her arms gone around him? She clung, shivering as he blazed hot kisses over her throat, found the fluttering, frantic pulse and sucked gently. Sensation shot through her and a choked cry escaped her. His mouth so tender and demanding, brought her near to madness. Teasing, tasting, exploring, until she turned her head and captured his lips with her own, fingers spearing into his hair as she took his kiss and offered her own.

And, oh! The taste of him. Hot, dark and elementally male as he possessed her mouth completely and everything in her leapt in response. Her tongue, dancing with his in a slow rhythm that resonated deep in her body.

Control. He was close to losing it and he must not. James forced himself to break the kiss. Very slowly he eased her back a little, rested his brow on hers and undid the top button of her nightshirt. Never before had he considered just how many buttons there were on one of his nightshirts. He did now. A second button, and then the third and fourth. The placket hung open and her breathing hitched as his fingers grazed over warm, silken skin, pushing the linen off one shoulder. Soft, so soft. His own breathing shuddered as he reached beneath the linen to cup the sweet weight of one breast. Her gasp tore at his control as he stroked his thumb gently over the nipple, ignoring the savage throb in his loins as it tightened in response. This would not, could not, be just for him. It should be for her. If it killed him, it would be for her.

He leaned forward to kiss her again and her mouth opened on a sigh. With a groan, he surged deep. Sweet, yielding and utterly his to possess. There had never been anything like this. Nothing like this hot, sweet mating of mouths that was more than anything he'd ever known and yet still was not enough. Could never be enough.

She needed more. What, she didn't know. Just more. Beneath her hands, muscles bunched and flickered. All that masculine power, restrained and leashed. For her.

She tugged at the sash of his dressing gown, and he stilled, breathed her name against her lips. 'Lucy?'

Doubt broke through the heat. 'Shouldn't I—?'

'Yes. God, yes.' His mouth brushed hers.

Reassured, she released the sash and pushed open the front of the dressing gown. He shrugged free of it, baring his chest to her fascinated gaze.

Beautiful. He was beautiful. She had always

thought that men were handsome. But he was beautiful. The firelight danced with shadows over sleek muscles, dark hair dusting his powerful chest and arrowing to his waist and below. Her breath caught and she reached out...hesitated, one hand an inch from his chest. He captured her hand and set it gently against his chest, over the flat nipple.

'Like that.' His murmur shivered through her. 'I'll enjoy it just as much as you did.'

She had wanted more. Now she had it. All that male strength and power. Hers to touch and explore. The hot, smooth skin, the swell of muscle flickering under her fingers, his harsh breathing, the jerk of his throat and the low groan as she circled his nipple, stroked it. She had done that to him, pleased him. And the knowledge melted her as surely as his hands and mouth.

'My turn,' he murmured, gathering up her nightshirt. 'Lift your bottom for me.'

He was already naked to the waist, the dressing gown draped at his hips. Once the nightshirt was gone... She obeyed, shutting her eyes, and the nightshirt was gone, lifted away. She was naked now, too, and she waited, bracing herself. It would happen now. She wanted this, wanted him, but...he would put her beneath him and...

Nothing happened. Puzzled, she opened her eyes.

He was staring at her, hands still gripping the night-shirt. His throat worked.

She followed his gaze, looked down at her breasts. They weren't very big. Was he disappointed now he saw her?

'They hurt you.'

His voice was hoarse, rough, and she saw what he saw; bruises where Wat had mauled her breast, another where his fist had slammed into her midriff.

'It was when they brought me up to the…the room where…the sale room.' She forced the words out. 'I found a chair and when they came for me…I hit one of them with it and it broke, so I stabbed the other in the stomach with the broken leg.' The words came more easily, as if telling him lanced a wound that threatened to fester. 'He was going to hit me in the face, but the other one said it would lower my value.'

'I should have killed them.' Low and hard. Then he took a deep breath, spoke gently. 'Sweetheart, I don't want to hurt you any more. I can wait.'

'I can't,' she whispered. 'Please. I don't want them, this…' she touched the bruise on her breast '…between us. Not now, not ever. I want to beat them, not let them come between us.'

Silence stretched between them. Then, very slowly, he loosened his grip on the nightshirt, let it fall and reached out. Her breathing seized as he skimmed the outer curve of one breast. Just his fingertips. So light a touch to have her breath ragged and her heartbeat race past frantic. Still with that maddening feather of a touch he traced the bruise and fire danced under his fingers.

'Forget them,' she whispered. 'Help me to forget them.' Her heart pounding, she reached out to stroke the hard line of his jaw. The faint graze of stubble teased her fingertips and he made an odd sound, turning his head slightly so that her curious fingers touched his mouth. She traced the curve of his lower lip with one finger and he groaned, opening his mouth to suck her finger inside and nip.

Fire shot through her and at last, oh, at last, he took her completely into his arms and her naked body knew the heat and hardness of his. She clung to his shoulders, felt the muscles bunch and flicker as slowly he lowered her to the mattress, followed her down. She had thought that she knew his strength. She had known nothing at all, until now when that strength was revealed, when she was fully vulnerable to it and could feel it leashed. For her.

He eased back a little and she held on, wanting to pull him back down, but he shook his head. 'Not yet, sweetheart. Let me look. Touch.'

And not just his hand. His gaze touched her deeply as he explored her body, found the curve of waist and hip, cradled her breast and stroked the aching peak.

Hot kisses blazed down her throat, to the upper curve of her breast, and she arched on a cry of shocked pleasure as his mouth, closing over the nipple, sucked gently. Fire shot through her, under her skin, as he released her breast only to take the other one and his hand cupped the curls between her thighs. Shock held her utterly still as that hand slid lower, found liquid heat and stroked gently.

His mouth on hers was all hot demand, a dazzling contrast to his wicked, gentle hand between her legs. She sobbed in mindless need as his fingers explored, teased and melted her insides to honey. She gasped, hips lifting as one finger slid into slick, aching need.

He groaned. 'You're so wet for me. Am I hurting you?'

'No. Please.' She twisted, pushing up against him, needing, burning. She didn't care if it was pleasure or pain. She only knew she wanted it.

He gave it to her, his mouth taking hers as with his thumb he found a spot just above where he penetrated her and pressed. Pleasure splintered through her and her shocked cry spilled into his mouth. Under her clutching, frantic hands, his muscles turned to steel and his mouth plundered hers even as his hand remained utterly gentle. Another finger slid in beside the first, easier now in the shocking wetness. Need seared her.

'James—please.'

His fingers moved and a tiny convulsion racked her so that she tightened about him and sobbed as liquid heat exploded.

His voice, low and shaken. 'Lucy, I can't wait.'

It was happening, and she should have been terrified at the fierce urgency as he shifted over her, all hot, hard, male weight, and his caressing fingers withdrew. She cried out, opening to him eagerly, her hips lifting, seeking his touch. It came, different this time. A blunt pressure that stretched her, held the threat of pain, and she understood as he pushed inside.

It was going to hurt and she didn't care. She wanted him. Wanted this slow invasion as he came into her until it seemed there was nowhere for him to go and she was stretched and panting and it wasn't enough, could never be enough.

A shaking finger wiped dampness from her cheeks. 'I'm sorry, sweetheart.' The pressure eased and she clung to his shoulders to hold him, keep him, but he took her mouth fiercely and thrust. Pain blossomed, sharp and bright, and he slid fully, deeply into her body.

She lay beneath him, dazed as her body struggled to accept his invasion. She had not known… How could she? How could she have known that something that had sounded so unlikely, so embarrassing, and had actually hurt, could be joy itself? That she could hurt and want in the same breath, the same heartbeat? That she could feel invaded, vulnerable and utterly safe all at once? She had not known how he would feel inside her. Hot and hard, and the pain had already faded to a tender memory. So deep that his every breath splintered inside her.

James fought to remain still, not to hurt her any further, as her body, so tight and wet, softened around him. She shifted under him, a silken caress that tore at his control, and he dropped his brow to hers.

'James?'

'Yes. Dance with me, sweetheart.' He slid one hand under her bottom, urging her against him, and rocked slowly, every heartbeat a hammer blow, his body cradled by hers. Nothing had ever been this good. If it lasted for ever it would not be long enough.

Her body answered, found and matched his rhythm and they danced in a harmony of delight. Desire, need, burned through him, yet he held back. It had never been like this, wanting a woman's pleasure more than his own, every movement, every soft cry, searing him soul-deep, as he possessed her and she possessed him. So deep that he knew when the firestorm was near, could feel it in the wild tension of her body, hear it in her frantic cries.

'Yes, come to me, sweetheart.' His hand slipped under her bottom, tilting her, and she screamed as the coiling tension broke and she shattered around him. His control snapped and he took her mouth as he took her body, riding her through the storm, until his own white-hot consummation broke and he spilled himself deep inside her.

He woke in the grey dawn, Lucy restless in his arms, small sounds of distress breaking from her. He drew her close, murmuring reassurance until she settled against him, relaxed, entwined with him. Her trust stabbed at him. What had he done to earn it? She had trusted him with herself, her innocence and her future. Trusted him utterly with no guarantees, with no more than a verbal promise.

He ached to make love to her again. And there was a surprise. Making love. Always, always he had ensured that it was sex. Just sex. This hadn't been. And wouldn't be. Not that he was going to be selfish enough to take her again no matter what he called it. He'd wiped the traces of her innocence from her last night. He could wait. His arms tightened.

'James?'

Her sleepy voice wound through him, as he pressed a kiss to her temple. 'Yes.'

'I dreamed, but then you were there and I woke.'

'Just a dream, sweetheart. Sleep now.'

'You're not a dream now.' Her voice drifted. 'It's real and I love you.'

Chapter Seventeen

The well-dressed woman with overly refined accents left Child's Bank a bare ten minutes after it had opened. She stepped out into Fleet Street, saw the waiting hackney and strolled towards it. From the sanctuary of her veil, she assessed the street, saw the fellow lounging casually against a railing pretending not to watch her.

Damn.

She resisted the urge to quicken her step, to bolt. If you ran, they chased. The important thing was to look confident. As she approached the cab the jarvey's shrewd gaze flickered over her, summed her up in a trice. 'I'll see yer money, luv.'

Irritated, Maud Atkinson fished coins out of her reticule and held them up. The jarvey put out his hand. Even more irritated, she gave them to him. Arguing would only draw attention to herself.

The jarvey slipped the coins away. 'Where to?'

'St Paul's.' She said it loudly enough to be heard

by the watcher. She'd tell the jarvey the real destination when they were clear of unwelcome ears.

'St Paul's, did you say, madam?'

At the familiar voice she froze, turned slowly with
a very convincing smile plastered to her face. 'Sir.
This saves me a deal of trouble.'

'Doesn't it?' Kilby's hat was pulled low and a muffler covered his lower face. He glanced up at the
jarvey and handed him a sixpence. 'Ludgate Hill.'

Maud's delighted smile eased a trifle—her Drury
Lane days had taught her the value of not over-act-
ing—and allowed Kilby to hand her into the cab.

He leapt up behind her and closed the door.

'Thank Gawd!' She let the refined accents, which
pinched as much as her too-tight shoes, drop with
relief. 'I'd no idea where to find you once the hunt
was up.'

'My apologies, Maud. The thought of you worrying touches me to the heart.'

She scowled. 'Well, I didn't know where to take
the money, did I?'

Kilby smiled. 'Ah, but I knew where to find you,
so all is well. You have it?'

She patted her reticule.

Kilby shook his head. 'So dependable, Maud. I
thought that money was lost. A wonder he didn't
cancel the draft as soon as the bank opened.'

Maud laughed. 'Warned him, didn't I? Told him his little dolly mop ud be right back where she started if he tried it.'

She preened a little as he inclined his head in admiration. 'Very wise of him. My thanks, Maud. Since I have the money, he's welcome to her.'

'Long as I get me cut.'

'Of course, Maud. Can you doubt me?'

Easily. But she held her tongue.

'Now, how have you got it?' Kilby opened a small satchel.

Maud opened her reticule and drew out a roll of bank notes. 'Got two thousand pounds for the girl. Ten per cent, that's two hundred.' She let a hint of belligerence creep in as she handed over the money.

Kilby raised his brows. 'Given that I'm on the run because your house was raided, I think some negotiation is in order.'

Maud glared. 'Wasn't my rat scuppered it!'

'Rat?' Kilby leaned forward. 'What rat?'

She had him now. 'Your rat. That little toerag, Fitch. He's the one brought 'em all down on us!'

Kilby's eyes turned to stone. 'Did he now? Well, well. And where is Master Fitch?'

Maud shrugged. 'Dunno. He ain't been seen. Hiding somewhere.' She doubted that there was a hole deep enough to hide Fitch and that suited her just fine.

'And Wat? Jig?'

'Taken. They're in Newgate. What about me cut?'

Kilby sighed. 'Yes, of course. Your cut. I hadn't forgotten. I'll add a little extra for your trouble.'

His expression impassive, James gestured Armitage to the chair opposite his desk. Armitage's eyes darted around the library and flickered over the black-clad man seated to one side. James nodded at the man. 'My lawyer, Kenton. He has an offer for you.'

Armitage licked his lips. 'Very well.'

Kenton spoke slowly, carefully outlining the terms and conditions of the offer; Five thousand pounds with no conditions upon it, if he agreed to stay away from Lucy and James.

Armitage said nothing.

'It is understood,' James said, 'that this money is a once-only payment.'

Armitage nodded. 'Yes.'

'And it has nothing to do with your daughter.'

A sneer twisted Armitage's mouth. 'Nothing to do with her? Did you bed her last night, Cambourne? You're paying me for—'

'I'm not paying you for her.' James tried not to think of the sweetness of Lucy's response, her words in the pale light of dawn that had lodged deep inside. 'If she decided to leave me tomorrow—' his heart shook at the thought '—if she had never come to me at all, this money would be yours. I'm doing it for her, but I'll put no constraints on her.'

Kenton looked as disapproving as he had when James had explained what he wanted. 'His lordship has drawn up a separate and, if I may say so, most generous settlement for your daughter's maintenance while she remains in his keeping.'

James gritted his teeth. It hadn't been like that. Lucy was his, in a way he couldn't quite begin to comprehend, but he said only, 'Once you take this money, Armitage, you have no further claim on either me, or your daughter. Ever.'

Armitage seemed to shrivel in on himself. 'You're paying me five thousand pounds to stay out of her life.'

James hardened his will, his heart. He had not expected to feel pity for the man, but he could not forget Armitage's horror and despair when he realised the price Lucy had nearly paid for his folly. And he had given them Montgomery.

'I want her safe.'

Armitage flinched as if at a blow. 'I had that coming.' He spoke like a man in pain. 'Very well. I've failed her all her life.' He straightened a little. 'I...

I thought to take ship, for America. How…how soon—?' He flushed.

'How soon can you have the money?' James anticipated the question. Was that all he cared about? The shame and regret no more than an act? He gestured to the lawyer. 'Kenton will arrange it now. Do you wish to see the settlement on Lucy?' Disgust like acid rimed his voice. The fellow ought to be trying to knock his teeth down his throat, but, no; he wanted his money.

Armitage didn't meet his gaze. 'As you said last night, Cambourne; I forfeited all rights to my daughter when I allowed her to become a pawn.' He looked up briefly. 'You will have provided for her generously, I do not doubt. She…she is not in London, is she?'

Armitage seemed broken, shattered, and despite his distrust, James spoke a little more gently. 'No.' Elizabeth had taken Lucy out to Chiswick while he remained to sort everything out.

Armitage ran a hand over his jaw. 'Safer…I should write her a note.' He flushed. 'Cambourne, may I have a few moments alone?'

James rose, the queer, unwelcome thread of pity tangled with his anger. 'As many as you like.'

Kenton rose as well, but Armitage's hand shot out. 'No. Kenton, I require your advice, if you would be so good? My will, you know?'

Kenton resumed his seat. 'Certainly, sir. Very wise if you are leaving these shores.' He glanced at James. 'If I might make use of paper, my lord?'

'Of course.' James nodded to Armitage. 'Good day, sir.'

'Yes. I'll leave the note with Kenton.'

An hour later Armitage was gone and James returned to the library to find Kenton packing his papers away.

'All done, Kenton?'

'Yes, my lord.' The man filed papers in his briefcase with swift precision. 'The note for Miss Armitage is on your desk.'

'Thank you.'

'He left a note for you as well, which you should read as soon as possible. It will—'

'Thank you, Kenton.'

Kenton cleared his throat. 'As to that, my lord, there are two copies of Miss Armitage's contract on your desk as well, but you may wish to reconsider the very generous—'

'I don't.'

'My lord, allowing her an annuity, and the use of Hawthorne Lodge, or a similar property for the term of her life, not merely the term of your liaison, is—'

'How I wished it to be drawn up, Kenton. That

will be all.' He hadn't meant to snap and Kenton looked affronted.

The lawyer took a deep breath and let it out. 'My lord, I should not be doing my duty to you if I did not urge you to read Mr Armitage's note and point out that the clauses you insisted upon to protect Miss Armitage after your liaison are more suited to the maintenance of a widow than a discarded mistress.' He bowed, picked up his briefcase and walked to the door. Pausing with his hand on the knob, he said, 'Good day, my lord. And for God's sake, read that note!'

The door closed behind him with a decided snick.

James rounded the desk and sat down. The note for Lucy lay on the blotter with the note to himself just below it. To the side were the two copies of the contract that would protect Lucy and ensure her well-being even after the end of their liaison.

He picked up a copy and started to read it through yet again. Maintenance, residence, allowance, care and education of any and all children of the union. It was set out in meticulous legal terms, carefully worded to make sure no one could find a loophole large enough for an ant to crawl through should something happen to him, or if they parted. At last he set it down. No wonder poor Kenton had been shocked at the terms. Even if he grew a tail and two heads complete with horns, Lucy, and Fitch for that matter, would be safe. He'd inserted every clause he could think of to achieve that. And it still didn't feel right.

She loves you.

He couldn't doubt or dismiss the truth of that, even if she had been half-asleep. Folly, Elizabeth had called it. Because men were only too ready to take advantage of a woman's vulnerability.

Fifteen minutes later when Fox strolled in, James knew what was wrong with the contract and Kenton had given him the clue. Which didn't mean the poor fellow wasn't going to be even more shocked. He'd be interested to see what his godfather thought.

He held the contract out to Fox. 'Tell me what you think.'

Fox strolled across the room. 'I took the liberty of asking Penfold to bring coffee.' He shook his head as he sat down at the desk opposite James. 'I've been at Bow Street, afraid there's bad news. They took your advice and watched the bank. A veiled, well-spoken woman presented the draft and was issued with the full amount as per your instructions. She left and got into a hackney with a man. The Runners followed, but the man got down at Ludgate Hill and they lost him. They came up with the cab at St Paul's and found the woman dead, her throat cut and the money gone.'

James grimaced. 'They lost Kilby? Very well. At least he has the money.'

'You're taking it calmly.' Fox took the contract.

'If he's got the money, then Lucy is safe.' James ignored Fox's faintly amused look. 'But Hunt's brother goes without justice.' And that ate like a canker at his guts. Hunt needed to know that Gerald had been fully avenged.

Fox started to read. 'What's this—? Oh, I see.' He was silent for moment, scanning the terms. 'Well, as to that, they've got two fellows on the kidnapping. With young Nick's identification they've got them on assaulting him, as well, and one was persuaded to roll on his friend about Moresby in return for a lesser penalty on that charge. So they've got them on young Moresby's murder.' He looked up. 'And since kidnapping is a capital charge anyway, neither will escape the noose.'

It wasn't enough if Kilby escaped, but it might have to do.

'They're still being questioned, though,' Fox said, reading. 'Once they realise the only way to save their necks is to roll on Kilby, we might get enough to run him to earth. Also, I got your note about Montgomery so I stopped in at Brooks's. Dropped a word or two in a few interested ears. Should be enough to cook his goose.'

A tap on the door heralded Penfold with the coffee. James poured them each a cup and waited patiently while Fox went through the contract a second time. At last he set the papers down. A stray sunbeam gilded them, dust motes dancing golden in its path.

'Well?' James demanded.

Fox sipped meditatively. 'Very generous.' His voice was utterly neutral, the sort of voice that might have been hiding a herd of elephants, let alone his true thoughts.

James's teeth ground together. 'Is that all you can say?'

Fox's brows rose comically. 'What did you want me to say? That you're a damn fool and—'

'That it's the wrong sort of contract!'

James leaned across the desk, picked up both contracts and tore them up. Standing up, he tossed the shredded papers into the fire. The flames set upon them with an enthusiastic whoosh so that they curled and shrivelled into ash.

'Well, that was dramatic,' Fox said drily. 'But what does it mean?'

James sat down. Fox might think he'd run mad, but—

'You are considering marriage, are you not?' Fox's level tone gave nothing away.

James let out a breath. 'No. I'm beyond considering, sir. Dare I hope—?'

'A moment, lad.' Fox leaned his elbows on the table, steepling his fingers. 'Before Elizabeth left this morning I asked her permission to tell you something.' His eyes crinkled. 'I don't often give you advice; you so rarely need it. And this isn't precisely advice, since you've got there on your own. But, would it help to know that Elizabeth and I married seven years past?'

If one of the marble poets or philosophers had hopped down from his place and hit James over the head, he couldn't have been more dumbfounded. Seven years?

'Shocked you, have I?'

Was he shocked at the marriage itself? Or shocked that no one had known?

'Why have you told no one?'

Fox shrugged. 'Elizabeth did not wish it.'

No, Elizabeth would not have wanted to face the inevitable storm of gossip, the snide digs, society's outrage—

'I nearly lost her, James.' Fox spoke softly, as if remembering a pain too great to bear.

That did shock him. 'What?'

Fox's mouth hardened. 'Remember the Coutts business? The idea that Miss Fanny would be a suitable bride?'

'Well, yes.' He'd thought the idea insane. Fanny

Coutts could not have been more than twenty-two at the time, over twenty years Fox's junior.

'She was going to leave you over that?' That surprised him far more than their marriage.

'Saying she intended to step aside would be closer,' Fox said. 'For my sake,' he added softly. 'I couldn't bear the thought.'

'So you married her.'

Fox nodded. 'I never wanted her to know that sort of pain and insecurity again, to think that I might account a fortune of more worth than herself.'

Yes. He could understand that. He had not fiddled with that blasted contract merely so Lucy could feel secure. That was why it had never felt right. Because the one thing you couldn't nail down in a contract was love.

Fox continued. 'I have persuaded Elizabeth that we should make it known before we leave for France this summer.' He heaved his bulk up. 'So you may rest assured that any murmurs over your marriage to a woman with whom you might, just possibly, have anticipated your marriage vows, will be drowned out in the thunderclap of my announcement.

James started to laugh. The news of Fox's marriage to Elizabeth was going to rock society to its roots.

'In fact,' Fox continued, 'they'll all blame me for setting a damned poor example as your godfather.'

James snorted. 'I wouldn't be at all surprised. However...' he held out his hand '...many congratulations. It's far too late to wish Elizabeth happy, because clearly she is, but I hope that you and Mrs Fox will attend my wedding?'

Fox smiled. 'Of course. Now, take yourself off to Chiswick and propose to the lady.'

James grinned. 'Probably the best advice you've ever given me.'

'I shouldn't wonder,' Fox said.

The door opened. 'Lord Huntercombe, my lord.'

By the time James had seen Hunt, sustained a visit from the magistrate handling the aftermath of the brothel raid and sent instructions to Kenton likely to give the lawyer apoplexy, late afternoon was closing in and he still hadn't read Armitage's note. Cursing, he placed it in the box of paperwork he was taking out to Chiswick, along with the note for Lucy, and ordered his carriage.

Half an hour later as the carriage rattled out of London James finally read Armitage's note. It was brief, admirably direct and he had to read it twice to understand fully the implications of Armitage's decision. Shaken, he stared out into the softening light.

I hope, sir, that you will not think me ungrateful in giving these instructions, and that you will not think I did not trust you to provide suitably for my daughter...

His every unthinking, arrogant assumption had been turned upside down and inside out. Armitage had forced him to face the question Elizabeth had posed: would Lucy choose him if she were truly free?

Chapter Eighteen

He hadn't come to her. Lucy rolled over, telling herself it was the unfamiliar room and bed keeping her awake. That and the moonlight pouring through her window, along with the breeze fragrant with roses. Nothing else. A strange place, moonlight and a breeze. Of course, she could do something about the moonlight and breeze by closing the window and drawing the curtains.

He had said farewell to her tenderly that morning, promising to arrive by early evening, and indeed, his carriage had gone by on the main road. But he had not come. Instead he had sent a brief note saying that he would call in the morning.

And with that, she admitted to herself that her sleeplessness had nothing to do with a strange place, moonlight or the fragrant breeze. She shut her eyes in despair. After all Elizabeth's warnings, after all her own self-administered warnings, she had fallen in love with a man who could never be fully hers. Worse, she had told him.

She was his mistress. Perhaps he wished to remind her gently that *he* ordered their relationship and that love had nothing to do with it. On his side at least.

A muffled crash from the next room jerked her out of her reflections. She sat up.

'Fitch? Is everything all right?'

'Yeah. Fine, Lu. It's nothin'.' His voice was a little breathless.

'All right. Goodnight.' She settled down, but was upright almost immediately. Was he throwing things at the wall, drat him? She let out an annoyed breath as she pushed back the bedclothes and got up, sticking her feet into slippers. It was all very new to him, but he couldn't be permitted to wreck the place.

Treading quietly, all the better to catch him in whatever mischief he was perpetrating, she slipped over to the door and opened it.

James swirled the brandy in his glass, stared at the leaping, crackling fire and tried to remember just *why* he wasn't in Lucy's bed.

Because you're going to give her her father's letter in the morning.

He was going to give Lucy her freedom and hope she would stay. Because now, when Armitage of all people had set her free, he finally understood that a choice between himself and destitution was not a real choice.

He had not forced her, had not constrained her; circumstance had done that for him. Lucy had to know that she was free *before* he asked her to marry him. And definitely before he shared her bed again.

It was the right, decent and honourable thing to do. Unfortunately his heart wasn't convinced, his body was in open and uncomfortable revolt, and his supposedly rational mind was wavering. Nor could he banish the conviction that he ought to be with her right now, keeping her safe.

He took a swallow of brandy, barely registering, let alone appreciating, the fine spirit. Doing the right, decent and honourable thing would be a great deal easier if he could just forget how sweetly wanton and responsive she was with him…he could more easily forget his own name. He set his glass down on the wine table and picked up his book. Damned if he'd waste the brandy, which he wasn't even tasting, on getting drunk. When he proposed to Lucy he didn't want to feel like something the cat had dragged in and mauled.

He set the book aside and rose. Maybe a walk around the park. It wasn't late, he could visit her, drink tea with her, and…and come home just as restless. Or not come home, he admitted. His honourable intentions were struggling.

Desire baulked had never before been a problem.
An annoyance, perhaps. But not a problem. Right
now it was a beast to be reckoned with, especially
when coupled to the irrational prickle of fear that
had haunted him since getting her out of the brothel.
A light tap at the door stopped his pacing. 'Come.'
Field opened the door. 'Beg pardon, my lord. A
messenger from Bow Street brought this. Urgent,
he says.'

The prickle became icy. James strode across the
room and snatched the proffered note. He broke the
seal, took in the contents in a glance, and the ice
condensed to lead in his gut.

'Oh, God!' It was a strangled prayer. Kilby's
men, Jig and Wat, had turned King's evidence and
agreed to testify against Kilby to avoid the hang-
man's noose. Six hours later they had been found
dead in their cells, their throats cut.

The one thing Kilby won't tolerate is a traitor.
Kilby would come for the boy.

Lucy set her hand to the doorknob of Fitch's room,
reminding herself that it was all alien to Fitch. That
he wasn't used to living in any sort of comfort, or
having much furniture, let alone things he had to
be careful of, and that he wasn't used to being con-
fined. A gentle remonstrance would do for now.
She opened the door and walked in. 'Fitch—'

'Lu! No! *Run!*'

A blur of movement caught the edge of her vision. Shock paralysed the scream in her throat as a powerful arm whipped around her neck, dragging her back. She fought, scrabbling with one hand at the arm across her throat, while with the other she reached back, scratching for her attacker's eyes.

'Be still, bitch, or I'll slice you right here and now.'

The cold kiss of steel on her throat was a lethal promise.

'Lu!'

The terror in Fitch's voice steadied her. The boy stood on the far side of the room by the open window, clutching his left arm, blood seeping between his fingers.

She dragged a breath past the choking pressure on her throat. 'Fitch. Get out the window. *Now!*'

He didn't move and her captor laughed, the sound mocking in her ear. 'He knows better than that. He moves wrong and you're dead.' The blade's pressure eased. 'I'm Kilby. We haven't met, although I had the pleasure of observing Maud Atkinson examine you before the auction.' His voice became meditative. 'Very nice, too. Although I've no doubt Cambourne has cooked *that* goose by now.'

Her gorge rose… Kilby, the man who'd had Lord Huntercombe's brother murdered, had James's cousin beaten and arranged for her sale…he'd

watched while that woman verified her virginity…
'Now, Fitch,' the urbane voice continued, 'you
choose—will you let her die? I only want you.'

'Miss? Miss? Is ever'thing all right up there?'
The maid Maria's voice floated up from downstairs.

The knife pressed closer, even as the arm across
her throat loosened slightly. 'Tell her everything's
fine,' murmured Kilby. 'You really don't want her
up here. Just be another body.'

Lucy's breath shuddered in. This was going to
be her only chance. 'It's…it's fine… M-Molly. Just
Master Fitch being naughty. You and Sarah go back
off to the big house to bed. I won't need you again
this evening.'

There was a moment's silence.

'Ah, right you are, miss. See you in the morning,
miss.'

'Good.' Kilby's voice remained low, but the knife
eased off a little. 'Very wise of you.'

Lucy prayed that Maria had understood. There
was no Sarah and Maria's bed was off the kitchen,
not at the main house. Assuming the maid had understood, how long would it take her to run for help?

Kilby forced her further into the room, to the left
along the wall. Her hip smashed against something,
forcing a cry from her as Kilby swore. Rolling her

eyes, she saw they had knocked into a table that held a single, lit candle.

'Now, Fitch,' Kilby almost crooned, 'come along like a good boy and she goes free.'

'Don't, Fitch!' Lucy choked out. 'He's lying.' Kilby wouldn't risk her raising the alarm. Nor would he leave a witness to murder.

'Stupid bitch!' Kilby jerked her head back against his shoulder and the room spun as she gasped for breath, tearing at his arm.

'Lu!'

'Stop struggling, or I'll cut your face to show him who's in charge!'

But the arm loosened a little and air raced past the raw choking in her throat. Slowly she lowered her hands, fighting to think, not just breathe. She had to distract him long enough to get loose. Give Fitch a chance to run without getting herself killed. They bumped the table again and she saw the candlestick wobble. That was how fires...

She went very still.

Relief nearly dropped James to his knees as he saw the slight figure come through the gate from Hawthorne Lodge into the park. He'd gone via the stables to collect Digby and carriage pistols for the footmen.

'My lord! See there?' Digby, at his shoulder, spoke quietly.

Thank God...

The cloaked figure began to run towards the main house and his blood iced. Something about the way she moved...

''Tis Maria, I reckon.' The footman, David, waved. 'Here, lass!'

He'd kept his voice low, but the girl heard, swerving towards them and picking up pace. She was gasping when they met.

'Thank God...'tis you...m'lord. Something's wrong. Heard...something upstairs. Called out, I did, after what I heard about last night... She called me Molly...told me and Sarah to go off to bed at the big house.' She leaned on David, dragging air into her lungs.

James forced logic through the numbing fear. 'But there's no Sarah and you're assigned to sleep at the Lodge.'

Lungs constricted, Lucy reached for the table, sliding shaking fingers over the satiny surface.

'Let her walk out the door.' Fitch's face was white and blood still dripped from his arm. 'I swear I'll come quiet.'

Kilby laughed. 'Lying little rat. Think I don't know you'll fight once she's clear?' His arm jerked and Lucy lost contact with the table. 'No, you come right here, boy. Then I'll let her go.'

She found the table again and prayed Kilby wouldn't feel the shift of her arm as her fingers brushed cold metal.

Fear congealed every vein, clogged his throat, as James slipped up the dark stairs on stockinged feet, his men armed at his back. Step by step they crept upwards, keeping close to the wall.

Please, don't let a tread creak. Please let me be in time. He had sought justice and revenge and unleashed this whirlwind. If Lucy or the boy died...he pushed the thought down, kept his bone-deep fear beneath the icy fury...

'Come now, Fitch.' The unfamiliar, educated voice held only friendly encouragement,

James froze and gestured for stillness, gave the signal to wait.

'That's right. A little closer and I'll let her go.'

'I got your word?'

The boy's voice cracked a little as James breathed a silent prayer of thanks; they were both alive.

'Fitch! No! Don't—'

'Shut up, bitch!'

Now the voice was all snarl and Lucy's choked cry stabbed into James as he crept closer. He couldn't see Lucy or Kilby, it sounded as though they were to the left of the open door, but he could see Fitch, framed in the doorway... Signalling his men to keep still, and moving an inch at a time, James slid his stockinged feet over the wooden floor.

Fitch's gaze flickered to the door as he took a step closer to where Kilby must be.

'Don't even think about the door, Fitch,' Kilby rapped out. 'She'll die before you're through it. That's it, take another step.'

'You want me closer, get the knife away from her throat.'

Fear sliced straight to James's gut, as Fitch's gaze touched him briefly and slid away. The boy had seen him, had given him all the intelligence he could.

'See? It's not touching her now. I've lowered it completely. Come on, Fitch. You were the best I ever had. I'll make it quick for old times' sake.'

Fitch took another step. 'You want to put that fire out first, Kilby?'

'What...? *Bitch!*'

The roar of fury ripped into a howl, followed by a feminine cry and a crash.

'Now!'

James charged into the room, pistol in hand.

Lucy was on the floor, struggling to rise. Kilby stood between them, his coattails ablaze as he twisted and turned, screaming and batting at himself, and Fitch dived for the knife he'd dropped. He rolled and came up on the balls of his feet, the knife alive in his hand, death, cold and intent, in his eyes.

'Fitch! No!'

At James's shout the boy hesitated as Kilby turned screaming. James brought the pistol to bear, cocked it and fired.

Kilby staggered a little, then stood, a faint expression of surprise on his face as the red stain blossomed on his chest. For an instant he swayed, then fell with a crash, flames engulfing him.

'Hell!' James grabbed the counterpane off the bed, flung it over the burning body, smothering the flames with Digby's aid. A groom snatched up a blanket and helped roll the body in it.

Fitch stood watching, knife in hand, as the fire was extinguished.

Lucy scrambled to a sitting position and James felt his heart settle back into something approximating its normal position from where it had been lodged in his throat. He rose and turned to the boy.

'My thanks, Fitch.' His voice shook. He wasn't sure he'd ever be able to forget the image of Lucy, a knife at her throat and only the boy's courage between her and death. 'Always.'

'It…it were Lu,' Fitch said, his eyes never leaving James, his voice dull. 'She set him on fire.' Light danced on the blade still in his hand and James realised the boy was trembling.

'I was going to kill him,' Fitch whispered. 'For Lu.'

Very slowly James reached out, took the skinny wrist and eased the knife from his grip, passing it to one of the grooms. 'I know.' He'd shot a wounded, unarmed man to prevent it. He could only hope that saving the boy from making the kill would absolve him.

'It were my fault. I shoulda known—'

'No!' Lucy was beside them, her nightgown torn, hair dishevelled. 'You could have saved yourself! You could have got out of the window, even before I came in, but you knew he'd kill me. You stayed!' She gripped his shoulders and shook him. 'You stayed. Distracted him. James! *Tell* him!'

James laid a hand on Fitch's shoulder. 'Fitch, the fault wasn't yours, it was mine. But you and Lucy stood by each other and saved each other.'

Fitch stared at him. 'Your fault? How d'you reckon that?'

'I was warned that Kilby didn't tolerate traitors,' James said quietly. 'I should have realised he'd come for you. Will you forgive that?'

Fitch scratched his elbow, frowning. 'Well, yeah. You're a fair shot with that pistol. Wouldn't mind learning how to shoot. I can throw a knife pretty good, but Kilby winged me throwin' arm first thing.'

Digby came forward. 'We'll get that fixed up, lad. Time enough for his lordship to teach you to shoot when it's healed.' He glanced at James, at Lucy. 'With your leave, I'll tend him tonight. Plenty of room in my quarters.' He gestured to Kilby's body. 'Get that mess out of here, lads.'

Lucy shuddered and told herself not to be missish. Kilby could no longer harm anyone, but if Digby took Fitch for the night—and she agreed he should—then she would be alone here.

'Right.' James's crisp, decisive voice was her only warning. An instant later he'd swung her up into his arms.

'What—?' It came out as a startled squeak.

'I'm taking you home.' He strode towards the door.

She caught the grin on Digby's face over James's shoulder. 'But, you can't! I mean—'

'Don't bother telling me what I can and can't do.' They had reached the stairs and James started down. 'You're not staying here tonight and that's final.'

Chapter Nineteen

There were things he needed to say, things he had to tell her. But the words were not there. Not so that they would come out. He didn't know how to think them, let alone say them. All he could do was show her.

Not until he reached his rooms and kicked the door shut behind them did he find coherent thoughts. *This is where she belongs. With me. Always.*

His gaze fell on his valet, standing in the doorway to the dressing room, his jaw somewhere about his waist.

James dredged up a single, useful word. 'Out.'

He could have saved his breath. The dressing-room door closed behind Marsham as he spoke. He let out a shuddering breath as he walked across the room to set Lucy down beside the bed.

She looked about, her eyes wide and wondering. 'This is your room, your bed.'

'Yes.' He shrugged out of his coat and it dropped to the floor. Marsham would have a fit. Fifty fits.

There were practicalities involved, of course. No one else was in residence. This was likely the only bed made up, the only room prepared. Otherwise discretion dictated...

He consigned discretion to hell. Discretion now would be an insult.

She bit her lip. 'I shouldn't be—'

'Yes,' he said, dropping his cravat somewhere near the coat, his eyes never leaving her flushed face. 'You should.' She had been going to say that she shouldn't be here. Not in his room, not in his bed. Because of course a man's bed was reserved for his wife. And he had taken her as his mistress.

'But—'

He silenced her with his mouth. Kissed her deeply, fiercely, possessively. Kissed her so that she melted against him, her mouth all his, her body moulded to his. Kissed her until there was nothing else but the woman in his arms, in his heart.

Shock slammed through Lucy as James's mouth took hers, consumed it hungrily. Need blazed from him. She knew it in his mouth on hers, the hands that trembled as they framed her face, held her captive for his kiss, felt it in the muscles in his shoulders that bunched and flickered beneath her hands. And need leapt in her to answer his.

'This is exactly where you should be.' His mouth

trailed fire over her jaw, her throat as, button by button, her nightgown surrendered to his swift, shaking fingers until it hung open to her waist. 'This…' his mouth found the scrambling, frantic beat in her throat, lingered, sucked, so that her body arched against him on a gasp of pleasure '…right here, in my bed, is precisely where I want to love you.' He pushed the gown off her shoulders and the room dipped and whirled as he swept her up in his arms and tumbled her on to the bed.

Here, in my bed, is precisely where I want to love you… Lucy's heart cracked a little further as Elizabeth's warning words came back.

Never mistake sex for love, no matter how tender he is… Better not to even call it making love. Not even in your head, in fact, least of all there… Never delude yourself that a man's skill in bed is about love…

She was a fool and she was going to break her own heart, but she couldn't help what she felt for him. Not now, not here, perhaps not ever.

James gazed down at her, tumbled naked on his bed, her copper curls loose on her shoulders, creamy, rose-tipped breasts taut, lips softly parted. Need raked him as he shed his own clothes with shaking hands. The need to make love to her, to show her that it was more, more than he had admitted, more than he had ever wanted to admit, more than he had known was possible. To show her that this was where she belonged.

He came to her and she opened to him, her arms clinging, drawing him down to the soft cradle of her body, to her mouth that took his in a wild delight. His hands raced over her as much to reassure himself that he hadn't lost her as to claim. He found her, creamy wet and soft, ready for him, and her pleas were temptation incarnate as he traced the hot, liquid folds.

Not yet.

His blood pounding, he slid down her body, kissing, devouring. He wanted everything. Wanted to give everything, take everything, until there was nothing left. Until she was his utterly and he was hers. Pushing her thighs wide, he trailed light kisses over them, inching closer to her secrets while she sobbed and writhed. Her scent, hot, aroused woman, burned through him, and he pressed his mouth to her.

The impossible, silken caress speared her with dark pleasure that spilt through her in waves of heat. Shock held her as much as the heavy arm over her belly, anchoring her while he loved her, destroyed her. Tension coiled tighter, brighter, and she fought to move, to reach for the end, until at last he released her, surged up her body and drove into her. She broke at once, shattering on a scream as he plunged deep in her clenching body again and again. His release came swiftly and he braced over her, shuddering as he spent himself.

With a groan, he collapsed on her so that they lay in a sweaty, sated tangle of limbs. Tears filled her eyes as he pressed a tender kiss to her temple and she held him, still trembling with aftershocks of passion, loving the weight of him, the beat of their hearts steadying.

Another kiss to her temple. 'Mine,' he murmured. 'And I'm yours, sweetheart.'

Her heart filled, ached, as she kissed his shoulder in reply, not trusting her voice.

James left Lucy sleeping soundly in his bed, dressed and walked down to the stables, passing the peacock who uttered his wailing cry and spread his tail to strut after his wives. Damned if he knew what use peafowl were—beyond providing occupation for the gardener's boy who had the unenviable job of clearing evidence of the birds' existence from the terraces. But his mother had loved them, and Lucy thought them beautiful, so the wretched creatures were safe for another generation.

The stables hummed with activity. Grooms scurried back and forth with wheelbarrows and brooms, mucking out and feeding horses. Digby was bent over checking the offside fore of a chestnut gelding, but he set the hoof down, straightening as James approached.

'Morning, m'lord.' He cast a knowing eye over his master and his mouth twitched a little. 'All's well?'

James felt his ears burn. 'Yes, thank you.' He'd only himself to blame if his entire staff knew what was in the wind. Digby knew him well enough to put two and two together.

'Young Fitch helped Maria carry Miss Lucy's belongings up to the house this morning, early-like, m'lord. Saw her heading over and went to help. From what he said they put 'em in the countess's rooms.' A smile lurked in the shrewd eyes. 'Congratulations.' And he clapped James on the shoulder. 'Took your time over it, didn't you?'

James managed a laugh. 'I haven't actually asked her yet.' The confession was out before he even knew it was there.

'Right.' Digby raised his brows, turned back to the chestnut, running a hand down the nearside foreleg and picking up the hoof. 'Reckon they call that putting the cart before the horse.'

'Something like that. Is Fitch about?'

'Oh, aye. In the end stall grooming Puck.

Puck was the little Welsh grey he kept for his elder sister's children to ride when they stayed here.

'Thought he could try riding him later. Seems to me...' Digby scraped out the hoof '...the lad should learn to ride, one way or another.'

Digby never pried. Exactly. 'He should. I'll take him out myself later.'

Setting the hoof down, Digby looked up. 'That's the way of it now, is it?'

'It is, yes.' People would say he'd taken leave of his senses, that he was a candidate for Bedlam, but it felt right. All of it. As long as it was what Lucy wanted.

Fitch was muttering while he cleaned out a hoof. 'You gotta lean all of yerself on me? Ain't like you ain't got three other legs!'

Leaning on the half-door, James grinned. 'My nephews make the same complaint about him.'

Fitch looked up, shoving his surprisingly clean hair out of his face. 'Yeah? Dunno how they'd know, seeing as they must be gents.'

'They know how to look after a pony,' said James, opening the door and stepping in. Puck came up to him and nosed hopefully at his pockets. 'Sorry, old chap.' James rubbed the silken nose. 'Another time.' He smiled at Fitch. 'When Toby and Jeremy come they share him and take turns to muck out and groom. Just like you are.'

Fitch looked at him curiously. 'You keep a pony just for them?'

'It means they aren't tempted to try one of my horses. You'll like them.'

Fitch cleared his throat. 'Right.'

How the devil did you explain? Ask a boy if he'd like to be... Like to be—what? A gentleman? Your ward? Especially when you weren't planning to give him a choice.

'Lu all right, is she?'

James let out a breath. And there it was. As easy as that. 'She's fine. Asleep when I left her.' At the narrow-eyed look Fitch gave him his cheeks burned. He ploughed on regardless. 'I have a question for you, Fitch.'

'Yeah?' The boy had turned away, picked up a soft brush from an upturned bucket. He began with Puck's face and the pony closed his eyes in equine bliss.

'About Lucy.' From the set of the boy's shoulders he was paying close attention. 'Do I have your permission to ask her to marry me?'

The brush fell from the boy's fingers as he turned to stare. 'What?'

'I want to ask—'

'I got that bit—' Fitch staggered as the neglected

pony gave him a shove. 'Don't get why you're askin' me. Got a dad, don't she?' He spat in the straw. 'Reckon he'll jump at it.'

James nodded. 'I don't doubt it. But I'm asking you. Her brother.'

Fitch's breath caught and James saw the skinny throat bob. 'I ain't—'

'In every way that counts, you are,' James said very quietly. 'Do you object?'

Fitch scowled fiercely. 'Not so long as it's what she wants.'

James leaned on the manger. 'If she accepts, that would make you my brother.'

The scowl deepened. 'Ain't going to persuade her just so's I can call brothers with you.'

James waged an unsuccessful battle with a grin. 'I didn't think so. But if she doesn't agree I'll make arrangements for you to become my ward—in a brotherly capacity.'

Fitch bent down for the brush, taking an inordinate amount of time fumbling in the straw while Puck blew in his ear.

Finally he stood up. 'S'pose that means I go to school.' He was still scowling, but his hands on the pony's face were gentle.

'It does,' James agreed. 'A tutor at first, anyway.'

'What about this stupid pony?'

'Oh, he'll be here when your lessons are over. I

might have to find a couple more for Jeremy and Toby. Three boys and one pony is asking for trouble.' James tactfully strolled over to the door and looked out into the stable yard as Fitch wiped an eye. 'Digby thought to give you a riding lesson later, but I said I'd see to it.'

Fitch nodded slowly. 'S'pose that'll be all right, then.'

'I suppose so.'

'Better keep on here, hadn't I?' Fitch said.

'Yes. Come up to the house when you're ready for something to eat. I'll be about somewhere. Just ask one of the footmen.' He opened the half-door.

'What if I can't do it?'

James looked back. 'Can't do what?'

'Read...or...or write. What—' Fitch looked more ferocious than ever '—what if I can't stop stealing?'

'That's a risk,' James said. 'What if you'd run last night?'

'That's different.' Fitch kicked at the straw.

'No, it's not,' James said. 'You took risks for her all along. Last night you risked your life for her.' The boy was actually blushing. 'Changing your life may be a damn sight harder than facing a knife, but you'll do it.'

'Right.' Fitch's eyes were suspiciously bright. 'Reckon you can tell Lu I've give me blessing, then.'

* * *

James's staff wouldn't let her return to Hawthorne Lodge after breakfast.

'His lordship's compliments, miss. He asked for you to stay here.'

She felt awkward in the house, although none of the servants seemed at all shocked by her presence and the fact that she had spent the night in their master's bed. They made sure she had everything she could possibly need. When she asked about walking in the garden, Maria had smiled and shown her the way to the lily pond.

Low hedges of box formed a knot garden to enclose and protect fragrant herbs all around the pond in the sheltered, walled garden. In the centre of the pond a slender boy in bronze wielded a bow. Cupid, she supposed, although she had always thought of Cupid as small and fat. A fish flashed silver between lily pads and vanished into the depths. A rustic-looking seat had been placed beside the pond in the drooping shade of a weeping cherry. A blackbird hopped between clumps of sage and then took off, flying low across the garden in a blur of wings, a worm dangling from his beak.

She sat down on the bench and sighed in pleasure. The seat might look rustic, but it had been carefully thought out. The seat was just the right depth and height, the back at precisely the right angle. Here in the embrace of the cherry tree she allowed herself to remember the night that had passed…and dreamed.

'My mother would have liked to see you here.'

The deep voice jerked Lucy out of the dream Elizabeth had warned her against and that she had promised herself never to dream. She opened her eyes and her heart tripped and fell a little further into love at the smile in his eyes. Tenderness and the memory of the passion they had shared. Was it possible to keep falling deeper and deeper into love?

'May I join you?'

He was asking? This was his home, his garden, his seat. And she was his mistress—a woman his mother would have been horrified to see here.

'Of course.'

He sat beside her, took her hand. 'Mama had this seat built, and the statue of Eros installed.'

'Eros? I thought it was Cupid.'

He pulled a folded, sealed paper from his pocket. 'Eros is the Greek god of love. Cupids are small and fat.' His mouth twisted. 'Eros is a far more dangerous individual, too close to Eris, the goddess of chaos, if you ask me.' He offered her the paper. 'For you.'

She took it and thought for a fleeting moment that his hand shook. 'What is it?'

He rose and went to stand with his back to her, staring at the statue. 'Read it.'

She opened it and her stomach lurched as she recognised her father's hand. Hurt, anger, bitterness, a hopeless tangle, welled up inside her. She wanted to tear the note to shreds and drop the pieces in the water. An apology, no doubt—one she neither wanted nor would believe. A plea for forgiveness, an assurance that it had all been an accident... James had asked her to read it.

There *was* no apology, no plea for forgiveness, no explanation, or excuses. She had to read it again for the words to sink in and a third time to convince herself that it wasn't a hoax.

Finally she managed to force words past the choking lump in her throat. 'Have you read this?'

'No.' His voice was clipped, strained. 'But I am aware of the gist of its contents.'

'He says he had a run of luck the other night—'

James swung around sharply. 'A run of *luck?*'

She nodded. 'Yes. I thought you said—'

'Never mind. Go on.' He turned away again.

'A...a run of luck. And that he has settled the money—five thousand pounds—on me. That...that it is mine, in trust.'

'Yes.'

She could hardly breathe. 'It's an independence, enough to live on.'

'Yes.'

Yes? Was that all he could say? Could he not see what this meant to her? That she was free? She swallowed, looking at the rigid back, the hands clasped, clenched, behind him. Perhaps he knew exactly what this meant and was breathing a sigh of relief.

'I no longer have to be your mistress, my lord.'

He turned at that. *'My lord?'* There was an edge to his voice, an odd, shuttered expression in his eyes.

She stood up. 'It is true, is it not? With this money I can live not in wealth, but independently.'

'Lucy.' He took a single step towards her and her heart leapt.

He stopped. 'Yes. It's true.'

This then, he thought, was pain. Knowing that he had lost her. His whole world was crumbling and there wasn't a damn thing he could do about it. He had dared to hope that Elizabeth was right and that Lucy had given herself for love, that she had meant those sweet words in the dawn.

'Is the rent at Hawthorne Lodge more than I can afford?'

'Rent?'

She looked a little uncomfortable. 'I would rather pay rent. If it is too much, will you help me find somewhere smaller?'

He bit his lip. 'If that is what you wish.' Just breathing hurt now.

'Somewhere close, so if you wish to…visit me—'

'Visit you?'

He struggled for words. 'Lucy, I can let you go.' Even if it destroyed him. 'But…it has to be a clean break. Continuing to visit you as a…a friend, not your lover would be—' He broke off. Torture? Insanity? Try impossible.

'But you could still be my lover. If…if you wanted me.'

He wondered if he was insane already. 'Lucy, you said you didn't want to be my mistress, so—'

'I said I didn't *need* to be your mistress.'

'Precisely, so—'

'I can still take a lover, can't I?'

She wouldn't be his mistress, but she still wanted him as her lover. Deep inside hope flickered and leapt to a flame. He went to her and drew her with him back to the seat under the cherry. 'Yes, but think.' He forced himself to say it. 'With five thousand pounds safely in trust, you could marry.'

She paled, her eyes over-bright. 'No. Not that. Never that.'

'Why not, sweetheart?'

Her mouth trembled as he took her hands in his. 'Even if I could fall in love again, do you really think any man would want me, if it weren't for the money? I'd rather be alone.'

Even if I could fall in love again... His heart threatened to burst.

'What about marrying a man who loves you? A man with far too much money for five thousand pounds to be any sort of temptation?'

Lucy's world tilted on its axis. He *couldn't* mean what she thought he meant.

'Lucy?'

She stared up at him, into the storm-dark eyes.

'Fitch gave me his blessing, if that helps.'

'Fitch?'

His smile tore at her. 'As the closest thing you have to a brother, I asked his permission to address you.'

'My lord—*James*, then…' as the glint in his eyes turned dangerous '…you *can't* marry me. I'm a walking scandal!'

'Eros,' James said, raising her hands to his lips and kissing them, 'doesn't give a flying damn about scandal and nor do I.' His fingers tightened on hers. 'Do you want me down on one knee?'

She didn't, but before she could say so he was kneeling before her.

'Sweetheart, for God's sake, put me out of my misery and say you'll marry me?'

The garden blurred, went misty. 'James, this is insane. You can't marry me. Even Mr Fox will be horrified.' But her fingers clung to his, and her heart, oh, her heart was singing and dancing that he could even think of asking her.

He raised her hands to his lips. 'I'm going to take that as a yes. If Fox is all that's worrying you, let me reassure you that we already have his blessing.' His fingers tightened on hers. 'And even if he hadn't, I'd still want to marry you, because I love you.

Her heart seemed to forget what it was supposed to be doing. Everything in her and of her, past, present and future, contracted, distilled, to this single point in time and space.

'You've never said that before,' she whispered. 'Not even when you were courting me, or—'

'Courting you?' His hands nearly crushed hers. 'Lucy, I didn't court you; I seduced you. And, yes, I was absolutely scrupulous about not telling you that I loved you. Even when you told me. Can you forgive me for that?'

'Forgive you?'

'For seducing you, taking advantage of you, and being too stupid to tell you that I loved you.'

'And you want to marry me.'

'More than I want to breathe.'

A smile wobbled on her lips and in her heart. 'You'd better keep breathing. Elizabeth told me once that you'd never say you loved me unless you meant it.' She leaned forward and kissed him. 'Yes,' she said softly.

* * *

St Anne's Hill
November 20, 1802

My dear James,
Thank you for your letter. Elizabeth and I are safely home after our sojourn in France. I am amused to hear that your cousin William has accepted your marriage at last. I am not at all surprised that his wife and young Nick had something to do with that. Susan was always a sensible female and it was clear from Nick's conduct last spring that he is turning out very well.

You will be interested to know that we saw Montgomery in Calais. I have heard that he has decided to live on the Continent.

Very pleased to hear that Fitch is doing so well at his lessons and will be ready for school next year. Clearly a lad of parts.

E. has received a letter from Lucy, inviting us to stay with you in Cornwall at Christmastime. Naturally E. will reply to her, but we will be very glad to come down.

I shall not refer to anything else she mentioned, except to say that I am delighted that the two of you are so very happy together and

that it did not take you as long to realise the value of what you had as it took me.
Your affectionate friend,
Fox

* * * * *

If you enjoyed reading this
look for Huntercombe's story.
Coming soon!

MILLS & BOON®

Why shop at millsandboon.co.uk?

Each year, thousands of romance readers find their perfect read at millsandboon.co.uk. That's because we're passionate about bringing you the very best romantic fiction. Here are some of the advantages of shopping at www.millsandboon.co.uk:

* **Get new books first**—you'll be able to buy your favourite books one month before they hit the shops

* **Get exclusive discounts**—you'll also be able to buy our specially created monthly collections, with up to 50% off the RRP

* **Find your favourite authors**—latest news, interviews and new releases for all your favourite authors and series on our website, plus ideas for what to try next

* **Join in**—once you've bought your favourite books, don't forget to register with us to rate, review and join in the discussions

Visit **www.millsandboon.co.uk**
for all this and more today!